SHERLOCK HOLMES

ADVENTURES IN THE WILD WEST

OTHER WORKS BY
JOHN S. FITZPATRICK

Sherlock Holmes: The Montana Chronicles
The Casebook of Sheriff Pete Benson

SHERLOCK HOLMES

ADVENTURES IN THE WILD WEST

BY
DR. JOHN H. WATSON, M.D.

AS EDITED BY
JOHN S. FITZPATRICK

RIVERBEND
PUBLISHING

Published by Riverbend Publishing, Helena, Montana

ISBN 978-1-60639-113-6

Printed in the United States of America

1 2 3 4 5 6 7 8 9 10 VP 28 27 26 25 24 23 22 21 20 19

RIVERBEND PUBLISHING
P.O. Box 5833
Helena, MT 59604
1-866-787-2363
www.riverbendpublishing.com

DEDICATION

To my wife, Connie, who has spent 49 years patiently looking after and encouraging me, and with whom I have shared
a happy and productive life.

ACKNOWLEDGMENTS

A work of this type necessarily involves contributions from many people. First and foremost, I wish to thank my long-time associate Kay Haight for her outstanding secretarial assistance, critical insight and positive encouragement and to Barbara Effing, longtime friend, for her copy editing. Chris Cauble at Riverbend Publishing read an early version of the manuscript and offered many valuable suggestions for improvement, and I am very grateful to all of my reviewers for their assistance.

For favors big and small, thanks also go to my brother Gene Fitzpatrick for assembling information about Spokane, Washington; Tiffany Ipock for explaining the Washington system of land title recordation; Tammy Copelan and Liz Stepro with the Wallace District Mining Museum for providing information and photographs about Wallace, Idaho; Karen Sherve and Sandra Jonas for supplying information about Susanville, California; and Neil Colwell for sharing information and publications which documented the history of the Washington Water Power Company.

John S. Fitzpatrick

DISCLAIMER

This is a work of fiction. In general, names, characters, places, and incidents are products of the author's imagination or are used fictitiously, and are not to be construed as real. Any resemblance to actual events, locales, organizations, or persons, living or dead, is coincidental. However, in these stories a number of the characters named in the story are based on actual people who lived near the turn of the century, although their use herein is completely fictitious. Many of the locales are also real, although the author "adjusted" geography and historical chronology a smidgeon to fit the story's plot. The reader should not interpret these writings to be historically accurate.

PHOTOGRAPHIC CREDITS

DEVLIN FAMILY COLLECTION
    1.   Mr. Michael (Mick) Devlin

LASSEN COUNTY HISTORICAL MUSEUM
    2.   Steward House Hotel

MARCUS DALY HISTORICAL SOCIETY
    3.   100 Block of Main Street, Anaconda, Montana

MONTANA HISTORICAL SOCIETY
    4.   East Broadway Street, Butte, Montana
    5.   The Grand Opera House, Butte, Montana
    6.   Merrill Avenue, Glendive, Montana

NORTHWEST MUSEUM OF ARTS AND CULTURE/
EASTERN WASHINGTON HISTORICAL SOCIETY
    7.   Mr. Daniel Chase Corbin

SHERLOCK HOLMES AMERICANA COLLECTION
    8.   Miss Valerie Ann
    9.   Miss Abigail Mayfair
    10.   Mr. Edward McNay
    11.   Miss Greta Uleland
    12.   Messrs. Thomas Bellingham and Stephan Coopersmith
    13.   Mr. Rinaldo Capelli

WALLACE DISTRICT MINING MUSEUM
    14.   Sixth Street, Wallace, Idaho

WIKIPEDIA, THE FREE ENCYCLOPEDIA
    15.   The Telharmonium
    16.   Phoebe Apperson Hearst
    17.   William Randolph Hearst
    18.   La Hacienda Del Pozo de Verona

CONTENTS

PHOTOGRAPHS

DIAGRAMS

Introduction

In the fall of 1994, Marion Geil, librarian at the Hearst Free Library in my hometown of Anaconda, Montana, called me and told me that she had found an old manuscript that she wanted me to see. When I asked for more details, she was uncharacteristically vague and would say little more than it was quite old, and given my reading propensities, I would find it quite interesting. My curiosity was piqued, but it was three weeks before I was able to make the trip to Anaconda, arriving the day before Thanksgiving.

Marian then revealed her find—a collection of stories and case notes written by Dr. John Watson, M.D. chronicling a series of adventures undertaken by Sherlock Holmes during visits to the western United States in the 1890s.

Marian had already concluded that Watson's work required some edits, then "must be published so that the world will know of Holmes' many exploits in the United States."

I could not have agreed with her more, and she then surprised me by handing me a copy of the various manuscripts while telling me that she wanted me to edit Watson's work.

Honored by her confidence, I reluctantly accepted the task. Then almost immediately, I dropped the ball and allowed the press of my career coupled with the need to raise two sons to delay the task before me. After a series of on-again, off-again editorial efforts, I put Watson's work in the cabinet bottom of an end table for safekeeping and its presence slowly receded from my mind. More than a decade passed before a stop in a used bookstore, where I saw an old copy of *The Adventures of Sherlock Holmes* on the shelf, rekindled the memory of Watson's manuscript in my possession. Unfortunately, the document was nowhere to be found and I cursed myself for my cavalier attitude toward the work. Several months later, quite by chance, I rediscovered the manuscript in a basement filing cabinet sandwiched between a file folder of political bumper stickers and a series of sociology bibliographies dating back to graduate school.

By 2008, I had worked through several of Watson's stories and published the volume *Sherlock Holmes: The Montana Chronicles* which detailed several of Holmes' adventures in southwestern Montana. This volume continues that work but includes tales of Holmes' work in other states as well.

While in the United States, Holmes was principally in the employ of Marcus Daly, President of the Anaconda Copper Mining Company, but Holmes' reputation and Daly's referrals soon led him to a number of cases that did not involve working for Daly's great mining enterprise. These tales are presented here.

John S. Fitzpatrick

The Unrelenting Case of Mr. Cahill's Telharmonium Plans

"Watson," Sherlock Holmes said, "if you're free this afternoon at four o'clock, you may wish to join me in the second floor parlor where you met Miss O'Sullivan.[1] I am sure this meeting won't be quite as enchanting as her company, but I sense that it will provide us with a puzzle that will stimulate our minds."

We were finishing our luncheon in the Collins Café down the street from the Montana Hotel where we were domiciled during this latest trip to Montana. We came to Montana the past spring at the request of Mr. Marcus Daly, President of the Anaconda Copper Mining Company, to assist with sev-

---

1 Editor's note: Holmes was referring to the parlor on the second floor of the Montana Hotel in Anaconda, Montana. The room was used for small social gatherings and it was there that Watson met Miss O'Sullivan as documented in a case entitled "The Tammany Affair." See *Sherlock Holmes: The Montana Chronicles* as edited by John S. Fitzpatrick, Riverbend Publishing, 2008.

eral matters of interest. Since then, Holmes had been offered numerous inquiries but, as usual, he would only take those which captivated his imagination, turning the rest over to Sheriff Fitzpatrick. Obviously, something in this latest matter had caught Holmes' eye. "What seems to be the problem?" I asked.

"We'll have the particulars this afternoon, but based upon the brief conversation I had with our prospective client, it appears to be a matter of some stolen plans for a new type of musical instrument which uses electricity to produce sound."

Modern technology. It was one of Holmes' greatest interests. He was forever reading about, studying, or experimenting with new technology, always on the watch for something that would be of assistance in criminal detection.[2]

"Who will we be meeting?"

"A young gentleman by the name of Thaddeus Cahill, from Washington, D.C.," Holmes said as he stood up from the table and departed, leaving me both the opportunity to have another cup of coffee and, as usual, pay the check.

I joined Holmes just before our guest arrived, having spent the afternoon at the library reading the newspapers followed by a walk down to Lucien King's, a stationer whose shop carried an excellent array of tobacco products. I

---

2 Editor's note: While Holmes' prowess as a consulting detective rests primarily in his acute observational skills and powers of both inductive and deductive reasoning, Holmes used science whenever possible to gather necessary facts. He was among the first to use fingerprints in his search for villains. That technology played a critical role in solving "The Case of the Boulevard Assassin."

purchased several cigars. I had no sooner sat down to enjoy one when a deep voice behind me said, "Mr. Holmes and Dr. Watson, I presume. I am Thaddeus Cahill."

He had a serious look about him. His movements were quick and definitive, suggesting a man who had much to accomplish and no time for twaddle. His physical appearance was undistinguished, being about medium height and build with thinning brown hair and a rounded face which, while serious, was not unfriendly. Cahill took a seat on the divan across from Holmes and me.

"I cannot tell you, Mr. Holmes, how difficult it was to find you. I cabled your flat in London several times to no avail. Only luck brought me here where a chance encounter with a copy of last Friday's Anaconda Standard showed me that you were in Montana of all places."

"I endeavor to not let my opponents know when I am gone from London," Holmes answered. "I don't want the criminal classes to think that should I take a holiday, they get one as well."

"Well put, Mr. Holmes. Nevertheless, I would have thought that a man of your station would have an associate to look after your mail and other communications."

"I do, my brother Mycroft, but he is always of the opinion that unless the matter is of the highest concern to the Crown the matter can wait, and he is usually correct. Now, enough about me. Do you like the cat?"

"What?" Cahill said showing surprise.

"You seem to be living with a cat, probably a white angora who has developed an affection for you," Holmes said.

"Indeed, she is the property of the woman where I am boarding, and yes, the cat and I get along famously. You can tell that from just looking at me? Your powers of observation are impressive."

"The success of the detective," answered Holmes, "very much depends upon seeing that which all are capable of seeing yet they do not observe. So, pray, please tell us about this problem you have."

"I have invented a revolutionary instrument which I call the telharmonium," Cahill stated. "It makes music using electrical impulses instead of vibrating a string or column of air. With one instrument I can duplicate an entire symphony orchestra."

"At the risk of appearing foolish," I said, "how can one instrument replace fifty to a hundred instruments that make an orchestra?"

"Excuse me, Dr. Watson. I always mistakenly assume that people I am talking to about my work are as versed in music or the propagation of sound as I am. Let me start from the beginning."

"Please," said Holmes.

"You gentlemen are familiar with the operation of the telephone," Cahill said. Holmes certainly was; I was not, although I had used the device on many occasions since coming to the United States.

"My instrument works on the same basic principle as the telephone. When you speak into the mouth piece of a telephone, the air pressure created by your voice presses against a diaphragm in the mouthpiece. As it moves up and down with the changes in air pressure, the diaphragm causes an electrical impulse to go down the wire. At the receiver end, the process is reversed with the electrical impulse causing the diaphragm to move up and down creating sound."

"All right, I think I understand." I said. Holmes nodded in agreement.

"Every musical note has a unique frequency," Cahill said. A look of puzzlement must have crossed my face. Cahill continued, "Frequency is simply the speed with which an object vibrates. Middle C on the piano vibrates 261.6 times per second. A in the fourth octave above middle C vibrates at 440 hertz or 440 times per second. A hertz is one vibration per second. With a horn or a pipe organ, the thing that vibrates is the column of air in the instrument. The faster the vibration, the higher the pitch of the note. Conversely, the slower the vibration the deeper the sound."

That made sense, I told myself. I was confident that Holmes understood, so it probably didn't mean much if I did not.

"With my instrument," Cahill said, "the telharmonium, the sound is created by a series of electric dynamos which contain tone wheels. These wheels have bumps and grooves on the surface so that when they spin they give off the frequency of just one note. An electrical receiver picks up that set of vibrations, converts it into an electrical impulse very similar to the telephone, and sends it down the wire to a speaker where it issues forth as music. Whenever the telharmonium operator presses a key, it releases the note down the wire."

"Fascinating," Holmes said as he reached for his tobacco pouch and pipe. I could not tell if Holmes was genuinely intrigued or bored.

Cahill went on. "With the telharmonium I can install a tone wheel to match every note that can be played by any instrument so I can literally create the sounds of a full symphony orchestra with one machine and one or two musicians."

"So it's a device to rid the world of symphony orchestras," I interjected with a smile on my face.

"I doubt many people would think of doing that," Cahill replied in earnest. "My plan is to create an instrument that can send music along electric wires to homes or businesses, a lot like a telephone. For example, if a homeowner wanted to listen to music he would simply turn on his receiver and out would come the music."

"People can do that right now using a gramophone," I said.

"Very true, Dr. Watson," Cahill replied, "but with my telharmonium, the sound quality will be infinitely better and one can have music all day rather than for fifteen minutes at a time with a record player."

"How far along are you with the invention process?" Holmes asked.

"I have fully developed the theoretical concept and have completed a full set of construction blueprints. In addition, each of the major components of the telharmonium has been physically tested to insure that they work as planned. My next step is to build a small-scale version of the instrument to show investors. Once that is done, I will be able to raise the capital necessary to complete the full-scale instrument."

"What are we talking about for size?" asked Holmes, continuing with his inquiry.

"The test instrument will have a little more range than a typical piano with ninety-six keys over eight octaves versus eighty-eight keys on a piano. All the equipment will fill a large room, twenty feet by twenty feet, I am guessing, and

TELHARMONIUM KEYBOARD

will weigh between 14,000 and 16,000 pounds."

"Impressive," Holmes said with a thoughtful look on his face. "Something clearly designed for a fixed installation. And you say the full-scale machine will be bigger?"

"Infinitely so, Mr. Holmes. The full-scale machine will be able to produce thirty notes per octave. It will have multiple keyboards like a pipe organ. I don't really know at this time how much room it will take, but it will be sizeable."

"Thank you for explaining the nature of your invention," Holmes said. "Could you now go back to the beginning and explain the nature of your problem?"

TELHARMONIUM DYNAMO ROOM

"Certainly," Cahill answered. "I believe someone has stolen the plans to my invention and will patent it as his own device. Furthermore, I believe the thief is in Butte, Montana, at this very minute. That's why I came here from the east coast."

TELHARMONIUM WIRING ASSEMBLIES

"How did this theft take place?" I asked, anticipating Holmes next question.

"My invention is no secret. A lot of people in the music world know about my work and most are very encouraging. For the past several months I have been contacted by a variety of people either wanting to invest in my enterprise or buy an instrument from me when they become available. About a month ago I was personally visited by two such men. One was Adam Bial, who is one of the co-owners of the Koster and Bial Concert Hall in New York City. He wanted to buy a telharmonium for use in their concert hall."

At this point, Cahill paused to drink a swallow of beer which the bartender had recently placed at his elbow. He continued, "Two days after meeting Bial I was visited by a man calling himself John Elitch of Denver, Colorado."

"Yes," Holmes said. "I know the man. Creator of Elitch Gardens along with his wife Mary. A consummate show-man and fine gentleman as well. Please continue."

"We had a short conversation. He too wanted to buy a telharmonium but unlike Mr. Bial, seemed quite impatient. It was as if he seemed to think that I was already producing the instrument and it was a simple matter of loading one on the next freight train."

"Did you show either of these gentlemen your blue-prints?" Holmes asked.

"No," responded Cahill, "but their presence is hardly a secret. The living room of my apartment is also my office. I have a drafting table in the corner and big map case which suffices as a file cabinet for my design drawings. It's no secret where the drawings are kept."

"I trust that your home was then illegally entered and the drawings taken," Holmes offered.

"Not exactly," Cahill said. "I left Washington, D.C. for a trip of several days' duration to Baltimore and Phil-adelphia."

"And Bial and Elitch knew you would be gone?" Holmes asked.

"True. I told both of them, independently of course, that I needed some time to think over their offers and would reply by post after I returned from my travels. When I got back home, the door to my apartment was unlocked. I dis-tinctly remembered locking it so I asked the landlady if she knew why it was open and she said, 'I guess that photographer you hired must have left it open by mistake.'

"I asked her, 'What photographer? I never hired any photographer.'

"She then told me, 'He arrived Thursday morning after you left. He pulled up in a wagon that said Mason's Portrait Photography on the side. The photographer came to my door and introduced himself as Joseph McIver and showed me a copy of a letter from you directing me to assist the photographer in any way possible.'"

"A very ingenious method of entry into your abode," Holmes noted.

"Indeed," Cahill answered. "According to Mrs. Shaw, the landlady, Mr. McIver brought in three bags of camera equipment into my apartment and started taking pictures of my drawings. When she asked him why I was having that done, McIver supposedly told her that I was just being careful. The photos would be stored in another building in the event there was a house fire or other catastrophe which might cause me to lose my drawings."

"Again, a most ingenious thief," said Holmes, "and, I might add, a very smart idea for people like yourself and Watson to protect your life's work. Thinking about it, John, it would be an excellent idea for you to back up all your case files and store a copy in the vault of our bank in case someone like Moriarty invades our domicile on Baker Street.[3]

---

3 Editor's note: The first recorded incident where the concept of backing up files and storing them off-site for security purposes, which is now routine practice for people and businesses with important documents on their computers.

"Pray, please continue, Mr. Cahill. I apologize for my digressions."

"That's perfectly fine. As a matter of fact, I immediately hired a photographer and copied my drawings and put them into safekeeping. To be frank, I never thought about the consequences of a fire in the rooming house where I live. More importantly, if the photographer had not left my front door unlocked, I might have never known that anything was amiss. I rarely see Mrs. Shaw and the matter of the mystery photographer taking pictures of my drawings might never have been raised."

"What have you done since then?" Holmes asked.

"I asked Mrs. Shaw for a description of the photographer but it wasn't very helpful—short man, maybe five feet six inches tall, one hundred thirty pounds, brown hair, no moustache, nice smile. That could be almost anybody. Next, I went to every photographic establishment in Washington, D.C. and across the river in Arlington. There is no such photographic studio by the name of Mason's Portrait Photography operating in the Washington, D.C. area. No one admitted to having been sent by anyone to my apartment to take photographs of my drawings.

"Having no luck solving this mystery in Washington, Mr. Holmes, I decided to travel to New York and question Mr. Bial," Cahill said. "Mr. Bial was a gracious host. I met him in his office at the theater where I tried to elicit any type of response indicating that he knew about the burglary of my apartment. My effort was to no avail and I finally just asked him if he had sent someone to surreptitiously copy my documents. Mr. Bial was horrified by my suggestion and protested that he had nothing to do with such chicanery. His response seemed genuine and I believed him. It also put me on the train for a trip to Denver and a confrontation with Mr. John Elitch."

At this point Cahill momentarily paused his narrative to gather his thoughts and take another sip of beer. "Ten days ago I arrived at Elitch's theater unannounced and was ushered into his office immediately. Imagine my surprise when the man behind the desk who stood up to warmly greet me was not the same man who had presented me Elitch's business card two weeks previous. I was confused and ended up stammering out the reason for my visit. Elitch told me that he hadn't been back to Washington for several years, did not employ or send anyone back to visit me, and confessed that he had never heard of the telharmonium. He went on to insist that whomever had given me his business card was both a fraud and a poor forger. The card I had received at my home had Elitch's name misspelled, with two l's rather than one.

"Suffice it to say, Mr. Holmes, I was shocked at the deception and disappointed that my trip to Denver was a complete waste of time. However," Cahill continued, "back in my hotel room as I prepared for dinner I experienced a lightning bolt of inspiration. After concluding his business with me, the fraudulent Elitch made a telephone call from the instrument in the hall outside Mrs. Shaw's apartment. I happened to be coming down the stairs toward the front door of the building and I overheard him say 'Butte, Montana.' Then it struck me that when he had arrived at my home another man was in the carriage with him. I never paid much attention to the second fellow, but I do recall that he had brown hair and seemed slight of build. With that knowledge I came to Butte rather than returning to Washington, D.C."

"Have your inquiries in Butte proved fruitful?" Holmes asked.

"In part," Cahill replied. "I visited all of the music halls and theaters in Butte without success, although I was not able to meet the managers of either the Renshaw Hall or the Grand Opera House. According to the people I talked with, both gentlemen were out-of-state on travel. These two theaters interest me greatly. Both are large, successful establishments and out of all the theaters I surveyed, these would be the only two which I believe could fund the construction of a telharmonium."[4]

"How much would that be?" I asked, my curiosity piqued.

"I believe the small-scale prototype, which I call the *Mark 1* and plan to build in the near future, will cost a minimum of fifty thousand dollars. The full-sized machine will be double or triple that."[5]

"A lot of money," I commented in a state of complete disbelief, wondering how anyone could take that kind of risk on an unproven technology.

"Then yesterday it happened," Cahill announced. "I was

---

4 Editor's note: The reader should understand that at this time Butte, Montana was about the same size as Los Angeles, Seattle, and Portland, fully electrified, a wealthy and cosmopolitan city where modern technology represented by the telharmonium would be right at home.

5 Editor's note: Cahill built three versions of the telharmonium, each being larger and more sophisticated than its predecessor. The first instrument, the *Mark I*, weighed seven tons; the *Mark II* weighed twenty tons and cost $200,000 to construct.

EAST BROADWAY STREET, BUTTE, MONTANA

riding the trolley on Broadway Street and as I looked out
the window, I saw him."

"Saw who?" Holmes asked as his eyes flashed with
interest.

"The man who came to my apartment saying he was
John Elitch. I got off the trolley at the next corner and
went in search of him, but he had disappeared. When my
papers were copied without my consent in Washington, I
cabled you in London without success. Last week I read
that you were here in Montana. Can I count on your help

to find the man who has stolen my invention?"

"Admittedly," Holmes said, "There are some points of interest in the case. Using a camera as a method of business espionage and theft is most ingenious. It may well give rise to a new brand of forgery. Yes, Mr. Cahill, with Watson's assistance I will look into this matter for a few days to see if we can assist you."

"Excellent, Mr. Holmes," Cahill replied, clearly happy that someone had taken an interest in his problem. "I can be reached at Mrs. Ellen Cammick's Rooming House at 77 East Park Street in Butte."

The next day Holmes and I traveled by train to Butte and took rooms in the Southern Hotel, a common place of residence when visiting the mining city.

That evening we attended a production of *The Hypocrite*, a melodrama produced by Paul Merritt, at the Renshaw Opera House.[6] We arrived early and Holmes excused himself while I found our seats. I knew he was inspecting the building, looking for a place to secrete himself after the performance so that he could make a detailed inspection of the building later in the evening after the staff had departed and the building was closed for the night.

The performance was uninspired but was time better

---

6 Editor's note: The Renshaw Opera House was constructed in 1881 and 1882 by Robert Renshaw. A hall on the second floor was used as the theater. John Maguire was its first manager and he hired Edgar Paxson, who later achieved fame as a western artist, to paint scenery for the Renshaw Opera House and several other theaters that Maguire was managing in southwestern Montana towns. Several of Paxson's original scenic backdrops survive to this day in the Opera House Theater in Philipsburg, Montana. The Renshaw Opera House building still stands in Butte, the ground floor occupied by the Terminal Food Center. The theater hall upstairs is unused.

spent than sitting in a hotel room reading a newspaper and waiting for tomorrow. After the final curtain Holmes bid me good night and slipped away into the crowd.

At breakfast, Holmes seemed to be in a thoughtful mood. All he said about his previous night's work was that the Renshaw was a well-built theater, modern in every sense of the word, and there was no evidence that he could find which indicated that the photographs of the telharmonium drawings were in the possession of Mr. Renshaw, the owner of the hall. He then told me to prepare for another night on the town, this time at Maguire's Grand Opera House on Broadway Street, about a block west of our rooms.[7]

"Watson, if I could prevail upon you for some assistance this morning, I would be grateful."

"Certainly," I replied, always happy to play a role rather than be a mere observer in Holmes' investigations.

"Here is a list of five photographers who offer their services in Butte. I would like you to visit each of them today."

"And what do you want me to ascertain?" I asked while looking at the list which contained their names and business addresses.

"See if any of them fit the description of brown hair, clean shaven, and slight build."

"Then I can immediately cross off Miss Brennan," I said.

"No, visit her as well," said Holmes. Just to be sure. While you are doing that, I will meet Oliver Toth. He has business

---

7 Editor's note: The Grand Opera House was constructed in 1885 at 50 West Broadway Street by John Maguire. It seated 1,200 people. The stage was reported to be twenty-seven feet wide, twenty-eight feet high, and thirty-five feet deep. The house orchestra numbered seven members. It was destroyed by fire in 1912 and the Leggat Hotel was built on the site.

to conduct with Mr. Renshaw on behalf of Sir Reginald."[8]

After Holmes departed to prepare for the meeting with Robert Renshaw, the proprietor and manager of Renshaw Hall whose facility Holmes had carefully searched the night before, I enjoyed another cup of coffee, thought up a cover story for why I was searching out the services of a photographer, and looked over the list Holmes provided me.

L.S. Hazeltine, 422 S. Arizona
George Hertz, 61 W. Park
A.J. Dusseau, 104 N. Main
H.G. Klenze, 122 N. Main
Mrs. L.L. Brennan, 6 E. Park

All were within walking distance of the hotel, Hazeltine being the farthest distance, about six blocks to the southeast by my estimation. I would start with him and work my way back uphill finishing with Mrs. Brennan.

I decided to tell each of the photographers that I was looking for a photographer to do my daughter's wedding in September, and after the conversation got started, I inquired whether they would do the work or if it would be handled by an assistant.

Hazeltine was a big man, at least six feet tall with side-

---

8 Editor's note: Watson's notes indicate that Oliver Toth was one of many fictitious persona that Holmes adopted when he disguised himself to observe or interview a subject. Holmes, his brother Mycroft, and the British Foreign Service created several businesses, staffed by Foreign Service operatives, which provided a façade for Holmes and others undertaking undercover work for the Crown. Sir Reginald Curtiss, to whom Holmes alluded, was also a fictitious character. Curtiss was the alleged managing partner of Caledonian Import Brokers.

burns, and I quickly dismissed him from the list. Hertz was blonde turning toward gray and Dusseau likewise was an older gentleman and completely gray. Dusseau had an assistant, slight of build and clean shaven with brown hair, a very comely lass who fell one attribute short of being our man.

I was pleased to meet so many fine men and frankly, felt poorly that my actions were fraudulent in character, but I would be able to answer Holmes' entreaties when he saw me later in the day.

I lunched in the Chong Wa Restaurant and sampled Chinese food for just the second time in my life, both of which had occurred in Montana. My military adventures had taken me to the Indian subcontinent and Africa, but never to the Orient. I suspect that there are many Chinese restaurants in London, but more than likely they are in the poor sections of the East End where a man of my position would be unlikely to go. No doubt Holmes knew all about them.

Following my noon hour repast, I continued on with Holmes' mission and quickly crossed H.G. Klenze off the list. His coloring was appropriate, but he was middle-aged with a thick German accent.

I was down to Mrs. L.L. Brennan, a stout woman in her fifties, with gray hair and a pair of bifocals perched on the end of her round nose. Upon entering her shop I knew my timing was impeccable. Mrs. Brennan was instructing a young man whom she addressed as Joe, who was slight of build, brown hair and no mustache—in other words, a perfect match to the description of the photographer provided by Cahill. After Mrs. Brennan went into the back room to get me some information, I engaged the young man in conversation, introducing myself to him as John Tompkins and him to me, as Joe Quinn. I quickly learned that he was Mrs. Brennan's assistant and had been "learning the photography trade," as he put it, for over a year and he hoped that he would be able to start his own shop in the near future.

I complimented him on his ambition and then turned the subject to travel, saying, "This is truly a remarkable country, Mr. Quinn. My wife and I decided to come over early just so that we'd have the opportunity to see the United States in all its glory. I always thought of London as being a busy city, and it is, but tame in comparison with New York. Your capitol, Washington, D.C., is just magnificent. Have you ever had the opportunity to go there yourself?"

To both my wonderment and delight, Mr. Quinn imme-

GRAND OPERA HOUSE, BUTTE, MONTANA

diately said, "Yes. I was there a little over a month ago with a friend. We only had a few days, but you are quite correct, it is a beautiful city."

There was no sense in me pushing a conversation about Washington, so I steered the conversation to Pittsburgh, America's industrial power house, and our trip across the plains to Butte. I knew that Holmes would be pleased. One piece of the puzzle appeared to have fallen in place.

Holmes met me in the hotel dining room and I quickly reported my success. "Capital, Watson," he said. "That is excellent news. Did Mr. Quinn say who his friend was?"

"No, and I thought it impolite to pursue the subject. I assume that we can always follow the young man after work to determine with whom he keeps company."

"Good thinking, my friend. Right now he is the only certain fact we've yet to accumulate in this investigation."

"I take it that your meeting with Mr. Renshaw was unsuccessful."

"Decidedly so," Holmes replied. "Renshaw has no knowledge of the telharmonium. He had never heard of the machine, was astounded to learn that music could be produced by electricity, and showed absolutely no interest when I told him that Caledonian Imports had a client who was willing to pay five thousand dollars for a set of plans for the machine. In fact, Renshaw said to me, 'It wouldn't make any difference if you were offering a hundred thousand dollars, Mr. Toth, I know nothing about that of which you speak. I can't help you.'"

Holmes continued, "I then asked Mr. Renshaw if there was any other person in town familiar with the music business that I might contact. He thought about it for a minute and said, 'Perhaps you might wish to meet with John Maguire, proprietor of the Grand Opera House music hall on Park Street. He's my rival, but we are friends. He pays more attention to what is going on in the music world. If it's in fashion, he will know about it.'

"Inasmuch as I was already dressed for the occasion, I walked over to Maguire's establishment. He wasn't in, but I could hear hammering and sawing. When I asked his clerk about it, she said Mr. Maguire is improving the building's electrical system.' So tonight, as promised, we will again attend the theater and I'll be able to see what improvements Mr. Maguire is making to his Opera House."

That evening's entertainment featured the Huntington Broadway Company in a play entitled *The District Attorney*. It was a far more lively performance than what we had seen the night before at Renshaw Hall. Holmes disappeared at the final curtain to secret himself and, again, investigated the interior of the hall without the owner's knowledge.

The next morning Holmes reported that his nocturnal foray had borne fruit. He said, "Maguire may be improving the electrical service for the building, but you don't need to heavily reinforce the floors to install additional wiring and that is what he has done. New beams eight inches square spaced two feet apart now support the floor under the southeast corner of the building. Obviously, he plans to install something quite heavy there."

"Will Mr. Toth be visiting Mr. Maguire today?"

"Indeed," replied Holmes. "I am told that he will be in the office this morning by nine o'clock which doesn't leave me much time to get into disguise."

Holmes left me to my wiles. I took a long walk along Park and Broadway Streets looking in various shops. The array of goods and services for sale was certainly remarkable for a city on the remote frontier.[9] After lunch I treated myself to several chocolate candies from Mrs. Rosenstein's Confections, just down the street from our hotel, and then decided that I wanted to get a bird's eye view of the city so I ambled over to Main Street and climbed the hill to its crest where I entered the City of Walkerville. From there I followed some railroad tracks until I got out on a point of land below a mine, I later learned it was called the Diamond, and I could look down over the entire city. It was a beautiful, warm day and for Butte the air was clear. A light but steady breeze from the west had pushed the smoke, which belched forth from the power houses at the mines and from the furnaces in Butte's copper smelters, out of the valley.

From where I stood, I counted over fifty mines and would have counted more, but I kept losing track of those that I had counted previously.[10] At 4:00 p.m. the steam whistles blew, and a flood of miners flowed out of the mine gates headed to a battalion of saloons in the downtown area for some liquid refreshment.

I visited three saloons that afternoon and each had working men standing three deep from the bar. It was a sight to behold. Holmes told me later that Butte had five operating breweries.

---

9 Editor's note: At the time of Watson's visit, the population of Butte was about 44,000 people. It was by far the largest city in Montana at that time.

10 Editor's note: The 1896 *Butte City Directory* identified 164 mines in and near the city.

Back at the hotel I found this message from Holmes:

> *Please retrieve Cahill from his residence and dine at the Fashion Café at 7:00 p.m. tonight. Find an unobtrusive place in the back where Cahill can see the floor. Toth expects to meet with the quarry.*
>
> *Do nothing unless I summon your help. I suspect Cahill will recognize the man Toth will meet.*

S.H.

I did as instructed. Cahill and I were in our seats at 6:45. Holmes, disguised as Toth, arrived five minutes later and took a table near the front door. Just after seven, a young man in a black suit and wearing a derby hat entered the café, surveyed the room, and then went to Holmes' table. Cahill confirmed that it was the same man who had represented himself as John Elitch in Washington, D.C.

Holmes rose, shook hands with the gentleman, and returned to his seat. Holmes ordered dinner; his companion did not. They talked briefly, shook hands again, and the young man departed.

Without acknowledging Holmes, I escorted Cahill from the restaurant and took him home. He was in an anxious mood and wanted to call the police. I advised to the contrary and told him emphatically, "Holmes' methods are frequently unorthodox but almost universally successful. If he felt a police presence was needed this evening he would have arranged it. You asked for his help, Mr. Cahill. Now, trust him."

I returned to my hotel and found Holmes still dressed

in mufti[11] and asked why he was still dressed as such.

"Because Mr. Toth has another meeting tonight at ten o'clock," Holmes replied.

"Obviously, your visit to Mr. Maguire was fruitful," I remarked.

"Provocative at this point, Watson. I was afraid that my meeting with Maguire was just a waste of time. Like Renshaw, he claimed that he had never heard of the telharmonium and he showed little interest in the conversation until I mentioned my willingness to pay five thousand dollars for a set of the plans."

"He took immediate interest, did he?" I asked.

"Not to the casual observer, but I noticed a twitch in his left eyebrow when I mentioned the money. It was there a second time and a third, every time I brought up the sum I was willing to pay. Then he got up from his chair, offered me his hand, and wished me the best of luck. When I reached the door of his office to leave he called out to me and said, 'Mr. Toth, I presume this is your first visit to Butte.'

"'It is,' I answered," said Holmes.

"'Then I hope that you will enjoy its best. Might I recommend that you seek your dinner tonight at the Fashion Café? It's east of here about two blocks distant. Being Friday, tonight they will feature either baked haddock or cod. The fish comes to them encased in a block of ice. You would believe it was just fresh caught. Go about seven o'clock after the dinner crowd has thinned out. I can guar-

---

11 Editor's note: The term "in mufti" means "in civilian clothes" as opposed to military dress. Watson uses the term in this context to mean "in disguise."

antee you a very fine meal indeed.'"

"A rather oblique way of setting up a meeting," I commented in reply.

"No, Watson. A very careful one," Holmes said, a small smile curling up at the edge of his mouth. It's Maguire's way of distancing himself from whatever might transpire, or if something goes awry and the police are summoned. He did nothing more than recommend a good place to eat."

"Who was that young man who met you at the café?" I inquired.

"He said his name was Henry Glennon. When I asked him about his relationship with Maguire, Glennon said, 'I have no relationship with Maguire. I deal in special artifacts; Maguire runs an opera house.'"

"Do you believe him?"

"You know I don't engage in conjecture. But we may know tonight after we meet Glennon. Oh, and Watson, bring your trusted Webley."

Apparently Mr. Glennon did not impress my friend as a man of character. Holmes wanted me to bring my revolver.

The sun had passed the horizon but twilight lingered as we left the hotel. The sky was aflame with pink, orange, and magenta hues reflected in the broken clouds that lay to the west. We walked a short distance on West Quartz Street.

"This should be it, Watson. Let us now reconnoiter the surroundings."

We circled the block and walked down the alley to come up on the back side of the building. Holmes said it was called the Fiske Rooming House, but it looked quite decrepit and unused. I saw lights in two windows on the ground floor from the front and nothing from the alley.

There were two entrances to the building. Lest someone be monitoring the front door, we crept into the structure through the rear entrance and quietly climbed to the third floor in search of Room 310.

Holmes left me near the back stairs and slowly crept down the hall as silently as a leopard stalking a deer. He checked each of the doorways very carefully. When he reached the end of the hall, he turned around and just as softly moved back in my direction pulling himself flat against the wall next to a doorway to my left. He motioned that I should walk down the hallway and knock on the door on the right side, across from where he had positioned himself.

Suddenly, an enormous chill ran up my spine. Holmes was using me for bait in what I feared might be a lethal game of cat and mouse. Nevertheless, I did as I was summoned to do, making sure that I sounded like a company of cavalry as I marched down the hall. I found the door and banged on it three times. It started to open from the force of my blows and then I heard the sound of the door behind me. I half-turned only to be hit by a crushing blow from behind which pushed me through the door and onto the floor of the room. I expected another blow, but instead heard a gasp followed by a grunt, the sound of a man being strangled. I turned over to see Holmes with a chokehold on my assailant who was much bigger than Holmes. I rushed to my feet and drove my right fist into my assailant's solar plexus as hard as I could. He went limp. Holmes pulled out a pair of handcuffs, secured the fellow, shoved a handkerchief in his mouth, and dragged him back into the room from which he had rushed.

There was no electricity in the building. Holmes lit a match, found a kerosene lamp on a table next to the wall, and brought forth light.

It took our assailant about ten minutes to revive, at which point Holmes told the man that he was going to remove the cloth from his mouth and then ask him some questions. If he attempted to yell or flee, his compatriot—meaning me—would shoot him in the head.

I pulled out my Webley and parked the barrel about two inches from his left eye.

This individual was not Henry Glennon, so Holmes began the questioning by asking the man's name.

"Jasper O'Meara," came the man's slow reply.

"Who sent you?" Holmes asked.

There was no reply. Holmes asked O'Meara the same question again. Once more, no reply. Holmes then shoved the handkerchief back in O'Meara's mouth and said, "I am going to take you over to see Sheriff Fleming. He'll have the answer beaten out of you sooner or later, and then you'll get twenty years in Deer Lodge for attempted murder."[12]

At that point, O'Meara shook his head no. I put the gun against his brow, Holmes removed the handkerchief, and O'Meara said, "Hank Glennon. He said a guy was showing up at Room 310 with five thousand dollars and I would get five hundred for cracking his skull and bringing Hank the money."

"Or you could make five thousand dollars and be out of Butte within the hour," I said.

---

12 Editor's note: The Montana State Penitentiary is located in Deer Lodge, Montana, about thirty miles west of Butte.

"I am not that stupid," O'Meara said. "Hank has a posse. He'd find me and the rest, well it wouldn't be pretty."

"Where are you to meet Glennon?" Holmes asked.

"At McEvoy's Saloon on East Park tonight at eleven."

Holmes heard enough. He fixed the handkerchief back into O'Meara's mouth and we marched him down the back stairs of the rooming house. I held him at gunpoint in the alley while Holmes disappeared, only to reappear about twenty minutes later in a wagon with two draymen. We loaded O'Meara aboard whereupon the wagon took him to an empty warehouse secured through one of Holmes' friends in Butte. There O'Meara could be securely and indefinitely detained.

At eleven o'clock I went in the front door of McEvoy's Saloon, saw Glennon at a table in the far corner of the room, and took a seat at a table nearby. Holmes came in the back door and quickly dropped himself into a chair across from Glennon and very quietly said, "I have a pistol pointed at your stomach. So keep your hands on the table, keep very calm, and speak very quietly."

Glennon nodded in reply. Holmes then said, "That was very stupid of you, Mr. Glennon. Your associate Mr. O'Meara is quite dead at this point and I doubt his body will ever be discovered. I don't have the position I hold with Caledonian Imports because I am a fool. But you are a fool, and it's going to cost you a lot of money. Do you understand?"

Glennon nodded yes again in reply. "Now," said Holmes, "you and I are going to get up very carefully and walk out the back door together. If anyone follows us my associates will deal with them. Then, you and I are going to get those plans and you will be delighted to exchange your life for those papers."

Glennon shook his head no, then said to Holmes, "I don't have the plans. They're locked up safe and sound. It will have to be tomorrow."

"I guess it will," said Holmes nonchalantly. "Enjoy the evening, Mr. Glennon. Your time on this earth is very short."

That was the first, and I believe, only time I saw Sherlock Holmes threaten anyone with their life.[13] I surmised that Holmes thought Glennon was accompanied by several henchmen that evening who were seated elsewhere in the bar, and Holmes did not want to risk trying to take Glennon from the saloon.

A few minutes after Holmes had departed, Glennon stood up and exited the front door with three other men trailing in his wake. I waited another fifteen minutes before journeying back to the hotel where I met Holmes in his room.

Holmes had removed his disguise and was pacing back and forth in front of the bed. I took the chair at the writing table, sat down, lit a cigar and waited for Holmes to advise me of the next steps in the plan. Holmes lit a bowl himself

---

13 Editor's note: Watson's original text goes on at some length on Holmes' threat to use force. He said, "It was so totally uncharacteristic of Holmes to use force when the hallmarks of his success were careful observation and logic but, admittedly the villains one encountered in frontier America were made of a more brutal concoction than those seen in the British Isles." Watson then qualified his remarks by saying that "his (Watson's) experience with the criminal classes of Britain had been largely confined to the drawing rooms and manor houses of polite society and not in the slums of London's East End whereas Holmes had experience with all forms of thuggery and would instinctively know when he could use reason with a suspect or would need to use harsher methods."

and after the tobacco was burning robustly, spoke for the first time since bidding me entrance to his room.

"I hid in the alley waiting for Glennon to follow me but gave up on the idea after a few minutes when he didn't come out the door. I left the alley on the east side of the block and turned down to Park Street where I saw Glennon and three of his associates standing in front of Mrs. Brennan's photography studio. His actions confirmed your earlier hypothesis that Quinn was working with Glennon. We go there tonight and see if we can find the photographic negatives."

An hour later we were in the alley behind the Brennan Studio. Holmes produced what looked like a railroad lantern with shutters on four sides. By opening one shutter, Holmes could concentrate the light on a small area, which in this case was the back door lock. We were quickly inside, Holmes in the lead. I could see little but the outline of Holmes in the darkness of the room. Then, there was the inescapable crunch of someone stepping on broken glass. Holmes halted and widened the aperture of the shutter on the lamp and shined it toward the floor. It was covered in broken photography plates. Holmes bent down, picked up a large shard of glass and examined it in the light. "We're too late, Watson. Someone has beaten us to the negatives of Mr. Cahill's plans."

"Who?" I asked more as an expression of surprise rather than a question. "Glennon?"

"No," replied Holmes. "Glennon is going to be as disappointed as we are. The plot thickens, my friend."

"Cahill," I said.

"No," Holmes replied. "I made sure that he was safely

engaged this evening to prevent his anger from compromising our foray. He is to dine with John Hendricks, Butte's Superintendent of Schools. We have an unknown third party who has entered the case."

At that very moment we heard sounds at the front door of the studio. "Quick, Watson, in here," Holmes said, pointing to a darkened doorway to my left. He closed the shutter to the lantern and we plunged back into darkness.

"Hank, I don't have enough time to print a new set of plans for that instrument." It was the voice of Joseph Quinn talking to Glennon. A light came on in the room which Holmes and I had departed, followed by "Oh, my God!" It was Quinn's voice again. We could hear him picking through the glass and then he reached the same conclusion Holmes had a few minutes previous. "Someone has broken all the plates for the telharmonium."

The next several minutes were used by Glennon venting his rage and Quinn his frustration. Finally, Glennon said, "I'll get the plans back and tomorrow, you're going to have to re-photograph them. I'd better get going and you'd better get this place cleaned up before Mrs. Brennan sees it." Quinn said something I couldn't hear. Then there were footsteps outside the room where we were hiding. The door opened and young Quinn stepped in looking for the light switch. He never found it—Holmes stepped out of the shadows and put him in a choke hold until Quinn was unconscious. Then Holmes and I beat a hasty retreat out the back door from whence we had come and returned to the hotel without further issue.

About half past eight in the morning the bellboy brought me a note from Holmes which said:

The day is yours. I shall return for dinner.

S.H.

By prior arrangement, we met at the Cottage Restaurant on South Arizona Street. Holmes thought it wise not to return to the Fashion Café or any others near our hotel on Broadway Street should Glennon have any agents about. Glennon had only seen Holmes dressed as Oliver Toth, but it was unclear whether he had paid any attention to me. As such, Holmes thought the extra caution worthwhile and I was loath to disagree.

Holmes told me that he had spent a good part of the day dressed as Gideon Reed[14] observing the Grand Opera House and reported that "Mr. Glennon entered the building a little after 9:00 a.m. and stayed about a half hour. He left the building with an angry look on his face and returned to his room in the Curtis Block, number 47 to be exact, on the fourth floor. After making arrangements to insure that Glennon was followed, Mr. Toth went back to see Mr. Maguire again."

Holmes then provided a verbatim rendering of Toth's meeting with Maguire, observing that "Mr. Maguire was not happy to see Toth again and reiterated that 'he didn't know anything about that new-fangled musical instrument you asked me about the first time you were here.' At that

---

14 Editor's note: Gideon Reed was another fictional character whom Holmes used in his forays in London's underground. Reed was a day laborer. Holmes used this disguise to blend in with working men on the docks and in the factories of London.

point Toth said, 'I don't believe in coincidences, Mr. Maguire. I told you that I was willing to pay five thousand dollars for a set of telharmonium plans. Then, you advised me to dine at the Fashion Café and low and behold, Mr. Glennon shows up from out of nowhere, interested in selling a set of plans for the telharmonium. Later that evening when I go to complete the transaction, one of Glennon's henchmen tries to do me in. Notwithstanding your pleas of ignorance, it is very clear to me, Mr. Maguire, that you are up to your hips in mud with Mr. Glennon.'

"Then Maguire replied, 'I don't know anyone named Glennon,' to which Toth replied, 'What name did the gentleman use this morning, just after nine, when Glennon entered this building and stayed a half hour?' Maguire looked away.

"'Mr. Maguire,' Toth continued, 'you may advise your associate Mr. Glennon that I will be at Buzetti's Saloon this evening at eight o'clock. If he doesn't arrive with the plans for the telharmonium, it will go badly for both of you. Good day, sir.'"

Holmes then surprised me and said, "This is not the type of case I envisioned when I took on Mr. Cahill's commission, Watson. I expected an intellectual challenge but have come to appreciate the fact that we are dealing with ruffians every bit as intelligent as Moriarty and just as ruthless as Sebastian Moran. I'll not rest well until he's behind bars."

That evening about 7:45 p.m. I took up position in Buzetti's Saloon at a table adjacent to one occupied by Holmes, who was again dressed as Oliver Toth, in anticipation of his meeting with Henry Glennon. I busied myself reading the newspaper. The time passed slowly as I read and re-read the articles and advertisements. I was reminded that horse racing was to begin tomorrow at Anaconda's track and was sorry to miss the event to which I had been invited by Major Thornton. I also noted that a baseball game was to be held this evening between Anaconda's lawyers and physicians. Holmes' friend Dr. Spelman would be pitching for the doctors.

Eight p.m. came and went without any sign of Glennon. Holmes remained patient. About twenty minutes past the hour John Maguire entered the front door, spotted Holmes in his role as Oliver Toth, and moved quickly to the table and sat down facing Holmes.

Maguire said, "Mr. Toth, I am glad to have found you here. I feared that I would be too late."

"And to what do I owe this fortuitous event?" Toth asked. "I was expecting Mr. Glennon."

"Glennon has disappeared," Maguire answered, "and now I need to find him as much as you do."

"Pray, please continue, Mr. Maguire," Holmes said.

"I haven't been forthright with you, Mr. Toth. I know about the telharmonium."

"A sudden attack of conscience, Mr. Maguire?"

"In part. Some conscience, some business. After you left my office this morning I went to the bank, had lunch and returned to the theater about two in the afternoon. My maintenance man, Hammond, was waiting for me outside the office. Hammond reported that when the building contractor's crew returned from lunch the plans were missing."

"So the remodeling of the theater that you're currently undertaking is to accommodate the telharmonium."

"Yes. I purchased a set of plans from Glennon several weeks ago and now they've disappeared and Glennon stole them."

"Why would he do that?" Toth asked. "Glennon has another set."

"No, he doesn't, or at least he didn't until he stole mine. When he came to see me that morning it was with a request to borrow my plans for a few days so that he could make another copy to deliver—to you, I presume. But I denied his request, telling him that I had construction underway and couldn't stop the work to accommodate his request. Glennon was quite angry when he departed. Then he returned during the lunch hour when the carpenters were absent and absconded with my plans."

"Now you want my help in finding Glennon," Toth replied, "after you arranged with Glennon to pick my pocket and leave me for dead in some ramshackle rooming house."

"I wasn't party to the attack on you. After you expressed your interest in having a set of plans for the telharmonium I did, indeed, contact Glennon and told him how to find you in exchange for a reduction in the sales price of the plans he sold me. Glennon agreed and the two of us went to see my lawyer to draw up the papers."

"Mr. Maguire, you may be the only man I know who does business with a scoundrel on the basis of a written contract."

"It's my way, Mr. Toth. When Glennon first approached me about the telharmonium I decided that I was interested, and further that I would only proceed on the basis of a written agreement. Knowing Mr. Glennon's reputation as a man who lives by his wits, I wanted to protect myself in case his behavior was anything but above board."

Maguire continued, "Mr. Curtis, a lawyer here in Butte and the owner of the building where Glennon resides, drafted the document. I agreed to purchase a set of plans for the telharmonium from Glennon for three thousand dollars, with five hundred dollars paid in cash on signing. To protect myself from any chicanery, the contract required that Glennon produce a bill of sale from the seller to certify that the plans had been obtained legally."

Toth then observed for Maguire, "I presume that when Glennon returned from his travels back east, he produced both the plans and the requisite bill of sale."

"Yes, he did," Maguire responded.

"Then why all the secrecy about the instrument?" Toth asked.

"I wanted to get it built and in operation before my competitors heard about it. Not only will it save me money in terms of the cost of hiring musicians at the opera house, I'll be able to sell subscriptions to deliver music to people's homes and businesses."

"How much of a reduction did you get from Glennon in exchange for telling of my interest in the telharmonium plans?" Toth asked.

"Fifteen hundred dollars," Maguire answered.

"You haven't paid him yet?"

"Not in full," Maguire responded. He received an additional thousand dollars when he delivered the plans to me and the balance was due when the machine was complete and functional."

"With the disappearance of the plans, you're out fifteen hundred dollars plus whatever you've spent thus far remodeling your theater."

"Correct."

"I assume that summarizes the business aspect of why you are here to see me," Toth said. "Pray, please tell me about why your conscience is now bothering you."

"It's very simple, Mr. Toth. When I told Glennon about you, I expected him to make arrangements with you to sell a copy of the plans. I did not expect nor countenance a plan to injure or kill you in an effort to steal your money. For that, I am truly sorry."

"Apology accepted, Mr. Maguire. Pray, please tell me what you propose from this moment forward?" Toth asked.

"I was hoping that we might join forces, find Glennon, and recover the plans for the telharmonium."

"Interesting proposition, Mr. Maguire. How far are you willing to go?"

"I don't understand, Mr. Toth."

"Are you prepared to bring Sheriff Fleming into the matter and prefer charges against Mr. Glennon?"

"Yes, absolutely," Maguire answered.

"Even when it will be shown that Glennon stole these plans from Mr. Thaddeus Cahill, the inventor of the telharmonium? That makes you an accessory to Mr. Glennon's theft."

"I had no idea that he stole the plans."

"That is no doubt true, Mr. Maguire, and if you possess the documents that you claim to possess, it is doubtful that you will be charged with a crime. But the plans, if found, will not be returned to you without Mr. Cahill's consent."

"Mr. Toth, I am an honest businessman. I saw an opportunity to improve my business and took it, only to discover this day that I am mired in deceit and associated with a man who will undertake the most vulgar of crimes. Notwithstanding the financial harm it will do to me to not be able to complete the telharmonium, I will not be a party to theft or murder."

"In that case, allow me to call Sheriff Fleming and we can find Mr. Glennon."

"You know where he is?" Maguire asked.

"Indeed, I followed him to his place of residence after he left your theater this morning and once that was known, made arrangements with the local Pinkerton Agency to have him followed. He's hiding out in Mrs. Annie O'Neill's boarding house in Dublin Gulch."

Within the hour Holmes had contacted the sheriff and Glennon was arrested and taken to the county jail where he was charged with conspiracy to commit murder and theft of the telharmonium plans.

Glennon denied everything.

Holmes revealed his true identity to both the sheriff and Mr. Maguire, and we both provided a detailed statement regarding the attempt to kill me and steal the money I was carrying to purchase the telharmonium plans.

The next morning Maguire gave his statement to the sheriff during which time he produced the contract documents he had signed with Glennon and a copy of the bill of sale for the telharmonium plans. Thaddeus Cahill was then called in to provide his statement. Cahill told the sheriff the same story he had told Holmes and me about the theft of his papers, and he denied that he had ever signed a bill of sale while admitting that the writing and signature on the document looked very much like his signature. Initially, the sheriff was skeptical of Cahill's testimony. He said that it sounded to him like a man who made a deal, then changed his mind and was now calling the buyer a thief.

Holmes asked him to persevere and hear the testimony of Jasper O'Meara, who had attacked us, and that of Mr. Joseph Quinn, Mrs. Brennan's photography assistant.

O'Meara corroborated Holmes' and my testimony regarding the attack and stated unequivocally that he had been hired by Glennon to do the job. The attempted murder and theft charge would be successful.

I departed at that point in the proceedings for another appointment, and Holmes told me later that Joseph Quinn, Mrs. Brennan's assistant, told the sheriff how he had traveled to Washington, D.C. with Glennon and had photographed Cahill's blueprints at Glennon's direction. The big break in the case came when Holmes asked Quinn, "You arrived at Mr. Cahill's residence in a wagon marked Mason Portrait Photography. Where did you get that wagon?"

Quinn answered, "We rented it at a local livery and Glennon painted the sign on the sides. He's a sign painter by trade and an excellent calligrapher as well. Mrs. Brennan uses him to craft special invitations and announcements from time to time."

After Quinn departed Holmes took out his magnifying glass and closely compared the bill of sale which Glennon had provided Maguire with Cahill's writing and was able to show the sheriff several small flaws in Glennon's forgery. Glennon was doomed.

That afternoon I met Holmes at the Fashion Café for coffee where I congratulated him on the successful conclusion of another case.

"Not yet, Watson," Holmes replied. "We've caught the

perpetrator of the first crime, but we haven't recovered Mr. Cahill's plans and, more importantly, we don't know who stole the plans from Maguire's Grand Opera House."

"You don't think it was Glennon," I said.

"No. Glennon was under surveillance by the Pinkerton operatives when the plans disappeared and he was nowhere near Maguire's place of business. We're dealing with a third party; no doubt the same one who destroyed the negative photographic plates which Quinn had stored in Mrs. Brennan's photography studio."

When we returned to the hotel, Mr. Cahill was pacing back and forth in the lobby waiting for us. "I received this from my landlady in Washington. It arrived there about an hour ago."

Holmes opened the folded paper which Cahill had thrust in his hand. It was a telegram which said:

Willing to return plans for $5,000. If yes, put American flag in window. Further instructions will follow.

"What am I to do, Mr. Holmes?" Cahill asked.

"Cable your landlady and tell her to put a flag in the window as instructed," Holmes answered. "This telegram originated in Denver. Someone in Butte has the drawings, and confederates in both Denver and Washington, D.C. helped him with this theft and ransom plan."

"Elitch?" Cahill wondered.

"No," Holmes answered firmly.

"But who then?" came Cahill's rejoinder.

"That we have to find out, Mr. Cahill, but I can assure

you that it is not Mr. Glennon. The plot thickens."

After Cahill departed, I pressed Holmes. "How can you be sure that Elitch is not involved?"

"Because he's an intelligent man, Watson. Cahill visited Elitch, and Elitch is not fool enough to deny any knowledge of the telharmonium and then wait a few weeks and offer to ransom the plans. No, whoever sent that cable thinks that Cahill is still in Washington, not Butte, and is probably trying to cast suspicion on Elitch. I go back to my original supposition. It is someone in Butte with confederates in two cities. This sordid affair is becoming so complicated that one might think Moriarity is involved."

Holmes' last statement unnerved me and I blurted out, "He's not, is he?"

"No, Watson. Mycroft seems to think he may be involved in a bit of intrigue in Bavaria."[15]

Later that afternoon, Holmes and I returned to Maguire's Opera House for another conference with the impresario and with his maintenance man, Adam Hammond.

Holmes started the conversation by asking Hammond, "How many men are working on the construction crew?"

"Four, Mr. Holmes," Hammond answered. "The builder, Rufus Whitman, and three carpenters."

"What are the workmen's names?"

"Michael Harrington, Thomas Shea, and Gustav Beck."

"Do you know the men well?"

---

15 Editor's note: This case was first reported to the public in 1997 with the publication of the book *Against the Brotherhood* by Quinn Fawcett, Forge Books. It deals with the effort of Mycroft Holmes, Sherlock's older brother, to defeat the Brotherhood, a 19th Century terrorist organization. Moriarty was not involved.

"Whitman has his office a few doors down the street. I see him from time to time. Beck is related to Simon Hauswirth in some way and is in Hauswirth's Saloon a lot of the time. I take a small beer there sometimes. I don't know the Irishmen. In fact, Mr. Holmes, I don't know any of them well."

"Do you believe that any one of these four might have stolen the plans?"

"No!" Mr. Hammond's answer was emphatic. "All four men left together for their noon meal and the plans were still on the builder's table by the backstage door."

"When was that?"

"A few minutes after the noon whistle."[16]

"When did you discover the plans were missing?"

"I didn't, Mr. Holmes. I was on one of the catwalks above the stage replacing some worn rigging when Whitman called out for me. It was a little past one. When I got down to the stage he asked if I had moved the drawings. I told him 'no' and together we looked in the workroom and they were gone."

"Were you in the theater during the noon hour?" Holmes asked.

"Not entirely. I walked around the corner to Cohn's to get some more of my pipe tobacco. I also talked with a couple of men out on the street, so I was outside the theater for about twenty minutes. Then I went down to the furnace

---

16 Editor's note: In Butte during that era various mines had steam whistles which were blown at different times during the day to announce the start and end of the work shift. The Stewart Mine, which was a few blocks north of Maguire's theater, also blew its whistle at noon.

room where I ate my lunch. I came back upstairs very near one o'clock."

"After you discovered the plans were missing, what did you do?"

"I went to see Mr. Maguire straight away and all six of us searched the building, but we found nothing."

"Was the back door of the theater locked?"

"No. Anyone coming down the alley could have gotten in."

"Where did the workmen go for their lunch?"

"Hauswirth's," Hammond said. "It's on the other end of the block near Main Street."

At that point I interjected myself into the conversation by noting, "I know it. It's a very lively place. Someone is always playing music."

"You are quite correct, Dr. Watson," Maguire said. It's very popular with local musicians. Simon Hauswirth plays several instruments and will abandon the bar from time to time to entertain his customers."

At that point, Holmes thanked Hammond for his testimony and dismissed him. When he had departed, Holmes observed, "We seem to have two options here, Mr. Maguire. The first is that Hammond has taken your blueprints, and the second, is that an unknown third party entered the building and took possession of them when the building was vacant during the noon hour."

"I can't believe that Hammond is involved," Maguire answered quickly. In fact, he looked irritated by the suggestion.

"How long has Hammond been with you?" Holmes asked.

"Three years."

"And where was he before?"

"He came from Denver."

"Perchance, did he work at a theater there?"

"No. He worked at the Adolph Coors Brewery."

"Excellent beer," Holmes observed to no one in particular, and then added, "Did he have any connection with the theater business?"

"The only connection that I am aware of is as a patron," Maguire answered. "Hammond said he went to the theater on several occasions when he lived there."

"Did he ever mention Elitch Gardens?" I asked.

"Yes, several times," Maguire said and then offered, "I too have visited Mr. Elitch's establishment. It's an outstanding theater and Mr. Elitch is an impressive showman."

At that point, Holmes moved his eyebrows in such a way as to advise me to abandon that train of thought. I relinquished the balance of the interview to him.

After we had departed the opera house, Holmes told me that he was going to the Western Union office to cable Mycroft in London, and further explained that he would be indisposed until late on the following day. Holmes asked that I return to Hauswirth's Saloon in the evening and again over the noon hour tomorrow to see if "anything of interest" develops.

The next day I gave Holmes a full report of my observations. "My evening foray into the saloon was quite entertaining. Several different musicians performed, but I saw nothing that aroused my suspicions. The only person I recognized in the crowd was Mr. Renshaw. He came in just before eight o'clock, bought a glass of beer, and sat down at a table right in front of the stage and paid very close attention to a threesome that was playing. A pianist, a banjo player, and fiddler. I reached the opinion that he was auditioning the men for a possible performance at his hall."

"Anything else of note?" Holmes asked.

"Not that evening, but today during the lunch hour it was a different story," I replied. "Just after noon the four workmen from Maguire's entered via the alley entrance just after noon and took a table near the center of the room. One of the men, a clean-shaven fellow going bald, walked up to the bar and gave Hauswirth an order. While he stood there, another fellow left his place near the front of the bar and walked down to talk with Maguire's man."

"What did this new fellow look like?" Holmes interjected.

"He was short of stature, with thin brown hair and spectacles," I replied.

"Go on," Holmes said.

"Hauswirth brought four schooners of beer and the three of them visited amiably for a minute or two. Then Hauswirth moved away to serve other customers and the man with the spectacles pulled a letter-sized envelope from the inside of his coat. He placed it on the bar in front of the workman, who slid his hand over it, palmed it, and placed it in his pants pocket. Then he picked up the beer and returned to the table with his mates. The man wearing the spectacles left the bar.

"A few minutes later, the accordion player finished his performance and sat at a table next to me. I complimented him on his performance and we began a conversation. I ended up asking him why so many musicians frequented

Hauswirth's bar. He said, 'Hauswirth is president of the Musicians Union in Butte so we all patronize his place. We play as a way of demonstrating our skills. It's sort of an audition. People looking for musicians come in and listen.'"

"As Renshaw did the previous evening," Holmes noted.

I continued. "Then I took it upon myself to ask about various people in the saloon and he confirmed that the man behind the bar was, in fact, Simon Hauswirth, and the fellow with the spectacles was Samuel Taylor, the treasurer of the Musicians Union."

"And the man who picked up the envelope?"

"The accordionist said that he didn't know his last name but he answered to 'Gus' and was good friends with Hauswirth."

"Excellent work, Watson," said Holmes. "From what you have described, it appears as if Gustav Beck received some sort of remuneration from Mr. Taylor."

"For telling the union about the telharmonium?" I offered in conjecture.

"Pray, please continue, my friend," Holmes replied.

"I've been trying to figure out who would benefit if Maguire's plans were to disappear and I've come to two conclusions—a party that wants to profit from the invention itself, perhaps by ransoming the plans back to Cahill, or a party that doesn't want to see the telharmonium constructed at all, such as the Musicians Union, many of whose members could be displaced by a simple machine."

"Excellent deductions, Watson. A similar idea occurred to me the night we discovered the broken photographic plates at Mrs. Brennan's studio. Tonight we'll test your theory by visiting the Musicians Union Hall. It's just across the street from Hauswirth's Saloon on the second floor of the Mantle and Bielenberg Building."

"Another private investigation after the lights are out," I commented, more to myself than Holmes.

"No," answered Holmes as he poured tobacco into his pipe. "I would like to interview the officers. From what I have learned about Mr. Hauswirth, his reputation is impeccable."

Back at the hotel, Holmes and I again encountered Mr. Cahill pacing back and forth in the lobby. He rushed up to Holmes and said, "I received another cable, Mr. Holmes. They saw the flag in the window of my flat in Washington," whereupon he handed Holmes the telegram. It said:

Bring money to Franklin Square tomorrow.
6:00 p.m. Plans will be returned.

"What am I to do now, Mr. Holmes?" Cahill asked.

"Do you have a friend or family member who could take your place in Franklin Square tomorrow?" Holmes asked.

"My lawyer would help," Cahill answered. "But won't they recognize that it's not me?"

"I doubt it, Mr. Cahill. I am certain that whoever is perpetrating this theft is here in Butte and working through an associate in Washington who has not likely seen you."

"So I am to have my lawyer bring the money to the man?"

"My heavens, no! The money will simply be stolen and you'll not see a return of the telharmonium plans. Cable your attorney and ask him to represent you in Franklin Square tomorrow evening. When he is approached for the money, have him deliver a telegram which says:

> *In transit to Butte, Montana to visit family. Reach me at Butte Hotel, three days hence.*
>
> *Thaddeus Cahill*

"I have no family in Butte," Cahill protested.

"You will by tomorrow," Holmes said. "We are simply buying time to catch the perpetrator, whoever that happens to be, but I am certain he is here in Butte."

That evening, just as the sun set, Holmes and I entered the building housing the Musicians Union Hall. The directory said the office was on the second floor. We made a stealthy advance up the stairs and down the hall to Room 23 on the back side. Voices could be heard inside the office, but it was not possible to understand what was being said. It was at that point that I upset our plan of attack. As I moved into position on the other side of the doorway opposite Holmes, I failed to notice a cuspidor on the floor and struck it with my foot. It went clanging down the hallway and the voices inside the Musicians Union office died down. Holmes tried the door; it was locked, so Holmes knocked loudly.

We could hear chairs being moved and hushed voices followed by a door closing, and a few seconds later we were granted admittance.

"Yes?" answered a man with gray hair as he opened the door.

"I am Sherlock Holmes, here to meet with the officers of the union," Holmes replied as he stepped into the room. He quickly surveyed its contents. All I could see from my vantage point was a back door in the far corner of the room and two more men, one of whom was Samuel Taylor, the union treasurer.

"Quick Watson," Holmes hissed. "Back down the front stairs. Our quarry has departed." Then Holmes bolted across the room toward the back door. I ran down the front stairs. When I reached the street, I saw a man dressed in a gray work shirt and Mr. Levi's dungarees enter the front of Hauswirth's Saloon. He was carrying what looked like a roll of paper. I followed and made it inside the front door just in time to see my foe disappear through the rear entrance into the alley. I rushed after him but the alley was devoid of life when I reached it. I decided that my quarry must have entered the door of the building immediately behind the saloon. The door was locked, so I raced around to the front of the building which I then recognized as the Curtis Block, where Holmes had said that Glennon roomed.

I quickly climbed the stairs to the second floor where a small office faced the stairway but no one was present. The center of the building was a large atrium which reached up past the fourth floor to a huge skylight. The rooms hugged the building's exterior walls. Each floor was surrounded by a promenade, edged by a balustrade of richly toned, dark brown pine. The second floor was largely occupied by offices. I saw signs for the Twin City Butte Mining Company; John Gannon Insurance Agent; Mrs. E.M. Hill, Music Teacher; and several others. Continuing up the stairs to the third and fourth floors I found Room 47 where Glennon was domiciled. There was no light shining from the transom above and I didn't expect there to be for Glennon was still ensconced in the Silver Bow County jail. I gently tried the door handle, unsure as to why I wanted to look in his room. It was locked. I circled the interior of the building and, to my surprise, there was no back stairway to the alley. The object of my pursuit, if he had entered the Curtis Block at all, had perhaps secreted himself on the ground floor and escaped when I left the alley. He never came through the ground floor of the building. The restaurant which occupied that area was closed.

I returned to the Mantle and Bielenberg Building only to find Holmes standing on the sidewalk outside the front door patiently, waiting my return, whereupon I told him of my unsuccessful pursuit.

"At least we know that he had the plans, Watson," Holmes said as he showed me a small triangular piece of paper which had obviously been torn from a larger sheet. "This is photographic paper," he continued. "Whoever disappeared down the back stairs caught the corner of page seven in the door as he scrambled to escape."

"Who was it?" I asked.

"I don't know," Holmes answered.

"Perhaps our musician friends up above may be forthcoming with a name," I answered.

"I think not. They disappeared after you and I vacated the building in search of the thief. We need to take this matter up with union president Hauswirth."

"Tomorrow then," I answered thinking we needed supper and rest.

"No, right now. He resides across the street in the rooming house his wife operates above their saloon."

A few minutes later Holmes and I were ushered into the Hauswirths' parlor which overlooked Broadway

Street, right above the entrance to the saloon. Mrs. Hauswirth was a congenial woman with a twinkle in her hazel eyes and a broad smile on her face. After offering us coffee she retreated to let the men have their say. Having seen Hauswirth downstairs at work behind the plank, I expected a more garrulous man. Instead, he seemed to retreat behind his spectacles as Holmes described the purpose of our visit.

"So very succinctly, Mr. Hauswirth, person or persons unknown purloined a set of plans for the telharmonium from Mr. Maguire's establishment and brought them to the union hall tonight, where he met with Mr. Taylor and two other gentlemen, both tall of stature, rather lean, one with a full brown beard, the other with long red sideburns. The man with the plans slipped out down the back staircase before we had a chance to see him."

There was an extended pause before Hauswirth answered, trying I am sure, to come up with a plausible explanation for tonight's events. He finally said, "It sounds like the two men with Taylor are McGarvey and Sullivan."

"You know them," Holmes stated.

"Indeed, they are musicians, not particularly accomplished musicians, but they are members of the union. Both of them work at the Mountain Con Mine, up the hill in Centerville, but they are basically lazy and want to get an office job where they won't have to work up a sweat. They have been hanging around the union hall a good deal the past several months and have become friendly with Taylor."

"Why would they be interested in pirating the plans to the telharmonium?" I interjected.

Again, Hauswirth paused. "To stop Maguire from

building that infernal machine. The union's relationship with Mr. Maguire is rather contentious. He would like to get rid of his orchestra, which varies in size between seven and thirteen men, but he knows that if he tries to hire non-union musicians his patrons will boycott his Opera House. So, what better way to solve the problem than by acquiring an instrument that can make all the sounds of an orchestra but which only requires one or two men to play? He reduces his costs for musicians, and so long as the telharmonium is being played by union members, the union cannot picket his business."

"Ingenious," I replied. "But to have the union engage in theft—"

Hauswirth cut me off decisively. "The union was not involved in any theft. I would never countenance such actions, but I may well have one or two miscreant members who would labor in the misguided notion that they were helping their brothers. The fact that you two gentlemen know of some involvement by them in this deed dooms any chance of success they might have enjoyed and will now subject the union to public scorn."

"What do you propose to do now that you know the facts?" Holmes asked.

"I am not sure," Hauswirth answered, "but I will look into it."

"If the plans are returned to me, no questions will be asked and no charges proffered. If not, the matter will be turned over to the sheriff, and his deputies can be very persuasive at drawing out any information someone might wish to hide. It will not be a comfortable time for Mr. Taylor or his two associates."

"And Maguire will continue building the telharmonium," Hauswirth answered.

"No," said Holmes quietly. The plans were stolen from the inventor before they were sold to Maguire. The plans will be returned to their rightful owner and Maguire loses the money he spent on the plans."

"Thank you, Mr. Holmes. That information may help me bring this matter to a happy ending."

Holmes advised Hauswirth where we could be reached and we departed for our hotel about a block to the east. I was certain that Holmes had resolved the matter successfully.

The next morning I awoke to a dreary sky and a heavy rain pelting my hotel window and the street below. I recalled that Holmes said he would be indisposed for much of the day, so after breakfast I seated myself in the hotel lobby and read my way through a pile of newspapers that I had purchased. I always read the Anaconda Standard, which has the largest circulation in Montana. It has excellent national and international coverage as well as regional news from all corners of the state. There was, fortunately, no mention of our recent activities. I did learn that the Japanese were continuing to protest the annexation of the Hawaiian Islands by the United States, and in Anaconda, the horse racing season had begun the past Sunday with six thousand people in attendance, a considerable feat, I thought since the town itself has a population of only ten thousand.

In the late afternoon, Holmes presented himself at my room carrying a message from Simon Hauswirth which asked us to meet him outside the Musicians Union Hall at 9:00 p.m.

At the appointed time, Hauswirth led the two of us up

the stairs to the union's office, whereupon we discovered that both the main office door and an interior door leading to a closet had been opened by force. The telharmonium plans which Hauswirth had locked away earlier in the day were gone.

Just when Holmes and I were both of the belief that the case was about to recede into the past, it was given a new lease on life.

Hauswirth was clearly discomfited.

"Who knew the plans were here?" Holmes asked.

"Just me," Hauswirth answered. "Taylor brought them to me at the bar. I carried them here around four o'clock and then went to your hotel to leave my message."

"Did you happen to see anyone who might have been observing you?" Holmes inquired.

"No, but I wasn't looking for anyone. I found Taylor this morning and told him to return the plans. I suspect that McGarvey and Sullivan are behind this."

After leaving Hauswirth to deal with the destruction of his office, Holmes and I walked to the county jail where Holmes made arrangements for the sheriff to search for McGarvey, Sullivan and Taylor.

The next morning, per Holmes' instructions, I met separately with Thaddeus Cahill and John Maguire to advise them that the telharmonium plans had once again gone astray. That mission accomplished, I returned to Hauswirth's Saloon, planning to enjoy a light repast and some good music over the lunch hour. The minute I cracked open the front door, I knew something was wrong. The saloon was empty save for Hauswirth behind the bar and the accordionist, with whom I had visited a few days previous.

A look of surprise covered my face and the accordionist explained. "Simon is being boycotted. The men learned of Maguire's plans to build some kind of new instrument that would put them out of work. They're not happy."

"I was just down at Maguire's Opera House," I said. "No one is down there."

"No," answered the accordionist. "They're not picketing his establishment, just boycotting Simon. They heard that Simon demanded the return of the plans from Taylor and now they think Simon betrayed them."

"I was such a fool," Hauswirth said. "When I asked Taylor to return the plans, he didn't protest at all. I should have smelled the rat. He's been after my job as president for a long time. The minute after Taylor turned the plans over to me, the three of them started telling the union members that I had sold them out and helped Maguire. Now, they have the issue they need and they'll take over the union at the next election."

"Which is two weeks away," the accordionist said.

I offered my condolences to Hauswirth and departed to advise Holmes of this latest development. This case certainly had some interesting turns. First, it was a simple theft, then a theft with a ransom demand, and now it's become part of a power struggle within the Musicians Union. What next?

Later that afternoon, Holmes and I met with Cahill at his room on East Park Street where Holmes gave Cahill his instructions for his newly planned arrival in Butte. Holmes had made arrangements with the Northern Pacific Railroad to have Cahill board the train at a siding about two miles east of Butte. When the Iron Horse and its trailing carriages arrived in Butte five minutes later, Cahill was to depart looking haggard from his two-day trip from Saint Paul.

"I am certain that someone will be watching for you to arrive," Holmes said. "It is important that you look like you've just completed an exhaustive passage from the east coast. Take a cab to your hotel. I've made arrangements for you to meet Mr. John Cahill, a miner here in Butte who has agreed to play the role of your brother."

The next morning Holmes and I were in place on the platform. He had disguised us using his considerable talents as a make-up artist, a craft he had mastered many years previously when he toured the United States as an actor. He had created a completely new persona for me by the name of Mortimer Cavendish. I had a mutton-chop beard, gold-rimmed spectacles, gray suit and matching derby hat. Frankly, I looked like some dandy who would normally be seen trying to ingratiate himself with some young damsel at a cricket match. Holmes appeared as Ivy Witherspoon, dressed somberly from head to toe in black and affecting a South African accent. We took up our stations at opposite ends of the platform. Then, who should appear coming around the east end of the station but Taylor, the treasurer of the Musicians Union, followed a few seconds later by Hammond who came out through the station doors. After the train had disembarked its passengers, Taylor climbed aboard with a small suitcase, apparently planning to leave town for a few days. Hammond met a comely lass who looked to be about twenty-five years old. She was traveling with a large amount of luggage and Hammond hired a porter to help get it all out to the street.

Cahill was among the last to disembark the train. A

few seconds later Taylor left the train and walked back inside the station. Admittedly, I was confused. Taylor didn't know who Cahill was, so his apparent effort to follow Cahill made no sense.

That evening, again in my civilian clothes, I started out for the lobby of the Butte Hotel across the street from where Holmes and I were staying. Holmes had asked me to take up position in the hotel lobby to observe who might be watching Cahill. At the corner outside the hotel I encountered Joseph Quinn, Mrs. Brennan's photographic assistant. He greeted me heartily, calling me Mr. Tompkins. He asked how the plans for my daughter's wedding were coming along.

I had not been present when Holmes and the sheriff interviewed him in conjunction with Glennon's arrest. He did not know that I was Dr. John Watson, then on a mission for none other than Sherlock Holmes.

Inside the hotel, I glanced into the restaurant and observed Cahill dining with his newly minted brother near the far corner of the room. Next to him was a single gentleman with a full black beard, which I presumed was Holmes, and closer to the door was Adam Hammond in the company of the woman he met at the train depot.

I stopped at the front desk and asked if Mr. Thaddeus Cahill had checked in and was answered in the affirmative. The desk clerk also commented that I was the second person to inquire about Mr. Cahill's arrival. I said nothing in reply but thought to myself, the other inquiry was made by the man Holmes wishes to apprehend. Now that he knows Cahill has arrived, it shouldn't be too long before the next ransom demand is made.

My prognostication was valid. The next morning, a little past ten o'clock, Cahill showed up at Holmes' hotel room with a note that told him to bundle five thousand dollars in hundred dollar bills into an envelope and deliver it to the McDermott Hotel at 4:00 p.m. and, further, to tell the desk clerk it was for Mr. Jones in Room 360.

Holmes and I registered separately as guests at the McDermott Hotel, I again dressed as Mortimer Cavendish and he as Ivy Witherspoon. We took up our observation posts in the lobby. Cahill arrived promptly at four o'clock, gave the envelope containing the money to the desk clerk, and was in turn handed a key to Room 360. We waited.

Suddenly, Holmes jumped up and dashed down the hall toward the back of the hotel. I followed, unsure what was happening, but found Holmes holding onto Mr. Quinn who was protesting loudly. Holmes patted him down and searched his pockets to no avail. He then ferreted Quinn into the manager's office, a small room behind the front desk, where he placed Quinn in the chair behind the manager's desk and told me to obstruct his way to the door.

Holmes then started removing pictures from the wall which separated the manager's office from the front desk area. Behind the third frame, a still life of a waterfall cascading into an emerald pool, Holmes found a hole in the wall. He reached in and withdrew a small parcel.

"The back entrance to the mail slot for Room 360, Watson," Holmes declared. "Cahill's envelope was placed in the box, and after Cahill departed the lobby, I observed another envelope appear in the box and Cahill's envelope disappear. Truly ingenious."

"Do you want me to call the sheriff?" I asked.

"Not just yet, old friend," Holmes replied. "I need to find Cahill's envelope. Otherwise, the sheriff will have nothing to charge him with."

It didn't take long. In a postal sack beneath a letter slot near the door, Holmes found a thick envelope addressed to Joseph Quinn, Room 46, Curtis Block, 25 West Park, Butte, Montana.

A minute or two later, we heard Cahill's voice calling for Holmes. I brought him into the manager's office where he quickly recognized Quinn as the man who had been driving the buggy which brought Glennon to his Washington, D.C. apartment. Cahill then said, "I found the plans, or at least I found part of them."

Holmes gave him the look which said to tell us more.

"He sent me on a wild goose chase all over the hotel. I started in Room 360, where I found a note which said to go to Room 202. From there I went to Room 247, then to Room 309, and finally down to a closet in the basement next to the boiler room where I found these," referring to the roll of telharmonium drawings in his right hand. "But it's not a full set. There are only twenty-three drawings here, not forty-seven."

"Do you have page seven?" Holmes asked.

"Yes," Cahill replied.

"See if it is torn," Holmes instructed.

Cahill rummaged through the rolled drawings before announcing, "No, it's just fine."

"How can that be, Holmes?" I asked.

"Elementary, Watson. This is not the set stolen from Maguire's theater. There are two sets of plans in the city. The case continues."

Quinn was turned over to a Silver Bow County deputy and Holmes, Cahill, and I made our way back uptown where we took up residence in Hauswirth's Saloon, the only customers in the place. Holmes was taciturn. He had solved the crime twice but had yet to conclude it.

When we'd received our libations from the bartender, I asked Holmes, "How long have you known that it was Quinn?"

"For several days Watson. Recall that after Mr. Cahill showed us the ransom note forwarded by his landlady in Washington, I went to the Western Union office to cable Mycroft on that matter he is dealing with in Europe."

"Yes, I recall that."

"While I was in the office, I also inquired if anyone had recently sent a telegram to Washington, D.C. No one had, so I asked about Denver, and that's where I 'struck pay dirt' as our prospector friends like to say. A cable had been sent the day before to a Rosabella Murphy with an address near Elitch Gardens. The clerk remembered the young man who sent it, and so described him as clean shaven with brown hair."

"Hammond," I interjected. "And, the woman forwarded the telegrams from Denver?"

"Yes. So I asked the Western Union to inquire about cable traffic between Denver and Washington, and two days ago was provided a list of transmissions on the day in question. There were seventeen, fifteen of which were directed to various offices of the U.S. Government or to commercial enterprises in the city. The other two went to attorneys resident in the city. I didn't think any of those parties were credible partners for an extortion scheme, so I asked Western Union to check their cable traffic in adjoining cities and they reported a transmission between Denver and Arlington, Virginia, across the Potomac River from Washington. It was received by a Gerald Quinn."

"A relative of our Quinn," I interrupted.

Holmes continued. "Who, I suspect, will be a brother or cousin of our young extortion artist."

"I am still puzzled about what went on at the hotel," I said to Holmes.

"As am I," said Cahill.

"After Mr. Cahill received instructions to drop the money at the hotel desk, I immediately assumed that the perpetrator was someone intimately familiar with the building so that he could retrieve the money and quickly escape. That suggested an employee, so last night I checked into the hotel dressed as my old companion, Oliver Toth, and while the guests slept I examined the hotel from top to bottom. I also had an interesting conversation with the night clerk who verified a suspicion of mine, namely that Quinn worked at the hotel. He does, three nights a week as the front desk clerk.

"No doubt he cut the hole through the wall from the manager's office one evening when he was supervising the front desk. His knowledge of the hotel building also extended to what rooms were occupied. He crafted the little wild goose chase around the building for Mr. Cahill to give him time to collect the money from the mail slot and escape. By the time Mr. Cahill discovered he'd only received half of his plans, Quinn would be safely back in his lodging or wherever he intended to make his escape." Holmes paused and drew on his pipe. "Had we not been involved in the case, he would have succeeded. Even if our illustrious client here had brought the sheriff into the affair, it's highly likely that all they would have done is monitor the building to see who withdrew the envelope from the mail slot. It likely would have taken overnight before anyone discovered the ruse. Further, should they have suspected Quinn in any way, a search of his person would not have revealed any money. It would have simply disappeared into thin air."

"Thank you, Mr. Holmes. It is all so complicated. I am amazed that you saw your way through it," Cahill said, "but we still have not recovered my plans for the telharmonium."

"True, but I expect we'll cross that bridge tomorrow when we talk with Mr. Gustav Beck. I suspect the sheriff will have him in custody by now."

"Gustav!" I said more loudly than necessary. "What does he have to do with it?"

"I would prefer to discuss it tomorrow, Watson, after we have the facts. It is purely conjecture on my part to speak further of this matter."

"Holmes, I beg of you, spare us of any further intrigue. You have a hypothesis. Advise us of your thoughts tonight, now."

"I share Dr. Watson's entreaty, Mr. Holmes. I'd like to get a good night's sleep knowing that we are close to the end of the trail in this matter," Cahill said.

"Watson, you know my methods. I don't speculate," Holmes answered.

"I do, Holmes, but Mr. Cahill is your client and it is he who is paying your fee. Certainly you can accommodate his inquiry."

SHERLOCK HOLMES: ADVENTURES IN THE WILD WEST

Holmes was clearly uncomfortable with Cahill's request. Had I asked him alone, his answer would have been a brusque "no."

"If you insist," Holmes answered. He then paused to collect his thoughts. His speech would be very deliberate, careful to expose his theory without ever admitting it as fact. At that point the bartender revisited our table and poured us another round of brandy.

After the bartender moved away, Holmes began. "Gentlemen, I am sure that you recognize that we have dealt with three separate crimes here. While the participants may be known to one another, each of these actions stand alone."

Cahill and I nodded in reply.

"Good," Holmes continued. "The first matter was the theft of Mr. Cahill's telharmonium plans in Washington. This crime was propagated by Glennon with young master Quinn as his associate. Glennon planned to reproduce and sell sets of plans for the instrument to whomever would pay. Mr. Maguire was merely the first of what Glennon hoped would be a long line of clients. It was Quinn's job to continue making duplicate sets of the plans for future sale. He was halfway through the second set when their partnership dissolved. That dissolution came about because of me, impersonating Mr. Oliver Toth. Toth showed up in Butte offering to buy a set of plans. For reasons still unknown to me at this time, perhaps it was my English accent, or perhaps because Quinn did not have a second set of plans ready, Glennon decided to transact his business with Toth violently, taking his money while sending his body to the grave. We foiled that plan and when Quinn discovered what Glennon had done, he decided to put their partnership to an end. He did not want to be party to murder and recognized, perhaps for the first time, what type of man Glennon really was. Quinn devised an ingenious scheme for saying goodbye. He destroyed the photographic plates containing the telharmonium plans and suggested to Glennon that the Musicians Union was behind it.

"Watson, the night you and I were closeted in Mrs. Brennan's dark room, we could hear snippets of Quinn's conversation with Glennon in the other room."

"Indeed," I replied, "but not enough to learn their thoughts."

"No," Holmes answered, "but I heard two names mentioned, the importance of which I failed to recognize at the time. I heard Quinn say Hauswirth and Hendrew, the president and vice president, respectively, of the Musicians Union. Once Glennon was arrested, Quinn played the part of a gullible associate who was hired by Glennon to photograph documents which Glennon was licensed to copy. Recall, it was his statement about Glennon being a sign painter and calligrapher that sealed Glennon's doom."

"Yes," I replied. "But surely you saw, Holmes, that Quinn was more than an innocent associate of Glennon."

"No, I must admit to complete laxity in my observation skills. I too was taken in by Quinn's boyish, affable, innocent manner and never pressed the issue with him or with the sheriff. My view began to change, however, when Mr. Cahill received the first ransom note. I knew instinctively that the ransom demand never came from anyone on the east coast. Initially, I thought it Glennon getting greedy again as he had in his dealings with Toth. It was an act that he could have put in motion before his arrest."

"Which brings us to the second crime," I interjected, "Quinn trying to sell the plans back to Mr. Cahill."

"Quinn wanted more money than what he had received from Glennon for his part in the theft. With Glennon in jail, Quinn cabled Cahill asking for money in exchange for the plans, but had the good sense to run it through two intermediaries. Quinn believed Cahill to still be in Washington, D.C. Inasmuch as the photographic plates were ruined, Quinn only had one opportunity to acquire some cash, that being to sell half a set of plans back to their rightful owner in exchange for five thousand dollars. I suspect that if Quinn had known that Mr. Cahill was in town and had played a role in Glennon's arrest, he might have added the parts together and determined it wasn't worth the risk. But, like Glennon before him, Quinn got greedy."

"Which brings us to the union," I said.

"Yes", Holmes said as he took a small drink from the glass of brandy before him and then followed that act by retrieving his pipe from his jacket pocket and putting it to fire before resuming. "Now we enter the realm of conjecture. It's my belief, Watson, and to you, Mr. Cahill, that Adam Hammond, the maintenance man at Maguire's Grand Opera House, set the union's involvement in motion."

"That's daft, Holmes," I replied. "Maguire said Hammond was a dedicated and loyal employee. He'd never undertake any action that would hurt his employer."

"On that latter point I am rather skeptical, Watson. The night when I searched the opera house after hours, I found several pieces of literature which I can only describe as radical unionism. There was also a letter from Rosabella Murphy then in Cripple Creek, Colorado, who lamented his need to leave town after the infamous strike of 1894.[17] When Hammond discovered the purpose for which Maguire planned to use the telharmonium, he went to Gustav Beck, one of the carpenters on the crew installing the machine, and told him what he knew. Beck, as it turns out, is Hauswirth's brother-in-law, and Hammond expected Beck to warn Hauswirth. At this point, I am unclear as to what happened. Perhaps Beck went to Hauswirth with Hammond's information, and Hauswirth told him that he wouldn't be part of any plan to steal from Maguire, notwithstanding how odious Maguire's actions might be to him. Or, knowing that Hauswirth is a man of rectitude, perhaps Beck went straight to Taylor. Taylor and his confederates McGarvey and Sullivan were quite happy to parlay with Beck. Using his information, one of them slipped into the back door of the opera house, stole the plans, and took them to the Musicians Union Hall."

"What were they going to do with the plans?" Cahill asked.

"I suspect that they simply planned to show them to a few key members of the union, the type of men the other

---

17 Editor's note: In 1894, the Western Federation of Miners struck the gold mines in and around Cripple Creek, Colorado, about twenty miles west of Colorado Springs. The miners were protesting the mine owner's plans to increase the work day from eight to ten hours with no change in the $3.00 per day daily wage. The strike lasted for five months and was marked by considerable violence. On two occasions the state militia was sent in to restore order. Finally, Colorado Governor Davis Waite negotiated a settlement to the strike which restored the eight hour day at $3.00 per day. The outcome of the strike was seen as a great victory for the union which quickly organized local unions throughout the region. The union's success was short lived. Continuing violence propagated by WFM miners caused the union's popularity and acceptance by the public to quickly wane.

members listen to, to demonstrate that they were looking after the members' welfare when Hauswirth was not. After the union vote was taken and Hauswirth ousted, the plans would undoubtedly have been destroyed."

"Who was the fourth man in the room that night you and I went to the union offices?" I asked.

"Gustav Beck," Holmes replied quickly. "You saw Taylor pay off Beck for his information in the saloon that afternoon, but something must have scared Taylor and he wanted to move the drawings to a safer location so he had Beck return that night. Beck escaped down the back stairs and disappeared into the night, although you gave chase admirably, Watson.

"Then Hauswirth recovered the drawings, probably by putting pressure on Taylor who delivered the plans to Hauswirth, who subsequently took them over to the union hall. He was observed, probably by McGarvey or Sullivan, and one of them removed the plans from the closet where Hauswirth had placed them for safekeeping."

"So, who has them now?" I asked.

"I don't know," Holmes said in reply. "Yesterday when I saw Taylor at the train depot, I contacted the sheriff and he was arrested soon thereafter, and Taylor gave up McGarvey and Sullivan. We'll see them all tomorrow at the jail."

The next morning Cahill and I joined Holmes at the county jail where Holmes and Sheriff Fleming interviewed Taylor, McGarvey, Sullivan and Gustav Beck. McGarvey entered the room with a limp and Sullivan's jaw was swollen, both men's injuries, no doubt, the result of the deputies "getting them in a talking mood," a phrase used by the sheriff previously. Holmes abhorred such violence, preferring to rely on logic and reasoning to solve his cases, but he did admit on one occasion that "the rough justice these American lawmen administer seems to be compatible with the type of villains they encounter." In Great Britain, excepting Ireland, of course, murder and assault are much less common than they are in the United States, and the need for "rough play," as I term it, is not necessary.

All four suspects were quite forthcoming in explaining the events of the past few days including their roles in the same, and with minor variations each endorsed the suppositions which Holmes had described to Cahill and me the previous night.

Gustav Beck confirmed that Adam Hammond initiated the process by telling him of Maguire's intended purpose for the telharmonium. He brought the news to Taylor who paid him twenty-five dollars for the information. McGarvey stole the plans from the opera house and Beck spirited them out of the union hall the night Holmes and I showed up at the door. McGarvey also removed the plans from the Musicians Union offices a second time after Hauswirth deposited them in the closet prior to returning them to Holmes.

"Where are the plans now?" Holmes asked McGarvey.

"Where they'd never be discovered," McGarvey answered. "I put them in the one place you lawmen would never look again. They're under the bed in Glennon's room over at the Curtis."

Sheriff Fleming dispatched two deputies to find and collect the plans but they returned empty-handed. One reported that the door was unlocked when they got there. Someone either had a key or picked the lock.

Following our business at the county jail, Holmes and I walked over to Maguire's Opera House to advise him of our findings, all of which was done in Adam Hammond's hearing.

Hammond admitted that he told Gustav Beck about the plans and put the chain of events into motion which led to the plans being stolen from Maguire. Hammond admitted to no wrongdoing and he confessed to having no knowledge as to where the unrecovered plans might be. To my surprise, given the volatile nature I had previously seen exposed in Maguire, the showman retained his composure and simply said to Hammond, "I will not have perfidy on my payroll, Mr. Hammond. You are discharged."

"The Unrelenting Case of Mr. Cahill's Telharmonium" concluded at that point. As we walked back to our hotel, I asked Holmes if he planned to continue the search and he simply replied, "No, Watson. I don't know where the plans are, but I don't think their absence threatens Mr. Cahill's venture in the future."

After saying goodbye to Cahill, who was both appreciative of the work which Holmes had done and generous in the stipend he paid, Holmes and I packed our bags and returned to Anaconda that afternoon.

Several days later when Holmes and I were enjoying a quiet dinner at Whatley's Café, my favorite eatery in Anaconda, I offered my opinion. "Holmes, your work on the missing telharmonium plans was simply brilliant, my friend. I don't ever recall when you've dealt with a matter that had so many different actors each pursuing an agenda unrelated to the others, no doubt one of your more complex cases."

Holmes was nonplussed, as I expected him to be. He replied, "Yes, we achieved a satisfactory result for Cahill, but I will go to my grave, Watson, wondering where those plans are."

"Frankly, I am just happy you were able to put Cahill back in business building his telharmonium. If it works as he insists it will, people in cities the world over will be able to enjoy music of all types for the modest investment of a telephone speaker and a monthly subscription fee for the music. Cahill will be a rich man indeed."

"Regrettably for Mr. Cahill, I don't share your opinion, my dear Doctor." After ingesting his last bite of Whatley's most delectable German chocolate cake, Holmes continued. "Mr. Cahill's instrument is already obsolete, but Cahill doesn't know it yet, displaced by Mr. Edison's marvel, the phonograph."

"Surely you jest, Holmes. The sound quality from the rotating discs—"

"Records, Watson. They're called records."

"Records then," I replied. "The sound quality is abysmal. You get music all right, accompanied by the most horrific scratching sound."

"No doubt that is true today, Watson, but it won't be true ten years from now. Once the population takes a fancy to an invention, be it a camera, printing press, electric light or whatever, the mechanics, inventors, and tinkerers swarm over it looking for ways to make it better. The same thing will happen with the phonograph. There will be a time in the future, Watson, when you'll be able to put a record on a phonograph and it will sound as if the symphony orchestra is in the room with you."

"You make a valid point, Holmes," I conceded.

"There's another thing that will doom the telharmonium, old friend—variety. With a phonograph you can purchase a stack of records and enjoy a variety of sounds and styles in music. With the telharmonium, you hear what is being played whether you enjoy it or not. I didn't have the heart to say this to Cahill myself, and I would hope that you do not either, Watson, should you further correspond with him to insure that your records of the case are accurate. The man has a dream. He needs the opportunity to try and fulfill it. It's why I took the case—so Cahill could build his dream."[18]

---

18 Editor's note: According to Watson's records, nothing more was ever heard of the missing telharmonium plans. Cahill's efforts to build the telharmonium were not delayed by the events in Butte that summer inasmuch as Glennon and Quinn had only copied his plans. Thaddeus Cahill was successful in raising investment capital to construct the telharmonium. The New York Electric Music Company was founded in the early 1900s and began selling subscriptions for music service, the predecessor of Muzak which fills the speakers of shopping centers and elevators with what is now termed "easy listening" music. Cahill's company failed. The instrument produced so much electricity that it created crosstalk between its distribution cables and adjacent telephone lines. The telharmonium faded from existence, the victim of its own technical deficiencies and successful competition from the phonograph, an invention which steadily improved as Holmes predicted it would, until it too was displaced by digital music available via compact disc or over the Internet.

The failure of Cahill's telharmonium was not, however, the end of producing music electrically. In 1934, Laurens Hammond patented the electric organ, an instrument which was to prove successful in both the household and commercial marketplace. The Hammond organ used tone wheel technology to create sound just like the telharmonium, although it did so by miniaturizing the technology so that it would fit within the cabinet of a small instrument that would fit comfortably in the living rooms of most American homes.

There is no evidence that Adam Hammond was in any way related to or had any association with Laurens Hammond. If Adam Hammond did, in fact, acquire the missing telharmonium plans in the final days of Holmes' investigation, there is no evidence that he did anything with them. The fact that Adam Hammond shared a last name with Laurens Hammond thirty years later must be considered a coincidence.

A Case of
Unrequited Love

It was a quiet and relaxing Sunday. Holmes had gone to Butte two days ago to look into a matter involving the theft of some silver bullion, but I had foregone the opportunity to participate when I heard that the case was likely to be plebian in nature and remained in Anaconda, Montana.

In England, Holmes would have never taken the case since it was clearly within the purview of Inspectors Lestrade or Gregson. But here in western Montana, Holmes felt a special obligation to our host Marcus Daly, President of the Anaconda Copper Mining Company, and took cases that were little more than a trifle for a man of his talent.

I attended Sunday services at St. Mark's Episcopal Church, a small chapel constructed of locally hewn sandstone, and followed that soul-refreshing moment by lunching with the St. Jean brothers, both of whom were medical men like myself. We then went to a baseball game featuring a team from Butte contesting a local nine. I rather like baseball. It's a far more lively game than our English cricket and seems to be more democratic in spirit. In the United Kingdom, cricket is played by gentlemen. In the United States, baseball is played by men from all walks of life. In the American west there is a convenient mixing of the social classes, very democratic and possibly very helpful in such a rugged land.

I had returned to the Montana Hotel, the billet for our stay in Anaconda, and was enjoying a cigar and snifter of brandy in the late afternoon when I happened to notice a most comely damsel make her way up the front steps of the hotel and enter the lobby. She wore a dark red dress which perfectly complimented her auburn hair. Upon closer inspection, she was no damsel. What I thought was youth was cosmetic in nature, and I assessed her to be a woman of my generation.[19]

As she approached the front desk, I turned back to my glass of brandy only to hear her ask the clerk for Sherlock Holmes. He responded, "Mr. Holmes is out, ma'am, but if you want to visit with his associate, Dr. Watson, that's him in the chair near the front window."

I heard the clap of her heels on the tile floor grow in crescendo as she neared me. I stood and faced her. "Madam, how can I be of service?" I asked.

"You are Dr. Watson?" she asked taking in the brandy and cigar.

"Indeed," I said and noticed that she hardly needed any cosmetics.

She seemed to hesitate and then replied abruptly. "I have a problem which requires Mr. Holmes' skill, a matter most delicate."

---

19 Editor's note: About 45 years of age.

"Unfortunately, madam, he has gone from the city, although I expect him to return tonight. May I take your name and I will send you a message when he returns?"

"What time do you expect him?" she asked. I was startled by her forwardness, which fell just short of impertinence.

"We have a dinner engagement with mutual friends at 7:00 p.m.," I answered, although I immediately questioned why I would divulge such information to a perfect stranger, comely though she may be.

"I'll return at 9:00 p.m. and meet you both here in the lobby." She then curtsied, an act most unusual in the United States, and glided out the front door.

Holmes was annoyed when I told him of my afternoon visitor, and the situation was made no better by me telling him that his prospective client was a "very attractive woman."

With the one exception of Miss Irene Adler,[20] Holmes was immune to the charms of the fairer sex, perhaps the only aspect of Holmes' character for which I felt sorry for him.

Our guest arrived promptly at 9:00 p.m. and Holmes quickly asked, "What may I do for a woman of your station?" I was used to Holmes' abruptness, but his manner here was cold.

"I need help with a most delicate problem," the lady replied.

"Madam, it is my vocation in life to fight evildoing and crime, not assist its propagation."

---

20 Editor's note: See "A Scandal in Bohemia," from *The Adventures of Sherlock Holmes*, originally published in *The Strand* magazine, July 1891.

I was shocked by Holmes' remarks. To suggest that a woman so fair could be involved in a criminal enterprise simply boggled my imagination.

Lady Fair replied promptly and with assurance. "How can you draw that conclusion after knowing me for less than a minute?" she asked.

"Quite easily," Holmes replied. In the next few seconds the powers of his observational skills would become apparent, and I, sadly, would be humbled by the erroneous conclusions I had drawn about her.

"First," Holmes said. "Your clothes are expensive and well-tailored, which purposefully displays your body to excellent effect. Likewise, your jewelry is also expensive but tastefully understated. That marks you either as a member of a noble family, the wife of a wealthy man, an heiress, or a successful business woman in your own right. Inasmuch as there is no wedding band on your left hand, there is and never has been a husband. Your speech marks you as an American, and while you possess great grace and charm, they are skills that you acquired later in life. One can learn posture, manners, and the fine art of conversation; few people can retrain the speech patterns or accents of their youth. You were raised in an Irish workingman's home in New England. Thus, you are not of noble birth, the wife of a rich man, nor an heiress.

"Second, your cosmetic use is expertly applied. It accentuates your natural beauty which is quite robust in its own right. The cosmetics mask the sallow pallor of your skin. You see little of the sun. Most business women, heiresses, and wives are about by day. You are a creature of the night.

"And finally, there is tobacco staining on your fingers.

You smoke cigarettes. When I add these three observations together," Holmes continued, "it is clear that you are indeed a successful business woman but one who operates a bordello. Is that not true madam, no pun intended?"

"You are quite correct, Mr. Holmes," answered the lady. She looked Holmes in the eyes. "You can be reassured that I had no intention of hiding my profession from you. In fact, it is the reason I am here, and I do not present myself before you to ask for your assistance in the conduct of my business. Rather, I need you to help me protect the reputation of a man very prominent in our government who made the mistake of making my acquaintance."

"I am sorry," Holmes began, "but I am—"

At that moment a group of about a dozen travelers entered the hotel lobby through the front door and disrupted our conversation. "Perhaps we should adjourn to the bar," I suggested.

"A woman would not be welcome there," answered our formidable female acquaintance, whose name we had not yet learned.

"They will make an exception in Mr. Holmes' case, once I explain that he is with a client and the lobby is not sufficiently private." At that point I temporarily absented myself to confer with the bartender.

We seated ourselves in a corner of the lounge, well away from the few men gathered at the bar, and ordered our drinks. The lady asked for sarsaparilla; Holmes and I, brandy.

At that point she retrieved a package of cigarettes from her handbag and lit up, exhaling the smoke into the air over Holmes' head, and with it dispelled any notion yet untarnished that she was a lady.

Holmes took out his pipe and lit it, without asking the woman for her permission. Then he took a sip of brandy. "Pray, please tell us how we can be of service," Holmes said. This was the calm, solicitous Holmes speaking, the side of him that I much admired.

At that point I interrupted. "We do not yet have the pleasure of knowing to whom we are speaking, Miss —."

"Miss Victoria Broderick, and I am known to all as Miss Victoria," she replied. "And, Mr. Holmes, you were correct in your earlier assessment of me. I am a New Englander by birth, the sixth of seven children born to a fisherman and later, a cannery worker. I own a small establishment, just six girls. We primarily cater to a professional class of men, few workingmen and no Negroes, Indians, or Chinese. My house, and the girls who work for me, are gentile in every respect."

Miss Victoria continued. "My current problem grew out of a trip that I took to San Francisco. I stayed at the Palace Hotel. There, I met a gentleman whose name I was familiar with from the newspapers. He is very much a self-made man with successful investments in many fields of enterprise and who has chosen to cap his career by being elected to the United States Senate. I speak of none other than Senator Sherman Price.[21]

"How did your introduction come about?" Holmes asked.

---

21 Editor's note: Sherman Price is a pseudonym. Watson's notes indicate that Miss Victoria would not reveal the Senator's name until Holmes and Watson had agreed to never disclose his name in any venue. Watson had himself used the name Price as an alias during his participation in a case known as "The Stockbroker's Clerk."

"I was dining with Mrs. Peter Padbury Klein. She is an old and dear friend whom I met while working in Deadwood. She left town, moved to Denver, and married well. Neither her husband nor her children know anything of her prior life."

"But Senator Price did," interjected Holmes.

"Yes," answered Miss Victoria. "He too was in Deadwood when we were there, but I never made his acquaintance. Since then, he has been a perfect gentleman throughout the years and protected her secret. While we were dining, the Senator entered the room and paused at our table to greet Mrs. Klein and she introduced us."

Miss Victoria stubbed out her cigarette and lit another. She continued her story. "I thought little of the incident until late the next afternoon when I received a note from the Senator inviting me to join him for dinner. Since I was uncommitted that evening, I accepted. Over the next four days I was his companion to the theater, horse races, and several meals. And, to be perfectly direct on the matter, I most emphatically did not share his bed. I enjoyed his company, nothing more. He is an engaging conversationalist and the exploits of his life are most interesting.

"After we said our goodbyes from what was, admittedly, a very fine time, I returned home to my business thinking that I would not see or hear from the Senator again. That proved to be a miscalculation on my part," Miss Victoria said as she stubbed out her second cigarette. "About four months later, I don't remember the exact day except that it was in early September, I received a letter from the Senator saying that he would be arriving in town to inspect some mines and talk with mine owners. He referred to it as 'a fact finding tour' in advance of hearings on proposed legislation affecting mining."

"You gave him your address?" Holmes asked.

"No, I did not," she replied. "At first, I was quite puzzled how he found me. Then, I recalled that when Mrs. Klein introduced me, she mentioned the city where I was living. I assume that he simply used the resources of his office to get my exact address.

"He arrived on October 9th. We spent three days together, again in a platonic manner. I did, however, encourage him to enjoy the connubial pleasures of my establishment, in part so that he would not have the energy to press the issue with me, and he pleased his senses with both Francesca and Valerie Ann.

"Four months later, the Senator returned again, but this time there was no 'fact finding mission.' He plainly told me that he missed my company. Again, we had three engaging days together and his physical needs were again met by Francesca and Valerie Ann, both of whom reported that he was quite robust in the physical expression of his masculinity."

Holmes took Miss Victoria's comment in stride. I, however, was shocked by her effrontery bordering on the edge of vulgarity.

"A week ago, I received a telegram from the Senator, saying that he was planning a return trip to town and wanted to see me. Actually, he said much more." Miss Victoria paused momentarily and looked straight at Holmes and said, "The Senator declared his love for me and said that he wanted to marry me."

I was stunned; so too was Holmes. The corner of his

mouth twitched involuntarily a couple of times, the only clue that the full impact of Miss Victoria's words had registered behind the otherwise implacable face he presented to her.

"When is he scheduled to arrive in Butte?" Holmes asked.

"He's not coming to Butte. He's coming to Wallace, Idaho.[22] That is where I reside."

Holmes busied himself for a few moments, withdrawing his pipe from his pocket and filling it with tobacco while Miss Victoria fished yet another cigarette from her handbag. Not to be left out, I withdrew a cigar from my breast pocket and when all three instruments of pleasure were aflame, Holmes continued the interview. "It seems to me, Miss Victoria, that you have all the means necessary to solve this problem yourself. Simply tell your suiter 'no,' and ask that he not contact you in the future."

"If it were that simple, Mr. Holmes, I would not have bothered you," Miss Victoria replied. "Telling the Senator 'no' is not the problem. I fear that the Senator's actions with me have come to the attention of his political adversaries who may either try to blackmail him or publicly humiliate him. That is why I have come to see you."

"Have you and the Senator been discreet?" Holmes asked.

"In Wallace, yes, but we openly kept company last year

---

22 Editor's note: Wallace is located in the panhandle of northern Idaho between Missoula, Montana and Spokane, Washington. It is the county seat of Shoshone County and sits in the middle of the Coeur d'Alene Mining District, the single largest silver producing area in the United States with over 1.2 billion ounces of silver mined in the area during the past 130 years.

when we were in San Francisco. Following the Senator's last visit, a man stopped one of my girls on the street and asked her if the Senator had gone home. She did not reply and told me about the event immediately thereafter. Presumably, the only people in town who knew the Senator was there were myself and my two girls. I have subsequently seen this man on the streets of Wallace near my establishment on several occasions. I believe that he is in the employ of one of the Senator's enemies and is in Wallace to keep a watchful eye on me to see if the Senator returns."

"What did he look like?" Holmes asked.

"He's average height with dark brown hair and moustache and wore a black hat and coat."

"Have you told the Senator?" Holmes inquired.

"Not directly," Miss Victoria answered. "I sent him a message through my friend, Mrs. Klein, the essence of which was that someone was monitoring his visits to Wallace and, further, it was imprudent for him to make any more visits to the Wallace area."

"Did you receive a reply?"

"Yes," Miss Victoria answered, "and he ignored my warning. In fact, he called Hillary, I mean Mrs. Klein, long distance on the telephone. My lord, can you imagine the expense involved in doing that? The Senator told her that 'no threat would deny him the woman he loved.'"

The Senator is married, I presume," Holmes said.

"Yes, with children, although they are all of the age of majority."

"So, you now find yourself being cast into the role of being a home wrecker," Holmes said with a touch of condescension in his voice.

"Yes," Miss Victoria answered. "It will certainly be depicted that way. I am of a mind, however, which says that if a man chooses to consort with whores, he is the home wrecker, not the working girl who earns a few dollars for fulfilling his desires. Society may not judge me such but, for myself, I do not fear society's opprobrium. There is no relationship between me and the Senator save a friendship. We have spent some time together in comfortable conversation. His love for me is totally unrequited. I have made a comfortable life for myself and have no desire to change it through matrimony. I have come to see you, Mr. Holmes, in the hope that you will return with me to Wallace, intercept the Senator, and use your considerable talent to help him see the folly of his actions and get him out of town. If that fails, then I need you to protect him from his enemies until he leaves the city—willingly or unwillingly."

Miss Victoria enumerated the word "unwillingly" in such a manner as to make clear her intention. Our conversation with her continued for another half hour, with Holmes' queries filling in some further details regarding her observations of the man she thought was following the Senator and how she accommodated the Senator in Wallace. As the conversation closed, Holmes said, "While you've given us an explanation of your lineage, Miss Victoria, I can't help observing that you are wearing a broach with the family crest of the McRae clan in Scotland. Perhaps a distant relation?"

Miss Victoria laughed and said, "I commend your knowledge of heraldic insignia, Mr. Holmes, but my possession of the broach has nothing to do with family bloodlines. My mother was a serving girl in the McRaes' manor house in Scotland. She financed her trip to America by stealing some of their jewels. Only two items are left of that legacy, my broach and another piece owned by a niece."

Holmes paused momentarily while he processed Miss Victoria's latest revelation. Her outspoken candor was remarkable. He looked at her and said, "I'm not in the habit of taking cases involving philandering husbands but will do so in this case, Miss Victoria, because your motives appear altruistic and the gentleman involved is a man of distinction. He does not need to have his reputation ruined even if it might be caused by his own indiscretions."

The next morning the three of us were aboard the train headed to Wallace, Idaho. As we neared our arrival, Miss Victoria explained that we were seeing the "new" Wallace. The original city had been almost completely destroyed by fire in 1890.[23] The community was located in a narrow canyon along the banks of the South Fork of the Coeur d'Alene River. I expected a town similar to Butte with the headframes of the mines dominating the landscape. Instead, the hills were covered with trees. Miss Victoria explained that most of the area mines were located in adjacent canyons and that Wallace, while home to many miners and mining companies, was the mercantile center of the region which the locals referred to as the Silver Valley. The town was currently at peace. There had been considerable labor conflict commencing in 1892 and occur-

---

23 Editor's note: Much of the city was again destroyed by fire in 1910 by a massive forest fire that consumed over three million acres of woodland in northern Idaho and western Montana. See *The Big Burn: Teddy Roosevelt and the Fire that Saved America* by Timothy Egan, Mariner Books, 2010.

SIXTH STREET, WALLACE, IDAHO

ring episodically thereafter, the barest outlines of which were known by me although Holmes was undoubtedly fully conversant on such matters.[24]

At Wallace we three disembarked separately. Holmes asked me to follow Miss Victoria at a discreet distance to observe whether anyone was monitoring her movements. In turn, she was instructed to move her parasol from one shoulder to the other if she encountered the man with the brown hair who was interested in the Senator. If he was

---

24 Editor's note: See *The Coeur d'Alene Mining War of 1892* by Robert Wayne Smith, Oregon State University Press, 1961, and *Coeur d'Alene Diary: The First Ten Years of Hardrock Mining in North Idaho* by Richard G. Magnuson, Binford and Mott Publishers, 1983.

discovered, I was to shift my surveillance to him and find out where he was living.

Our preparations proved unnecessary and Miss Victoria reached her business establishment without interruption. The mystery man was not seen. Holmes checked into the Carter House Hotel under an alias and I followed suit a few minutes later.

The next morning we walked about Wallace to get a better understanding of the town and its pattern of streets. The town was laid out in a grid pattern bordered on the north by the river and by steeply sided mountains to the south, with the business district concentrated in a small area around Bank, Cedar, Fifth and Sixth Streets. Miss Victoria's establishment was on Fifth Street midway between Pine and Cedar Streets. It was a nondescript, two-story red brick building, with a saloon on the ground floor to the east and grocery on the west. A doorway separated the two ground floor establishments and a stairway led up to Miss Victoria's place of business.

The town was much smaller than I expected with probably a thousand residents. It looked prosperous with seven hotels, two confectionaries, three bakeries, four grocery stores, three tobacco outlets, a brewery, and five saloons. I did not count the brothels. They were not evident during the day, but Miss Victoria later told me there were ten. I was amazed that there were more brothels than saloons.

We lunched with Miss Victoria at her establishment, making our entry through a rear door in the alley. Fortunately, the girls were not working at that hour and the house was quiet. We met Miss Victoria in her private quarters on a back corner of the building which overlooked a side street and the alley. A small bedroom was to the left of the entry hallway. The room was covered with a velvet, crimson wallpaper. A large dresser was just inside the door and, to my surprise, a single bed was pushed into the furthest corner of the room. It appeared as if Miss Victoria's representations about sleeping alone were honest. The parlor was at the end of the corridor. All I could see of that room was a divan pushed up against the wall below a high window which overlooked the alley.

She ushered us into her office across the hall from her bedroom. It was a windowless room that featured a heavy steel safe in the corner behind the door. Opposite the entryway was a large oak roll top desk with three oak chairs and a low table to its right. The desk was orderly with two short piles of paper thereon. On the wall to the left and above the desk was a rack holding a sawed-off shotgun and 30-caliber carbine. As I walked past her desk, I caught the gleam of a Colt revolver in the desk's top right-hand drawer. This was a woman committed to protecting what was hers. In addition to being well armed, the office was modern in every respect. A telephone was on the wall below the gun rack and a typewriter stood at the ready on the left side of the desk. Unfortunately, the right side was occupied by a large ashtray overflowing with cigarette butts and the room reeked with the smell of stale tobacco smoke, not the most inviting environment in which to eat lunch. Holmes, of course, showed no sign of distress, equally at home in a den of pickpockets, a whorehouse in Idaho, or a drawing room in Buckingham Palace.

After finishing our luncheon with Miss Victoria, Holmes asked to speak with the two women with whom the Senator had spent companionable interludes.

We met first with Francesca, a stunningly beautiful woman with long, lustrous jet black hair, an olive complexion, and dazzling brown eyes. She was relaxed and projected a naiveté which, I was to soon learn, was not naiveté at all, but stupidity.

Holmes started the conversation with some small talk to get her comfortable in his presence by asking how she had come to Wallace.

Francesca answered by saying, "On a train." Holmes, thrown back by the nature of her answer, sought to further explain his question by asking where she had lived before coming to Wallace.

Francesca said, "A lot of places. I don't remember their names."

The small talk was over so Holmes bluntly asked, "I understand you have entertained the Senator."

Francesca responded by first looking confused and then blurting out, "I don't do nothing with Senators. I am not that kind of girl. I only go with men."

I could see the frustration rising in Holmes when he replied, "Senator is his title, like Mister, or Missus for a woman. Do you recall a tall, thin man with a bald head and long gray beard?"

"No," she replied, "but he sure sounds nice."

Holmes continued, "I was given to understand that you had entertained him this past February."

"I don't remember things from a long time ago," Francesca responded, to which Holmes countered by saying, "Thank you for your time, Francesca. May I wish you a very good day?"

We departed Francesca's bedroom and made our way

MISS VALERIE ANN

to the one occupied by Valerie Ann. There couldn't have been a sharper contrast between the two women. Valerie Ann was tall, slender yet buxom, with reddish-blonde hair and lively blue eyes. She wasn't exceptionally pretty, but she projected energy and sadness at the same time. Her confident air reminded me of my wife Mary Marston, a woman who thought herself the equal of any man. She was reclining against the headboard of her bed, braced by a gaggle of pillows. I liked her immediately.

Holmes wasn't about to waste time on small talk. His mouth was pursed together and his movements brusque. He wanted to get something settled and asked, "Miss Victoria explained the purpose of our visit?" to which Valerie Ann nodded yes in reply.

Holmes continued, "I understand that you have entertained the Senator on two occasions?"

"Yes," Valerie Ann answered. "He is a most energetic and vigorous man, particularly given his advancing years. I would say that he was the equal of most men half his age." She then paused momentarily, looked toward me and then back to Holmes and finished by saying, "I enjoyed his company, and I say that of very few men."

"Did the Senator talk with you while he was here?" Holmes asked.

"Certainly, all men do," Valerie Ann answered. "Some seem compelled to explain why they are cavorting with a girl of my reputation. Others are simply hungry for some softer companionship.

"I have one customer, and a young man at that, who visits me every week and never touches me. All he wants to do is talk with a woman and imbibe of her scent. His loneliness must be excruciating."

Holmes seemed disinterested in her analysis and pushed on. "What did the Senator talk about?"

"What all men talk about in Wallace—mining. Some want to talk about hunting. Why a man would ever want to talk to a woman about hunting is beyond me, although I harbor the personal belief that it's to prove to themselves they are powerful men in both the bedroom and out there in the big raw world, even though they are largely common men of no distinction in the community."

Holmes' cynical side flashed for a moment by his saying, "Thank you for that most thoughtful insight into the character of the western American male. Now, would you care to be more specific about what the Senator said about mining?"

Valerie Ann yawned, and after excusing herself said, "They were mostly stories about his experience in the mines years ago. There was a comment or two about who he was going to see while he was in town. One of the fellows was at the Hecla Mine in Burke and the other two work for Bunker Hill in Wardner. Miss Victoria knows both of them very well and she can give you more information."

"Did the Senator say anything about investing in mining property?" Holmes asked.

"He's too late for that, I would think," Valerie Ann answered. "All the good properties are taken and have been so for years. The Senator knows that."

Valerie Ann continued. "Being here in Wallace, I have come to appreciate that there are three types of miners. The first type is the prospector. He's a dreamer in search of the fabled bonanza and when he finally discovers a rich pay streak he also discovers that he doesn't have the capital to actually develop the mine, so he sells out cheap to the second type—the capitalist—and then the prospector moves over the next ridge line or down the road to the next district to rekindle the dream. The Senator was a dreamer when he was a young man, but also one fortunate in his choice of friends, and he was able to attract the capital necessary to make him a capitalist.

"The capitalist is a businessman, and as a businessman he knows that he must produce his ounces of silver and pounds of lead at a cost below the market price of those metals or his business is gone in a flash of bankruptcy. Unlike every other business person in the valley, be it Miss Victoria running this whorehouse, the barkeeper pushing drinks across the plank, or the hardware store owner selling nails, bolts and tools, the mine owner has no control whatsoever over the sale price of the metal he produces. Miss Victoria can raise or lower the price of a woman at will, as can the barkeeper with his whiskey. Not so, however, for the mine owner. All he can do to succeed in his business is control his operating costs. Mine owners are singularly obsessed with cutting costs. Cost control is their destiny and because the miners and mill hands, in a word—labor—make up the largest cost component in producing silver and lead, the mine owners are very resistive to increased wages and will, whenever possible, try to cut them, which is why this valley broke out into open warfare between the miners and mine owners a few years ago. It's why things are still very tense, although that might not be visible to outsiders like yourself."

"A most interesting exposition on the economics of silver mining, Valerie Ann," Holmes declaimed. "I find it hard to believe that a mine owner would bare his financial soul while in his skivvies talking with a—" Holmes paused, realizing that he had just talked himself into a corner where the next word he uttered would be insulting.

"I believe the word you are looking for, Mr. Holmes, is trollop," Valerie Ann said graciously. "And, you are quite correct, the mine owners didn't provide me with that education. I got it from their superintendents, foremen, and bookkeepers. That young man I talked about earlier who simply comes here to converse is one of the mine's accountants."

Holmes was embarrassed. "Please forgive me for that last remark. My rudeness was unconscionable. Pray, please tell us about the third type of miner," Holmes added, wishing to move this conversation to its closure.

After accepting Holmes' apology, Valerie Ann said, "The third type of miner is the working man, one who needs a job to earn a living. A lot of today's paid miners started out with a dream of making it big in the gold fields, but reality crushed their hopes and now they work underground because it's the highest paying job they can find. The prospectors left Wallace a decade ago. The capitalists control the mines, and the miners work for them."

"And you serve them," I added.

"Not to any great extent, Dr. Watson. Miss Victoria attracts a high class clientele. The only miners who attend us here are those who exhibit the deportment and education of a gentleman. Also, most of the working men who frequent a bawdy house want to feel "in command" and superior to the girl they are using. I don't tend to elicit that type of response in my customers, although I do try to be pleasant to whomever Miss Victoria selects for me."

Holmes more humbly observed, "Your insight into the male condition is most profound, Valerie Ann. I am truly surprised that a woman of your obvious capacity has entered this profession."

"It wasn't a real choice, Mr. Holmes," Valerie Ann replied with bitterness in her voice. "My life is not your concern, is it, Mr. Holmes?"

Holmes demurred and quietly said, "No, it's not."

Miss Valerie Ann nodded and then said, "In answer to your question, I am here because I was orphaned at age fifteen and was in a place where I had no other way of surviving. I view this occupation as a temporary station in life. I am saving my money and hope to open my own business somewhere far from the Coeur d'Alenes.[25] And when I say a business, I mean a legitimate business, not another brothel."

"I understand that you were the first person to see or meet the individual who seems to be watching the Senator," Holmes said.

"Yes. I've seen him on several occasions, always near the railroad station. He seems to be monitoring both the westbound Northern Pacific coming from Missoula and the Union Pacific coming east from Spokane. He only stays long enough to see who gets off the train and then leaves."

"Thank you, Valerie Ann, and please excuse my earlier conduct," Holmes said. "It's been a very helpful conversation." With that Holmes rose and turned toward the door with me in his wake. Then he suddenly turned back toward the lady and asked, "If the Senator is not here to look for investment opportunities in mining, why perchance do you believe that he repeatedly comes back to Wallace?"

"I do not know, sir," came her swift reply. She too then rose to her feet from the bed and said, "Perhaps Miss Victoria can answer your inquiry. I believe she has known the Senator for twenty-some years going back to when they were both in Deadwood. They appear to be friends, and I use that word in the customary sense. Whenever the Senator is in town, he eats supper with Miss Victoria in her parlor and they talk into the night. Sometime around 10:00 p.m. he will take a girl for a couple of hours while Miss Victoria looks to the affairs of the house. Then, he returns to her parlor for a final drink with her before returning to his hotel."

---

25 Editor's note: Valerie Ann's reference here was to the Coeur d'Alene Mountains in northern Idaho where Wallace is located.

"Again, thank you," Holmes said, once more turning toward the exit. He then stopped by a dressing table covered with grease paint and the powders women the world over use to enhance their natural charms and said, "A most beautiful necklace, Australian opal and quite valuable, I am sure."

"Yes," replied Valerie Ann. "A family keepsake. If I could will myself to sell it, I wouldn't need to prostitute my body, but I cannot part with it." With that comment we finally said our goodbyes.

We returned briefly to Miss Victoria's office and made our plan for the day. She was to patrol the streets outside the railroad depot to see if she could locate the man shadowing the Senator and, again, I was to follow him if he made an appearance. In turn, Holmes would place himself inside the depot pretending to be a departing passenger and would clandestinely slip the Senator a note telling him where to meet us that evening.

Everything went according to plan. Miss Victoria found the mystery man and I trailed him while he followed the Senator to the Carter House Hotel. Holmes and I had taken rooms there as well, so contacting the Senator would be quite easy. From there, the subject of my surveillance walked east, stopped to buy some tobacco and then seemed to aimlessly walk the streets, perhaps just seeking some exercise, before returning to a rooming house on Cedar Street. I paused in my travels to window shop for a few minutes and give the subject of my pursuit time to return to his room so that I could enter the lodging and talk with the proprietor.

The proprietor was a plump, pleasant looking lady in her mid-forties who was sitting at a typewriter drafting a letter. She introduced herself to me as Mrs. Lawlor, and I to her as John Wordsworth, an alias I made up on the spot. I told her that I had been walking on Bank Street and saw an individual whom I thought I recognized as an old friend, Reggie Pemberton by name, whom I had last seen in the diamond fields of South Africa. He appeared to have entered this house. "Would that have been him I saw come through your front door a few minutes ago?" I asked.

"Heavens no, Mr. Wordsworth," replied Mrs. Lawlor. "The man who just entered before you is Mr. Daniel Sloan, from San Francisco."

I made my apology for taking her from her work and departed with the name of my quarry. Holmes was in his hotel room where I relayed the information which I had gathered. From there we walked over to the Western Union office so that Holmes could cable his contact in the Pinkerton Agency for information on Daniel Sloan. We then returned to the Carter House and knocked on the Senator's door.

The Senator greeted Holmes effusively. I was surprised but not shocked. How he and Holmes knew one another I did not know, but I am always surprised at whom Holmes knows personally—not just in the United Kingdom, but in Australia, Canada, South Africa, and especially the United States.

Holmes introduced me after which the Senator offered us a glass of whiskey from the bottle resting on the writing table. When the spirits had been poured he asked Holmes, "How is my friend Marcus Daly?"

Holmes replied, "The Anaconda Company is prospering, but there is no end to the political intrigue in the back rooms of Butte's hotels and saloons. There is a constant tug-of-war between Mr. Daly and his nemesis Mr. Clark, whom you know so well. As you might imagine, Mr. Daly took the loss of the state capital fight[26] quite personally, and he looks for opportunities to punish Clark."

"I can sympathize," said the Senator. "Clark can be a most difficult individual and I have come to realize that with Clark, a compromise means that he gets everything he wants and you get nothing."

"Senator, you have admirably summarized the character of the man," Holmes replied.

"There is a rumor that Clark will seek a Senate seat from Montana in the next election."

"Indeed," answered Holmes, "and it will be a hard fought battle."

"How do you see the contest?" the Senator asked.

"Without question, Daly will find a way to thwart Clark's ambitions.[27]

The Senator nodded in reply, but I sensed a sigh of relief with the prospect that Clark would not succeed in reaching the U.S. Senate.

---

26 Editor's note: In 1892, Montana voters went to the polls to select the site of the permanent capital for the State of Montana. Seven cities were in contention. No city received a majority. A runoff election was held in 1894. The City of Helena, backed by Clark, won the election over the City of Anaconda, which Daly had favored and which was the site of the great copper smelter he built there.

27 Editor's note: In 1899, W.A. Clark was elected to the United States Senate by the Montana Legislature amid charges of corruption and bribery. The U.S. Senate refused to seat Clark because of his role in the bribery of state legislators. Clark was re-elected to the Senate in 1901 and served a single term through 1907. When criticized for his bribery scheme, Clark is reported to have said, "I never bought a man who wasn't for sale." Clark's rival, Marcus Daly, had died in 1900 and was not present in Montana to thwart Clark's political ambition.

"Why have you come to see me, Mr. Holmes?"

"Information has reached the ears of your friends that you might be in some kind of danger."

"What kind of danger?"

"The kind of danger that destroys a political career," answered Holmes. "Questions are being raised about the propriety of your recent conduct."

"I am baffled by that insinuation," said the Senator. "I do not take bribes. My vote is not for sale."

"Pardon me, Senator," said Holmes. "I thought that since we were holding this conversation in Wallace, Idaho, the issue of propriety would be abundantly clear."

"You mean my business here."

"Indeed, but neither your mining nor political business, rather your business with a certain businesswoman in town."

The Senator looked dumbfounded, then drained his whiskey in one gulp. "There is no fool like an old fool, Mr. Holmes."

"This is not about your age or the fact that you might be looking for some excitement away from the marital bed. It has everything to do with her profession. A man may be forgiven a dalliance that becomes public, but a man of your position cannot be seen pandering with whores." Holmes' statement was defiant and there was no room for misinterpreting what he had said.

"I've pandered with whores in Nevada, California, the Black Hills, and Washington, D.C.," responded the Senator.

"But with more discretion than it is rumored you are using now."

"Mr. Holmes, we seem to be talking around the issue.

Let us put the matter squarely before us."

"As you wish, Senator. I will try not to be insulting."

"Please."

"Senator, information has been received that you have developed an attachment to one Miss Victoria Broderick that goes well beyond what usually transpires with such women."

"Most assuredly that is the case," replied the Senator, "and my intentions with Miss Victoria are entirely honorable. You may not believe this, but our relationship is entirely chaste. She is the most intelligent and engaging woman I have ever met and she has captured my heart."

Senator," answered Holmes sternly. "Your intentions are not what the public will judge. You will be castigated for publicly consorting with a whore. Your behavior would be considered unacceptable for a single man in your position, but since you are married, it will be judged as utterly reprehensible."

"I realize what she is, Mr. Holmes, and I have a plan to deal with that. I am going to move her from Idaho to Baltimore where she will develop a new identity and a new look before anything becomes public between us."

"Senator, if I know about your relationship with Miss Victoria, so too do others who are not likely to have your best interests at heart. We already believe that one of your enemies has an agent in Wallace."

"You are correct on that point," the Senator said. "That's why I found it so fortuitous that you wanted to see me. I am being blackmailed. Let me show you a note that was delivered to me this day." The Senator reached inside the breast pocket of his jacket and brought out a piece of paper and handed it to Holmes, who read it and passed it on to me.

The note was typewritten and said:

> *Senator,*
>
> *I know about you and Miss Victoria. Pay me $5,000 and I will say nothing. If not, I will contact the newspapers. You have three days to collect the money. I will send further instructions in three days' time.*

Holmes looked at the envelope and said, "It was posted here in Wallace. So it came from someone in town or you were followed."

"What shall I do, Mr. Holmes?" the Senator asked.

"For now, nothing, and nothing includes no contact with Miss Victoria until this matter is disposed of."

Holmes and I took our leave and quietly ambled over to Jameson's Saloon where we each ordered a glass of beer. I could see that Holmes' mind was wheeling with thought and I was anxious to discover what he was thinking so I asked, "What are your thoughts regarding the blackmail note?"

He paused for a moment and said, "You know I don't like to speculate, Watson, but I see four possibilities. First, the note could have come from Mr. Sloan, who would appear to be shadowing the Senator. Second, it could have come from Miss Victoria herself, but I feel that unlikely. If she wanted to extract money from him, the simple thing to do would have been to ask. In his frame of mind he's fool enough to grant her, her wish. Also, if she were involved, I question why she would come to us and ask our assistance. Third, someone in Wallace knows of the Senator's interest in Miss Victoria and wants to profit from it.

She said they've been very discreet, but who knows who, and how many people, the Senator may have informed willingly or unwillingly. And fourth, another party from the outside, like Sloan, has gotten wind of the Senator's amorous adventures and has followed him here to exploit the situation."

"What is to be done, Holmes?" I asked. "Sloan seems the most obvious perpetrator."

"Exactly," Holmes responded. "That's why I doubt he is the one. We need to get Mr. Sloan safely out of the picture. When that is done, we'll be able to deal with the various other possibilities."

"How do you propose to do that?"

"By getting him thrown into jail. Enough discussion for now. I need to call Sheriff Fitzpatrick back in Anaconda, and to do that I need to find a private telephone. The matter is much too complex for a cable. Then I'll need a disguise— something that will allow me to fit in as a new lodger in Mrs. Lawlor's boarding house." Holmes stood up in preparation for leaving the bar, then turned back to me and said, "Watson, you have a window facing Bank Street. I expect that Sloan will make another appearance about dinnertime so he can follow the Senator's movements this evening. When Sloan appears, notify me so I can get over to his boarding house while he's away."

Sloan appeared as predicted. Holmes then disappeared down the back stairs of the hotel, telling me that he would see me in the morning.

In the morning, per Holmes' instructions, I again watched the street outside the hotel for Sloan. He didn't disappoint, appearing a little after eight o'clock and taking up position a few doors down the street opposite the hotel entrance where he leaned against a store front and lit up a small cigar.

A few minutes later I saw a man with a full beard making his way down the street. I assumed it was Holmes dressed in one of his many disguises to effect the notion that he was a common miner or mill hand. He pulled a cigar out of his coat pocket, stopped before Sloan and asked for a match. Sloan was happy to oblige and soon lit Holmes' cigar. Holmes, in turn, gave him a nod of appreciation and returned to his walk.

Soon after Holmes rounded the corner, two deputies arrived in front of Sloan, talked with him a minute, then put him in handcuffs and led him away, I presumed to the sheriff's office.

Holmes momentarily reappeared and then was lost to my view as he returned to the hotel via its rear entrance. Fifteen minutes later he was in my room dressed in classic Holmesian attire.

"What did I just see happen?" I asked.

"Sheriff Fitzpatrick called his counterpart here with Shoshone County this morning to say that a man wanted for the theft of several thousand dollars in bearer bonds had been seen in Wallace. He then described me as a Pinkerton agent who would point out the thief. The sheriff was asked to apprehend and hold the thief pending extradition back to Montana."

"Where are the bonds?" I asked.

"In a dresser drawer in Mr. Sloan's room at the boarding house, where I hid them last night. When we get back to Montana the portrait of a new reality will be painted for

Mr. Sloan. Once he sees the artwork, he can choose to forget everything he ever knew about the Senator or take his
chances with a jury. I am certain he will develop memory
problems rather quickly."

"Brilliant, Holmes, elegant yet simple. And now?" I
asked.

"We have breakfast, enjoy a walk about this pleasant
little town, and return to Miss Victoria's establishment and
conclude this sorry matter."

We arrived at Miss Victoria's about mid-afternoon and
requested an audience with the Madam and Valerie Ann in
Miss Victoria's private parlor. It was a beautifully appointed
room with floral wallpaper consisting of several different
varieties of red, white, pink, and yellow roses intermixed
with green leaves over a light beige background. Two divans
and two overstuffed chairs covered in brown leather created a delightful seating area, punctuated by end tables upon
which were burnished brass lamps with Tiffany leaded glass
lamp shades.

After taking our respective places, with Holmes in a
chair and me in a divan opposite Miss Victoria and Valerie
Ann, Holmes began what I can only describe as a frontal
assault. "Why, Valerie Ann, did you send the Senator a note
demanding five thousand dollars in hush money?"

"I have no idea what you are speaking about, Mr.
Holmes." Valerie Ann's response was assured, and she
looked Holmes right in the eyes as she said it.

Holmes persisted. He pulled out the note which the
Senator had received. "This note was typed on the typewriter in Miss Victoria's office, and she has already informed me
that you know how to type."

Valerie Ann kept her composure. "If anyone typed that note in this building, it was probably her." She then turned her head toward Miss Victoria with an accusatory glare.

"You're making this much more difficult than it needs to be," said Holmes. "If you persist in your denials, I will turn this matter over to the sheriff and you will end up in prison. You know full well that Miss Victoria has no need to use blackmail to extract five thousand dollars from the Senator. All she has to do is ask. So what is your answer now, Valerie Ann? A confession to clarify and conclude this pesky little matter of blackmail, or an opportunity to discuss the issue with the sheriff?"

After some hesitation, Valerie Ann admitted she had sent the note to the Senator the previous morning before we met with her. Holmes then asked, "Why did you take that step?"

"Why else?" came a defiant reply. "For the money. I don't yet have enough money to start my business, and once Miss Victoria left the house to be with the Senator, I would be at the mercy of the next owner. I want out of this sordid mess and I thought I saw a way."

"Poor child. I would never do that to you," Miss Victoria said. "In the first place, I am not interested in getting out of the business. I want to get rid of the Senator. But even if I had wanted to start a new life with him, I wouldn't leave you here alone."

"So there is some affinity for your niece after all," Holmes remarked.

"You know about that!" Miss Victoria answered strongly as a look of anger flashed across her face and she turned to face Valerie Ann.

Holmes continued. "Valerie Ann never revealed your relationship with her. You did when you told me about the jewelry containing the crest of the McRae family, and more specifically, that you owned the broach and a niece had a necklace. I saw the necklace in Valerie Ann's room yesterday."

"Yes, Mr. Holmes, Valerie Ann is my niece," the madam admitted.

"I shudder to ask this of you, Miss Victoria, but did you bring your niece into this business?"

"She did!" answered Valerie Ann very forcefully. "I needed help after my parents died and she said she 'needed help' in her business. This life is not a choice I would have made had I been free to make a choice."

"There is a simple way of resolving this situation for the benefit of all concerned," Holmes said. "First, I am going to tell the Senator that the blackmail threat has been removed, and in exchange for no charges being brought against you, Valerie Ann, you are going to agree that you will never utter a single word about the Senator's relationship with Miss Victoria. The Senator has done you no harm."

"No!" answered Valerie Ann sharply. "If I am going to make that commitment, then I am walking out of this room with two things. One, I am finished with this filthy business; and two, my dear aunt is going to provide me with a going away present sufficient to allow me to start my business. I need three thousand dollars. Heaven knows she's made much more than that peddling my body."

"Miss Victoria?" Holmes asked.

The madam said "yes," but with some considerable reluctance.

"Get her the money now," Holmes ordered, and Miss Victoria went down the hall to her office and returned with a bundle of greenbacks and several twenty dollar gold pieces.

Valerie Ann took the money and disappeared from the room, then doubled back from the doorway and said, "Thank you, Mr. Holmes, Dr. Watson. Goodbye Aunty, I wish you no harm." Miss Victoria said nothing in reply.

At that point Holmes and I made our exit. Outside on the street, I said to Holmes, "You've had an active day, my friend. First jailing Sloan who is a political threat of some type to the Senator, then solving the blackmail demand, and freeing a young woman from the worst sort of bondage—prostitution. But, you've yet to solve the original problem that we came to Wallace to detect—removing the Senator from Miss Victoria's life."

Holmes was undisturbed. He said, "We'll resolve that matter tonight around 9:00 p.m. Now if you will excuse me, Watson, I have some cables to send. Brother Mycroft has a matter he wishes to consult with me about."

That evening we dined with the Senator, who was greatly appreciative of Holmes' efforts to remove the threats which had entered his life. The Senator was equally determined to see Miss Victoria that evening. Holmes demurred, telling him that the house was in turmoil over the departure of Valerie Ann and Miss Victoria was not going to open for business until after eight o'clock. Holmes suggested that the Senator go over around nine o'clock after Miss Victoria got things running smoothly.

Holmes and I accompanied the Senator on his walk to the establishment. As we turned the corner onto Fifth

Street, we could see that the building was surrounded by law enforcement officers. The girls were being led out of the building and put in a paddy wagon. Miss Victoria came out last, and at the foot of the stairs leading to her bordello a photographer took her picture.

The next day, the newspaper headlined a story entitled "Brothel Discovered Operating in City." It went on to describe that the police had raided the establishment and closed it down. Underneath the headline was a picture of Miss Victoria. Holmes noted that the wire service had undoubtedly sent the story with Miss Victoria's picture coast to coast.[28]

"Such hypocrisy," I retorted. "They didn't raid the other nine whorehouses in town. Why close her down now?"[29]

"Because they were instructed to do so by the powers that be," said Holmes casually. "Powers far larger than you and I, Watson, who care about the Senator's future. The Senator can no longer live with the illusion that he can take Miss Victoria out of Wallace, give her a new biography on the east coast, and then retire from public life with her as his wife. Her face is now everywhere, and his infatuation will soon be over."

After breakfast, Holmes received a telegram from the

---

28 Editor's note: Watson's notes indicate that Holmes had arranged the police raid on Miss Victoria's house of ill repute and, further, took steps to insure Miss Victoria's photograph went national. The *Coeur d'Alene Press* and *Spokesman-Review*, the two largest papers in the region, carried her picture a few days after the raid on her establishment.

29 Editor's note: Prostitution thrived, then survived in Wallace for over one hundred years. The last brothel in town, the U and I Rooms, closed in September 1990.

Pinkerton office in San Francisco regarding Sloan,[30] not that it now mattered. It said:

> *Mr. Sloan:*
>
> *Political operative.*
>
> *Currently attached to Senator Perkins.*
>
> *Consider unfriendly.*

Holmes, the Senator, and I all boarded the Union Pacific that afternoon for a short journey to Spokane, Washington where we would make further connections, the Senator to return to Washington, D.C. and Holmes and I back to Montana. The Senator was disconsolate, but his public reputation and political future were intact.

On our way to the station we observed a line of young women making their way back into the front door of Miss Victoria's house. Holmes hung back just a bit and whispered to me, "She'll be back in business tonight, the surge of moral outrage lasting less than twenty-four hours."

After finding our seats, the Senator excused himself to go talk with another fellow at the other end of the coach, and I asked Holmes, "I am puzzled by Miss Victoria's behavior in this entire affair. Was she really concerned about

---

30 Editor's note: According to Watson's notes, Sloan was taken back to Anaconda, Montana where he was given a choice, face charges for theft or abandon politics and get an honest job. Sloan opted for the second alternative and was given a job at the smelter in Anaconda where he stayed for several years. According to Watson, the bearer bonds which Sloan had been accused of stealing were in fact forgeries, a "theatrical prop" as Holmes liked to call them, but very productive for getting someone out of the way.

the Senator, or was it just about herself?"

"Who can discern what really goes on in the mind of the female of the species, Watson? I believe her motives were selfish, and not the least bit altruistic. Although she enjoyed the Senator's company—a respite perhaps from her usual interaction with men—she had no desire to leave her business, a point Miss Victoria made clear at the start of this case. She has become a very rich woman. Sooner or later her relationship with the Senator would have become known, and given Mr. Sloan's watchful presence, it likely would have come sooner. Once the scandal broke it would have drawn far too many eyes upon her business from all over the nation. Prostitution only exists with the tenuous sufferance of the police and the citizenry, and you can be certain that the politicians who inhabit Boise[31] would not hesitate to throw Miss Victoria to the wolves to protect the State's reputation. It's the powers that be, Watson, the powers that be."

---

31 Editor's note: Boise is the state capital of Idaho.

The Case of the Dastardly Deed

As much as I enjoy participating in Holmes' adventures, they exhaust me. I am a man regular of habit, and frequently find the hustle and bustle of Holmes' detective practice difficult to accommodate. Holmes, on the other hand, has a mercurial temperament and moves with the wind, without a schedule, and seemingly without any concern about what the next moment will bring. The air of nonchalance which Holmes affects is an act. His mind is always engaged, always anticipating the future, and always planning his next move. I find it rather astounding that we get along so well, our fundamental temperaments being so different.

As we boarded the train to leave Wallace, Idaho, having successfully dealt with the case I titled "A Case of Unrequited Love," I looked forward to a quiet passage back to Montana from whence we had come a few days earlier, allowing me time to catch up with my reading of the newspapers and, finally, to finish reading *A Connecticut Yankee in King Arthur's Court* which I had started a week prior. Since coming to the States I had immersed myself in American literature and had become quite fond of Mark Twain's writings.

It was not to be. On the train, Holmes was silent, almost taciturn, and, from experience, I took his disinterest in communication to indicate that he was thinking about some problem of which I had no knowledge. We arrived in Spokane, Washington in the mid-afternoon and took rooms in the Nagel House Hotel followed by dinner in the Manhattan Restaurant, a short walk from our hotel. I suggested to Holmes that we partake of an evening at the theater but he refused me by saying, "Not this evening, Watson. We have a meeting at 7:00 p.m. with Mr. Daniel C. Corbin.[32]"

"Who is he?" I inquired.

"A friend of Daly's,"[33] Holmes answered. "I received a telegram from Daly in Wallace last night. He asked that we meet with Corbin on some trifle."

Holmes doesn't work on trifles. He's got another case that will lead us only the Lord knows where. Well, so much for rest and relaxation.

Corbin was punctual and was accompanied by Mr. Henry Richards, whom Corbin described as a business associate.

---

32 Editor's note: Daniel C. Corbin was a railway builder and entrepreneur. Born in New Hampshire, he moved to Nebraska in the 1850s where he started a freighting business. He reached Montana in the mid-1860s and began a career of investing in mines and constructing short line railroads which linked the mines with the transcontinental railroads, particularly the Northern Pacific. In 1889, he moved to Spokane, Washington where he built railroads to serve the Coeur d'Alene Mining District in northern Idaho and the Kootenai region of British Columbia.

33 Editor's Note: Marcus Daly was a founder and President of the Anaconda Copper Mining Company. Daly knew Corbin through the latter's interest in the Helena Mining and Reduction Company which operated a lead and silver smelter near Wickes, Montana.

Corbin was slight of build with gray hair, gray moustache and goatee, and dark penetrating eyes. I judged him to be a man of energy. Corbin had foresworn the day's business attire and was comfortably dressed in dark pants and a white shirt with no tie or jacket. In contrast, Richards was attired in a charcoal colored wool suit noticeable for the excellence of its cut and the quality of its weave and, no doubt, uncomfortably warm on a day when the temperature had reached over ninety degrees Fahrenheit. He was a robust man whom I judged to be in his fifties with a receding hairline, sharply pointed nose, and a gray moustache to match the shade of his hair.

Holmes took Richards' hand in his and said, "I see that you are with the local electric light company."

"How could you possibly know that?" asked Richards while giving Holmes a broad smile.

"I observed that your shoes are wet. Dressed as you are in that fine suit, I doubt that you were watering the flowers of your wife's garden or fishing on the river. Since there has not been any rain in recent days to leave water in the streets, I deduced that you had recently visited one of the hydro-electric plants along the river edge before making your way to our lodgings."

"Uncanny, Mr. Holmes," Richards replied, "and completely accurate. I am, indeed, a business associate of Mr. Corbin, acting in the capacity of President of the Washington Water Power Company. Mr. Corbin is a major shareholder and I was at one of our generating plants, the Monroe Street Station, immediately before coming to your hotel. Your powers of observation are truly extraordinary."

"The world is full of obvious things which few people

DANIEL C. CORBIN,
Investor and Entrepreneur

observe," Holmes replied. Pausing for a moment to let Corbin and Richards drink in what he had said, Holmes continued. "I trust, that it's you who has need of my services Mr. Richards, not Mr. Corbin."

"Correct again, Holmes," answered Corbin, who had taken up residence in a chair to Holmes' left. "Our mutual friend, Marcus Daly, regaled me with the story of how you saved his prize race horse.[34] When Richards described the problem which has beset our business, I knew that you were

---

34 Editor's note: See "The Tammany Affair" in *Sherlock Holmes: The Montana Chronicles,* Riverbend Publishing, 2008.

the right man to help us sort out this dismal affair."

"Pray," Holmes responded, "please be seated, Mr. Richards, and give me the particulars of your problem."

Richards sat down next to Holmes on his right and I completed the circle by drawing up in between Corbin and Richards. Corbin was impatient, his hands in a constant state of flux. In contrast, Richards was composed. He paused for several seconds to collect his thoughts and finally said, "The matter that I bring to you today, Mr. Holmes, is a problem facing the Washington Water Power Company, not me in a personal sense. Our company was formed in 1889 to develop the immense hydropower potential presented by the Spokane Falls which are located just a couple of blocks north of your hotel. The company currently has two generation sites, one near Monroe Street which I mentioned previously, and another where Post Street meets the river. We've had these sites for several years and have invested quite heavily in the construction of our generation facilities—over a million dollars to date."

After pausing to unbutton his coat and loosen his necktie, Richards continued. "A week ago last Monday I received a visitor in my offices, a man by the name of Chester Parkinson. He said that he came to talk to me about the Post Street Station. I said, 'In what way can I help you, Mr. Parkinson?' He answered by saying, 'There is a small problem with that facility. You've built it on my property.'

"I was dumbfounded by his allegations, Mr. Holmes, but kept my composure and said, 'You are mistaken, Mr. Parkinson. The company acquired that parcel from the Nettleton family and their associates.'"

"Parkinson then responded by me by saying, 'I am well

aware of that transaction, Mr. Richards, and there is no problem with it except for the fact that W. H. Kotter, who sold the land to the Nettletons and Cochrans, also sold the same land to me three months previous.'

"I couldn't believe my ears, Mr. Holmes. We've had title issues with some of the properties along the river and always worked to clear title. Then, out of the blue sky, this Parkinson walks in with a claim that Kotter sold the property twice within a three-month period of time."

"It's preposterous, Holmes!" Corbin exclaimed, almost at a shout. "This Parkinson is a fraud. I know old Kotter and he is as honest as the day is long."

"Having described the problem to you, Mr. Richards, I am certain that Mr. Parkinson had an idea for a monetary solution to the matter," Holmes said.

"Of course, Mr. Holmes," Richards answered. "Yes, he said that his business affairs were elsewhere and he was simply interested in selling the parcel. He told me that he would quitclaim his interest in the land to Washington Water Power for one hundred thousand dollars. If that wasn't acceptable, then his attorney would contact the company about removing the generator. At that point, Parkinson became a little smug and said, 'Please, Mr. Richards, you don't have to take my word for it. Feel free to research this matter at the county auditor's office. They have the records for all of the transactions and you can see for yourself.'"

"Have you done that?" Holmes asked.

"Yes," answered Richards sheepishly.

"And what did the records reveal?" Holmes continued.

"That, that damn Parkinson has a valid claim to the land!" erupted Corbin. "But I smell chicanery!"

"Is that your view as well, Mr. Richards?" I asked, interjecting myself into the conversation for the first time.

"Yes, Dr. Watson. Something is amiss. We believe we purchased the land legally through purchasers who received it from Kotter and are at a loss to explain how our attorneys could have failed to notice that Parkinson was the legal owner, not the Nettletons."

"What does Kotter say?" asked Holmes.

"So far, we haven't been able to locate him," Richards replied.

"Interesting," Holmes observed quietly, but I could tell from the glint in his eye that his interest in the case had been piqued. "Anything else?"

"Yes, one thing," said Richards. "I asked Parkinson why he hadn't pressed his claim earlier. Water Power acquired that land almost ten years ago. Parkinson said that he had traveled to Wisconsin soon after purchasing the lot and he intended to return soon thereafter. Instead, Parkinson claims that he got engaged in a business transaction that proved to be eminently successful and kept him in Milwaukee until just a few weeks ago."

"Have you ever seen or met Parkinson before?" I asked.

"No," answered Richards. "In fact, no one around Spokane seems to know him."

"That's not unreasonable if he's been living in Wisconsin," Holmes remarked.

"True," added Richards hesitantly.

"Can you describe the man?" Holmes asked.

"Certainly," Richards said. "He's a tall man. I would put him at nearly six feet tall, medium build, with dark brown hair and a full, well-kept beard."

"Any distinguishing marks?" Holmes asked.

"Not that I can remember except, perhaps, for his eyes. His eyes were set very close together. Sorry, but I don't remember their color."

"Thank you," Holmes replied. "What have you done to locate Kotter?"

"Well, we did not conduct a search per se. I sent people around to his home once or twice a day. One of the neighbors—an elderly woman—said that she thought he had left town to visit family somewhere in California."

Holmes turned toward Corbin. "You mentioned knowing Kotter, Mr. Corbin. What is the nature of your relationship with him?"

Corbin answered, "I was one of his customers. He was a partner in a lumber yard before he sold out and retired after his wife passed away. I didn't see him socially, but I did business with him on many occasions and never saw the hint of anything untoward."

Holmes nodded and turned back to Richards.

"What would you like me to do?" Holmes asked.

"Investigate this matter and get to the bottom of it," Corbin interrupted. "If the deed is legitimate, the company will pay. If not, we'll send this Parkinson fellow to jail for fraud."

Then Richards said, "I concur and, Mr. Holmes, one other thing. We'd appreciate it very much if you looked into this matter very quietly so that it doesn't become an object of rumor about our fair city."

"We don't work any other way," Holmes answered. "You may count on our discretion."

"One more thing, Mr. Holmes," Corbin said. "We'd also

prefer it if you and Dr. Watson would assume other identities for the purposes of looking into this matter. If the famous Sherlock Holmes is discovered to be working on behalf of Water Power, I fear it might drive this Parkinson fellow away only to have him return when you've departed."

"And might raise questions with some of your shareholders and creditors, I assume," Holmes said.

"Well, yes, that too," Richards replied.

"Is Parkinson still in town?" Holmes asked.

"We believe so," Richards answered, "but neither Daniel nor I have seen him. When we met, he gave me two weeks in which to reach a decision and said that he would contact me."

"Interesting," Holmes mused for a second time. "Do you have a particular identity that you wish us to adopt?"

"Yes," Richards said. "Since we may need to meet with you periodically it would be better if you appeared to be associated with the electric energy business. So, I propose that you take the name of Charles Danforth, and Dr. Watson become Mr. Lawrence Fairweather. Those two gentlemen are with Westinghouse Electric and were recently assigned to our account. They have not yet come to Spokane so no one, save myself, knows who they are."

After our guests had departed I asked Holmes what he proposed to do.

"Nothing this evening, Watson, except perhaps to walk about this city and get to know it some. Tomorrow, we'll make our own effort to contact Mr. Kotter and drop by the county auditor's office to examine the deeds."

Kotter lived on 9th Street near its intersection with Elm, a residential area to the southwest of the business district. His home was a white bungalow with tall spruce trees on both sides of the front sidewalk. The back yard was surrounded by a picket fence, painted white as well. Yellow roses fronted the home beneath the windows facing the street.

We knocked on the front door but there was no response, so I followed Holmes to the back of the house. There a small porch shielded the back door from the weather. Upon entering the porch, Holmes withdrew a small case from his breast pocket, opened it to reveal a set of lock picks, and deftly used one to open the door.

We stepped into the kitchen. The room was stuffy, probably from having been closed for what was undoubtedly a long period. The room was orderly and clean, a pattern that was repeated in each room of the house.

In the single bedroom we found a dresser well stocked with underclothes, socks, and shirts. The closet contained several pairs of trousers, two suits, and a portmanteau. If Kotter had traveled to California, he appeared to have done so without taking his clothes.

In the corner of the living room, Holmes searched a desk, studied some papers he found, and then announced, "Our work is done here, Watson. We may retire from the premises."

Upon exiting the house, Holmes caught sight of the neighbor lady and called out to her. Soon he was quietly interrogating her about Kotter's whereabouts.

"I can only tell you what I told the other gentlemen who were looking for him," she replied. "Mr. Kotter hasn't been home for several weeks now. He does that from time to time, just gets tired of our little city and goes away for a while."

"Any idea where he might have gone?" Holmes asked.

"He doesn't confide in me," the neighbor responded. "He has a son, John, who lives in Eureka, California. He might have gone down there."

On our return to the downtown area we stopped by the Western Union office and Holmes sent a cable to John Kotter, Eureka, California, requesting information on his father's whereabouts. I could tell by Holmes' manner that this was merely a perfunctory act with little expectation that it would lead to anything of substance.

From the Western Union office we crossed the Spokane River, admired the view of the waterfall, and walked to the Spokane County Courthouse in search of the county auditor. In short order we introduced ourselves as Mr. Danforth and Mr. Fairweather, and he to us as H. N. Maguire. Holmes, playing the part of Danforth, explained the purpose of our visit but he didn't say we were from Westinghouse. Instead, he told Maguire we were with the Pinkerton Detective Agency which Maguire accepted at face value.

"It's nasty business, Mr. Danforth, selling a property twice!" Maguire exclaimed. "I would have never expected it from William Kotter. I've known him for many years and there has been nothing about him for me to doubt his character."

"Do you record the deeds?" Holmes asked.

"Heavens, no!" came Maguire's quick response. "That duty is handled by my deputy, Mr. Edward McNay. I haven't the patience or the eyesight to record deeds," he continued as he pushed the spectacles from the front of his nose back up to the bridge. "Edward is the calmest man I've ever known. He seems to actually enjoy the tedium of recording deeds."

"I am surprised that your office failed to observe that

Kotter had sold the same property twice," Holmes said.

"Quite understandable, Mr. Danforth," answered Maguire. "The office records hundreds of deeds every month. You can't expect my deputy to remember every one of them. I might also add that it is the duty of the purchaser to insure that the title is clear, and the attorneys for the electric light company were not as thorough as they should have been."

"With your permission, Mr. Maguire, I would like to talk with your associate, Mr. McNay," Holmes asked.

"That won't be possible today. He recently injured his foot, a very severe sprain I'm told, and he is unlikely to be in the office for several days."

"In that case, would you object to me looking at the books where the deeds are recorded?"

"No, not at all, Mr. Danforth. Let me arrange that for you." Maguire then excused himself and Holmes sat down to await his return.

Looking over the deed ledgers was not a job we could both do, so I absented myself from the premises and found lunch in the Owl Café on the corner of Howard and Main Street. The fare was undistinguished but acceptable, and it restored my energy level. I assumed that Holmes would be engaged with his research for the remainder of the afternoon so I took a walk along the shores of the Spokane River where I saw the property and generating station which were now the subject of our inquiry. In the late afternoon I stopped at the Western Union office to see if we had received a reply from Mr. John Kotter, but nothing had arrived.

I met Holmes for dinner at the LaBelle Restaurant and Holmes explained what he had learned during the afternoon.

"There is a podium where the deed registers are placed

when the deputy is recording the deeds. Each entry is entered into two books, one under the grantor's name and the other under the grantee. Within the Spokane city limits each title register is subdivided by quarter section of land and the individual parcels are recorded by lot number or a metes and bounds description. It took me a while to understand how the information was organized, but once I figured that out, it didn't take long to find the record of both deed transactions."

"So Mr. Parkinson has a valid claim on Water Power's property!" I exclaimed.

"I didn't say that, Watson. I found it interesting that the two deeds were recorded in different inks. The podium contained an ink well with a bottle of iron gall ink and a dipping pen. That pen and ink was used to record the sale between Kotter and the Nettletons, who sold it later to Washington Water Power. The deed between Kotter and Parkinson was recorded using a fountain pen and India ink."

"How can you tell that?" I asked.

"When one uses a dipping pen, each time the writer puts the pen into the ink well he picks up a quantity of ink which leaves an ink dot where the pen is first applied to the paper. There will be numerous such dots in a line of writing. With a fountain pen, the writing line is smooth."

"Is that significant?"

"Perhaps, perhaps not. I found other instances of entries made with a fountain pen although such entries are not common. It might be simply explained by Deputy McNay forgetting to use the dipping pen and using a fountain pen from his pocket."

"Were the writing styles the same?"

"Yes, absolutely the same," Holmes said.

"Did you see anything else of significance?"

"Indeed, I found two other incidents where a seller sold the same property twice. The first incident involved a man by the name of Maynard Rhinehart who sold a city lot on Main Street to a Jasper Harding, and also to Philip and Agnes Maynes. The second incident involves a fellow called William Sparrow who sold a tract of land south of the city to William O'Brien and also to Thomas, Edward, and James Thompson."

"And you've concluded—?"

"That something is seriously amiss," Holmes remarked as he pulled out his pipe and filled it with tobacco. After he'd put it to light he continued. "Duplicate sales of property are exceedingly rare. For it to occur three times in a small community like Spokane is most singular. Before we can conclude this matter for Mr. Richards and Washington Water Power we need to look into these other transactions."

The next morning we rented a buggy and called at the clapboard home of Mr. Maynard Rhinehart about three miles north of the city.

We were met at the door by a young woman holding a baby, while another youngster about age three could be seen in the room through the screen door. After introducing ourselves and asking for Mr. Rhinehart, she told us that he had passed away about a year previous. She went on to explain that she and her husband had purchased the property from the estate.

Holmes asked, "Do you know how he died?"

"Not really," was the woman's reply. "Some kind of accident. He was a man in his seventies, or so I am told, but you could speak to Mrs. Beck down the road another quarter mile on your left. She knew him a long time."

After making our apologies for disturbing her, Holmes and I drove to the Beck farm.

Mrs. Beck met us warily. Holmes concocted a story on the spot that he had been negotiating a property purchase with Rhinehart and suddenly the correspondence stopped. Mrs. Beck relaxed some and said, "That's 'cause he's dead."

"Oh my," Holmes replied. "Was he ill?"

"No. They found him on the floor of his kitchen. Looked like he fell and struck his head on the stove."

When Holmes looked at her questioningly, she filled in the silence by adding, "Nothing unusual in Maynard falling. He had a bad leg and it would go out from under him."

"I am still interested in pursuing the property acquisition I was negotiating with Mr. Rhinehart. Did he have any surviving family?"

"Maynard was a bachelor. His only family was a brother, Claude Rhinehart, who lives in Tacoma."

Holmes thanked her and we turned to leave when she suddenly asked, "Was it that lot down on Main Street that you were talking about with Maynard?"

"Yes," Holmes answered.

"You're the second person to come talk to me about that lot. The druggist, Philip Maynes, was out here not long after Maynard died and told me that Maynard had swindled him. I didn't believe it. Maynard wasn't that kind."

Further conversation with Mrs. Beck revealed little of substance. We took our leave, returned to the city, and enjoyed a light luncheon and glass of beer in the Eagle Beer

Hall near the pharmacy operated by Philip Maynes. After our repast we met Maynes in his store.

After Holmes explained the purpose of our visit, Maynes said, "A man by the name of Jasper Harding showed up here in the store last March and claimed that he owned the land under my store. I disputed his claim and told him that I had a deed, at which point he pulled out a copy of a deed as well, issued to him by Maynard Rhinehart. His deed predated mine by ten months."

"What did you do then?" Holmes asked.

"I contacted my attorney, V. A. Greenleaf, and asked him to look into the matter," answered Maynes.

"Did you check the title to insure that it was clear before you purchased the property?" I asked.

"No!" Maynes said tersely. "Maynard Rhinehart was a successful farmer, well known and well respected in the community. I met him at the Lodge."

"Lodge?" I asked, my confusion evident in the tone of my voice.

"Yes, we were both members of the Odd Fellows, Spokane Lodge 17."[35]

"Yes, we're familiar with the organization, Holmes said. "Please continue with your story."

"Greenleaf visited the county auditor's office and talked

---

35 Editor's note: The Independent Order of Odd Fellows was founded in 1819 by Thomas Wildey in Baltimore, Maryland. It is a fraternal organization which promotes an ethic of reciprocity and charity. The organization enjoyed considerable growth in the late 19th Century and by 1895 it was the largest fraternal order in the United States. It was also the first national fraternal order to accept both men and women as members in 1851 when it formed the Daughters of Rebekah.

with Edward McNay, the deputy who showed Greenleaf where Rhinehart had sold the same lot twice. Then he visited the notary, Howard Malette, who witnessed the transaction between Rhinehart and Harding. Malette didn't remember the transaction but verified that it was his signature on the deed.

"That's when I went out to Rhinehart's house. He died about three weeks earlier. I was hoping I might find someone in the family who could explain what happened and help get things right, but there was no one at the farm. I ended up talking with his neighbors, Thomas and Myrna Beck. They gave me the brother's name and I wrote him, but it didn't gain me any satisfaction. He wrote back and sympathized with my troubles, but said that he knew nothing about the matter and referred me to James Dawson, the attorney representing Rhinehart's estate."

"How much did you pay Rhinehart for the lot?" Holmes asked.

"Nine thousand dollars," answered Maynes.

"And how much did Harding want you to pay him?" Holmes asked.

"Five thousand dollars," Maynes replied, "and he would give me a quitclaim deed extinguishing his interest in the property."

"What did you do?" Holmes asked.

"Two things," answered Maynes. "I had my attorney file a claim against the Rhinehart estate seeking to regain the money I had paid for the lot. Then I paid off Harding and got his deed to the property. If I am successful against Maynard's estate, I may end up paying less for the land than what I paid Maynard."

"Can you describe this Jasper Harding to me?" Holmes asked.

"Tall, very thin," said Maynes in reply. "Gray hair and moustache. The hair was slicked back over his head."

"Any distinguishing feature about his face or hands?" asked Holmes.

"Not really. A very thin face, sharp nose, but I don't remember any scars or anything like that."

"What can you remember about his eyes?"

"Nothing, sorry. I can't remember making eye contact."

That evening we again dined at the Manhattan Restaurant. At dinner, Holmes was in a reflective mood and disinterested in conversation. When I raised the issue of Harding's description versus that of Parkinson—Harding had gray hair and a moustache compared with Parkinson's brown locks and full beard—he dismissed me gently with a "Not now, Watson, I need time to think."

While Holmes' company left much to be desired, the food was excellent. I had two large bowls of beef stew with fresh rye bread and copious amounts of butter. Holmes ate little, using his fork to toy with a generous slab of roast beef. I had just ordered rice pudding for dessert when Holmes got up and excused himself saying, "There is something I want to see at the county auditor's office, Watson. I'll see you in the morning."

With that, Holmes departed leaving me with the responsibility of paying the check while he engaged in one of his nocturnal forays planning to break into the auditor's office under the cover of darkness. I was delighted to stay behind. I never felt comfortable with that aspect of Holmes' practice and was always worried that at some time we would be apprehended and charged with burglary. I had two servings of the pudding and enjoyed a cigar before walking back to the hotel.

At breakfast Holmes was in a talkative mood and explained that he had been unable to access the county auditor's office the previous night. "When I got to the courthouse last night, the building's front door was wide open and I could hear voices within. A crew of workmen were painting the hallway on the ground floor," Holmes said.

"I would think the light would be too dim to paint at night," I said in reply.

"Quite to the contrary, Watson, the building was ablaze with light. In addition to the ceiling lights, the painters had brought in three pole lamps about six feet high made from pipe with a large globe on top of each. They had wired the lamps into the building's fuse box and had all the light they needed. The device was quite effective. Moreover, they were able to do their work without the building's employees and patrons underfoot and the awful smell of the paint will be largely dissipated by the time the building is opened this morning."

"Quite ingenious," I added.

"I tell you, Watson, the Americans will remake the world as we know it with electricity. Right now it's just light and big motors powering industrial equipment, but they'll extend electricity to every aspect of life. There will be electric machines to cook with, wash clothes and dishes, and even sweep the floor."

I was about to say, "Surely you jest, old boy," but stopped short and simply nodded in agreement. Holmes was technologically sophisticated and for all I knew, these machines may have already been invented.[36]

After our discussion of the future of electrical devices, Holmes advised me that we would spend the day examining the third duplicate land transaction and seek to find Mr. William Sparrow who had sold his property twice, first to William O'Brien and then again to three people named Thompson—probably brothers.

Sparrow's last known address, three years prior, was a rooming house on Division Street north of the Great Northern railroad yards. Our inquiries were for naught. No one remembered or claimed to know Sparrow. The house manager said she had purchased the business about eighteen months earlier and Sparrow was not among her tenants. From the rooming house we traveled to the office of the county coroner, where we discovered that there was no death record for a William Sparrow who, like W. H. Kotter, our initial quarry, seems to have simply disappeared.

In the afternoon Holmes and I visited the Thompsons at their blacksmith shop and forge where we learned that

---

36 Editor's note: Holmes' observation was correct, but it would take another twenty to thirty years before the electric appliances he envisioned were commonplace. The country needed to extend the electric infrastructure to homes and businesses, and the cost of electricity needed to substantially decrease before electric appliances were widely adapted. Watson was also correct about Holmes' knowledge of technology. A mechanical dishwasher was invented in 1886 by Josephine Cochrane and introduced to the public at the 1893 Chicago World's Fair. Electricity powered subsequent models. The first stove, actually an electric oven, was invented by Canadian Thomas Ahearn in 1892 and in 1905, Australian David Curle Smith patented a device which contained an electric oven with an electric plate on top, the design now used the world over for the electric range. The first electric clothes washing machine was introduced in 1908 by the Harley Machine Company of Chicago. It was invented by Alva Fisher.

they had been subject to the same treatment meted out to the Washington Water Power Company and to Philip Maynes, the druggist. They purchased property, in this case several hundred acres of land south of the city, only to be approached by a man claiming to own the property. In this instance, the claimant said his name was William O'Brien and he was described as a tall, thin man with sandy brown or "dirty" blonde hair, long sideburns the same color, beady eyes and thick eyeglasses. O'Brien was also described as a courteous man who calmly explained the facts to the Thompsons and asked for ten thousand dollars to go away.

We also learned that William Sparrow, who allegedly sold the land to both O'Brien and the Thompsons, worked for the railroad and had acquired the land from his mother after she passed on. The Thompsons also reported searching for Sparrow without success. In Edward Thompson's words, "The clerk at the railroad told us that Sparrow just stopped coming to work. No one has seen him since."

Later that afternoon, Holmes received a note from Richards asking that we meet him in his office at Washington Water Power. About four thirty we were greeted by a comely young woman in her late twenties who introduced herself as Abigail Mayfair, Mr. Richards' personal secretary. She had bright blue eyes and a wide smile. After taking our hats and offering a glass of lemonade, which we both refused, she ushered us into Richards' office and said, "Mr. Danforth and Mr. Fairweather from Westinghouse Electric." Holmes and I stepped forward pretending to meet Richards and Corbin for the first time. Richards was behind his desk, a large edifice made of cherry while Corbin sat in a leather chair to Richards' right.

After dismissing Miss Mayfair, Richards got right to the point. "Daniel and I are very anxious to know if you've made any progress on our little matter, Mr. Holmes. Sorry, Mr. Danforth."

"Will that be necessary in your offices?" asked Holmes.

"Perhaps not, but since it was I who asked you to assume a new identity for the purpose of this investigation, I should abide by my own rules."

"As you wish," Holmes answered, "and yes to your inquiry, I believe we have made some progress. I am certain that I know how the fraud has been perpetrated, but I do not yet know the names of all of the perpetrators, nor do I have the evidence necessary for a criminal conviction. I hope to have that information in the next day or two."

"What can you tell us, thus far?" Corbin asked.

"Three things," Holmes replied. "First, there have been three cases of a property being sold twice here in Spokane. The incident involving Water Power is simply the most recent and the most expensive. The other two transactions involved payments totaling fifteen thousand dollars."

"So the villains are stepping up their gluttonous demands," Richards observed.

"Yes, in a manner of speaking," Holmes replied. "They've found a more valuable property and an owner with the means to pay more, and they are exploiting that position."

"What else?" Richards asked impatiently as he bent forward over his desk.

"In each of the three cases we examined thus far, the seller of the property is now absent. Two seem to have disappeared, including Mr. Kotter who sold the property which your predecessor bought, and another man by the name of

Sparrow. The third seller, a farmer north of the city named Rhinehart, was found dead in his kitchen, either from a fatal blow or an accidental fall. That matter is not entirely clear in my mind just yet."

"Maynard Rhinehart was involved in one of these transactions?" Richards asked.

"You knew him?" Holmes responded.

"Yes. He had a very large vegetable garden and I visited with my wife on several occasions to buy his produce. He doesn't strike me as the type to be involved in chicanery."

"I doubt that he was, Mr. Richards," answered Holmes. "I don't believe that any of the sellers are guilty of fraudulent behavior. It is my considered opinion that they are all innocent, and the fraud has been perpetrated by other parties."

"Please tell us more," Corbin ordered.

Holmes responded, "Each of the sellers was a single man and none have family in the area. It looks to me as if a person or persons unknown at this point forged a deed in their names, ransomed the property to the rightful owner, and took action to make the seller disappear either by bribing him to leave town or, more likely, by killing him in cold blood."

"What?" exclaimed Richards loudly. Both he and Corbin were aghast.

"You heard me correctly, gentlemen. We are dealing with some very dangerous men."

"But you don't know who they are?" Corbin asked.

"Not just yet. I have some idea as to their identities, but I will not speculate at this time. I need more facts."

"What are we to do?" Richards asked.

"When were you to meet with Parkinson again?" Holmes asked.

"He said that he would call me when he returned to town this week. I could hear from him at any time."

"Excellent," Holmes said. "When he calls, ask if he'll accept a check or if he wants cash. I am certain it will be cash. Then, arrange to meet him in the evening of the day following his call."

"You don't expect us to actually pay him, do you?"

"Not the hundred thousand dollars he demanded, but enough to insure that he is arrested for a felony. After Parkinson calls, leave a message for me at the hotel with the particulars and Watson and I will assist you in preparing for the meeting."

After we left the meeting, I chided Holmes. "You weren't particularly forthcoming about the number of participants in this plot."

"No need to at this point, Watson. There are two for sure, one of whom is a master of disguise."

"You believe that Parkinson, Harding, and O'Brien are all the same man?"

"I do," Holmes answered. "Every witness who saw these individuals described his body structure in similar terms—tall and thin with beady eyes or eyes close together. One can't alter his basic morphology, but he can easily create a new identity with wigs, spectacles, false beards and moustaches. Those externalities are what most people see, so the disguise is successful, as you well know from my own practice."

"What are you going to do now, Holmes?"

"Tonight I am going back to the courthouse for another

look at the records. Hopefully the painters will have finished their work, or at least have moved on to another part of the building. I'd like you to go to the theater as you suggested three days ago."

"What am I to do there?"

"Look for an actor who is tall and thin with eyes close together. However, since our quarry may not be an actor, but rather someone in a supporting role, if you don't see anyone on stage who fits the description, after the show place yourself in a position that will allow you to observe the individuals who exit the stage door. If you find our man, follow him to his place of residence."

That evening I attended a Vaudeville performance at the Comique Theater on Main Street where I scrupulously examined the facial characteristics of the various actors in search of a tall, thin man with eyes close together. My efforts were in vain but I thoroughly enjoyed the show and reported the same to Holmes the next morning at breakfast.

Holmes was in an excellent mood. After devouring what was, for him, an exceptionally large breakfast of eggs, ham, toast and coffee, Holmes told me that during his nocturnal foray into the county auditor's office he had managed to inspect each of the suspects' deeds and discovered, as he had expected, that they were each drawn up by the same person, observing that "It was obvious, Watson, the o's and t's have a very distinctive style of loop. They are clearly from the same hand."

"Any idea who drafted the documents?" I asked.

"No, but it was not McNay, the deputy auditor. To be forthright, I expected to find that he prepared the false deeds just as he recorded the fraudulent transactions."

"So, McNay is not involved," I added.

"I didn't say that, old friend, just that he didn't author the fraudulent deeds. We'll soon discover his role because we are off to see him as soon as the cab I've hired arrives."

McNay lived in a residential area located on a bluff to the south overlooking the city's business district and the river which coursed through from east to west. It was just past ten o'clock when Holmes and I climbed out of the cab. Holmes instructed the driver to wait for us and we walked to the corner. McNay lived on 5th Street just one block east of Sherman Street where the trolley line was located. Holmes pointed to a brown house, second from the corner across the street from us, and simply said, "McNay's." It was a well-appointed neighborhood. The yards all had lawns, shrubbery, trees and flowers. Holmes asked me to wait for him while he "looked over the house."

He disappeared into the alley behind the structure and was lost to my vision for several minutes until he came back into view west of McNay's home and beckoned me to join him. When I reached his side, I asked what he had done.

"Disconnected Mr. McNay's telephone."

Baffled, I asked, "Why would you do that?"

"McNay is suffering from a sprained ankle, is he not?"

"Yes, that's what Maguire, the Auditor, told us," I said."

"If McNay is involved in this business, and I believe that he is," answered Holmes, "after we converse with him, his natural instinct will be to talk with his partner in crime, the thin man with the close-set eyes. By disabling his telephone, McNay will not be able to call him and he will be forced to seek him out in person. We'll be following close behind."

Moments later, Holmes was displaying a Pinkerton Detective Service badge to McNay while introducing us as Messrs. Danforth and Fairweather, in the employ of Mr. Philip Maynes.[37]

McNay did not want to talk with us, much less invite us into his home, but Holmes was insistent, finally suggesting that McNay's refusal to cooperate with the investigation would cast doubt on the propriety of his actions. We were reluctantly ushered into McNay's dining room and offered chairs on opposite sides of the dining table. To my surprise, there were two deed recording books on the table and a pile of papers in a basket.

It was a small home with a parlor facing the street on the east side of the house. Behind the parlor was the dining room, where a door led to the kitchen on the back corner of the west side of the home. In front of the kitchen was a bathroom and bedroom with windows on the front and side of the house. A narrow hallway running from the front foyer to the kitchen separated the two sides of the home. It was clean but spartan in appearance. There was no evidence of a woman's touch—pictures on the walls, figurines and other artwork or flowers. McNay was clearly a bachelor.

"Please excuse the paperwork, gentlemen," McNay said. "I made arrangements with Mr. Maguire to allow me to work at home. He delivered this stack of deeds for recording to me this morning. I was just about to start work when you arrived at the door."

---

37 Editor's note: According to Watson's notes, Holmes enjoyed a very close and mutually supportive relationship with the Pinkerton National Detective Agency. He was given the Pinkerton badge by the Agency and told to use it whenever he felt the need. Holmes repaid the confidence by referring a number of clients to the company, particularly those that had few "points of interest" and simply needed the services of a qualified investigator.

I observed a fountain pen on the table next to the deed registers. I am sure that Holmes saw that and more as his photographic eyes surveyed the table.

"Do you often work at home?" Holmes asked.

"No, this is the first time I've done so," McNay replied. "My foot is healing very slowly and I can't handle the rigors of the office just yet. At the same time, I am bored sitting here convalescing. I brought the work home to keep busy, that's all."

McNay had met us at the front door with crutches under each arm. His movements were quite facile and he moved around the room quickly and with grace. His right foot and ankle were quite swollen and I questioned whether he had suffered a sprain or fracture. The latter, I thought to myself, but this is no place to display one's medical knowledge so I said nothing.

"I don't want to keep you from your work, Mr. McNay, so if you'll excuse the intrusion and answer a few questions, we'll be out of your way," Holmes said.

"Please," answered McNay.

"I understand that you are the only one in the auditor's office who records the deeds?" Holmes asked.

"Yes, that's true."

"How long have you been doing that job?"

"About two years."

"Thank you, sir. As I stated at the door, the issue that brings us forth today is the duplicate sale of the same parcel of land by Mr. Rhinehart to both Mr. Jasper Harding and Mr. Philip Maynes. Did you record those transactions?"

"I am loath to confess it, but yes, I did," McNay answered.

"And you never observed that the same parcel was being

sold by the same seller to two different buyers?" Holmes pressed McNay with an aggressive tone to his voice.

"That's why I am loath to confess it, Mr. Danforth," Mc-Nay replied. "If I had seen the problem, I could have questioned the transaction and perhaps saved Mr. Maynes a lot of trouble."

"To hold a job like yours, Mr. McNay, requires a man of great precision," Holmes retorted. "You seem to be a very ordered and precise individual, and yet you blundered badly with two transactions that were separated from one another by only a few inches in your deed registers. How could that occur?"

"I am sorry, Mr. Danforth, I have no valid excuse except the press of work." McNay then motioned toward the pile of deeds in the basket next to his left elbow. "This is seven days' worth of deeds. There are thirty-two documents in the pile. Spokane is growing rapidly and there are a large number of real estate transactions each week. I cannot keep track of every document that crosses my desk, particularly when the transactions involving a single property are separated in time by many months or years."

McNay seemed to be keeping his composure. Holmes, in contract, was demonstrating a demanding demeanor, designed to pressure the interviewee.

Holmes continued. "The transaction involving Mr. Maynes was not the only instance of a duplicate sale of the same parcel of land being recorded by your office. I understand that a man by the name of Kotter sold the same piece of land to a Mr. Parkinson and to the Nettleton family which, in turn, sold the lot to the Washington Water Power Company. In addition, it appears as if a Mr. Sparrow sold a tract of land south of the city twice as well. Are you aware of those transactions?"

"Yes," replied McNay stiffly. "In both cases, the second person who purchased the property came into the office asking for verification of the validity of their deed, which I could not supply after discovering the land had been sold previously."

"Did you simply forget those transactions as well?" Holmes asked with a cynical tone in his voice.

McNay straightened himself in his chair and strongly answered, "I had nothing to do—" He broke his statement off as his voice rose in pitch. It was subtle, but he recognized that he'd made an emotional faux pas. Holmes waited while McNay collected himself.

His voice carefully measured, McNay continued. "I had nothing to do with those records. They were recorded before I joined the auditor's staff."

"I question that, Mr. McNay. Unfortunately, we can't question the sellers. One died in a strange accident and the other two are unaccountably missing, perhaps the victims of foul play." As he talked to McNay, Holmes bored his eyes into McNay's. McNay shifted his gaze toward me.

Holmes instantly saw McNay's reaction and said, "Excuse me Mr. McNay, I didn't properly introduce my associate, Mr. Fairweather. He specializes in criminal financial transactions. He'll be going through your financial history while I scrutinize every other aspect of your life."

"Why would you do that?" McNay asked. "I've done nothing illegal."

"I think differently!" said Holmes. "I believe that you accepted a bribe to record the transactions between Mr.

Rhinehart and Mr. Harding, which I believe is fraudulent. Mr. Harding extorted money from Philip Maynes using a bogus deed and you assisted that endeavor."

"Enough!" shouted McNay. "Enough of your calumny. I will not be accused of being a thief in my own home. You are to leave now, Mr. Danforth. Now!"

"As you wish," Holmes said with a smile and as we both stood up and turned toward the front door.

When we reached the street Holmes remarked, "A most productive visit, Watson. McNay is clearly involved in all three transactions. It's now just a matter of obtaining sufficient proof, and I believe we'll be taking another step in that direction in the next few minutes."

We boarded the cab that Holmes had waiting, drove down the street a block, turned around, and parked under the branches of a large maple tree where we could monitor McNay's front door. While we waited Holmes said, "My decision to revisit the Auditor's office yesterday was extremely well timed. If I hadn't done so, it would be well-nigh impossible to visit the content of those ledgers while they rest on McNay's dining room table." He then chuckled.

A few minutes later, McNay emerged from the front door on his crutches and moved rapidly for a man so impaired. He traveled west to the next street where there was a streetcar stop on the corner. We followed McNay's progress at a safe distance behind the trolley. When it reached the business district, McNay alighted on Riverside Street and we did the same thing, continuing the surveillance on foot.

To our mutual surprise and delight, McNay walked to Main Street and turned into the Nagel House Hotel where we had taken rooms. Holmes approached the desk clerk and asked where the man on crutches had gone. The clerk, a young man named James, said "Up to see his friend, Mr. Henry Barlow in Room 211."[38] Holmes was staying in Room 207 and I was farther down the hall in 224. I've since wondered, on many occasions, what was the statistical likelihood of us sharing the same hotel floor with our quarry.

Holmes told me to walk heavily down the hall to my room while he used the cover of my footsteps to surreptitiously step up next to Barlow's door and eavesdrop. He subsequently reported hearing the following to me.

McNay said, "Henry, we've got a serious problem."

"I figured as much for you to hobble all the way down here to see me. What's got your goat?" Barlow asked.

"I got a visit this morning from two guys who said they were Pinkerton detectives working for that druggist, Maynes."

"So what? That doesn't involve us. Maynes is suing Rhinehart's estate to get his money back."

"I don't think these two guys were really working for Maynes," McNay responded. "He doesn't have that kind of money to bring a detective all the way over here from England."

"What are you saying?"

"These two introduced themselves to me as Danforth and Fairweather, but I've seen Danforth before. At least I've seen a picture of him from when I was in England a few years ago. There was a story about him in a magazine called

---

38 Editor's note: Holmes made a habit of befriending hotel desk clerks, waitresses, bartenders, and other service personnel and always tipped them generously. They proved to be invaluable relationships allowing Holmes to obtain information that others could not, especially the police.

The Strand, where he solved a case involving some kind of treaty.[39] That Danforth is really Sherlock Holmes, and the big guy with him is his sidekick, John Watson."

"If what you're saying is true, then yes, you're right. Maynes couldn't afford his services. It must be those guys at Water Power. Richards surprises me. I didn't think he had it in him."

"What are we going to do?" McNay asked.

"Finish what we started. We've got a hundred thousand dollars on the table. I'll call Richards and demand the money."

"With Holmes on the case, he might find old man Kotter."

"Not a chance, Edward. I sent him away. Holmes won't find him. Of that, you can be sure."

"Has he been killed?" McNay asked.

"No, God no. Why would you say such a thing?" Barlow asked.

"He knew about all three cases with the duplicate deeds and indicated that all three sellers are either dead or missing. He speculated they might all be the victims of homicide. You told me there would be no violence."

"Keep your shirt on, Edward. Rhinehart is dead. He fell in his kitchen and killed himself. Don't you remember? As for Kotter and Sparrow, they both took the money and left town."

At that point Holmes was interrupted by the sound of footsteps on the stairs. He moved down the hallway and

---

39 Editor's note: McNay was referring to a case Holmes solved entitled "The Naval Treaty" which appeared in *The Strand* magazine in October and November 1893.

entered his room. A few minutes later I joined him. We left the door to his room ajar so that we could see McNay leave the building. After about twenty minutes McNay departed the hotel. Barlow escorted him to the lobby where they said their goodbyes. Holmes and I passed Barlow on the stairs as he returned to his room. No words were spoken and Barlow had no idea who we were. The meeting gave both Holmes and me a chance to memorize Barlow's features and he did, indeed, have eyes close together. He was also tall, thin, and clean shaven with light brown hair, blue eyes, and was much older than I expected, a man in his late forties or early fifties. I surmised we'd found the man playing Harding, O'Brien, and Parkinson.

In the lobby, Holmes again stopped at the front desk to talk with the clerk. Was that Mr. Barlow I just passed on the stairs?" he asked.

"Indeed, sir."

"The famous actor?" Holmes continued.

"Yes," James explained, "although he's retired from the stage now. He told me that he had appeared in several of Mr. Gilbert's and Mr. Sullivan's works when he was living in Philadelphia and New York. I've heard him sing. Mr. Barlow has a very strong voice."

"Thank you, James," Holmes said before turning and joining me at the front door.

"We'll need to go in disguise when we deal with Mr. Barlow in the future," Holmes said. "While he gave no sign of recognition when he passed us on the stairs, I don't know if, or how much, of a description McNay may have provided him about us. We will need to stay very close to him over the next few days."

We walked down the street toward the offices of Washington Water Power with Holmes making a small detour into a print shop where he gave an order to the clerk. A few minutes later we were in H. M. Richards' office.

"I expect that you'll soon receive a call from the man calling himself Parkinson," Holmes said.

"He's already called," Richards answered. "He called about ten minutes ago and I told Miss Mayfair that I couldn't talk with him until 4:00 p.m. I wanted your counsel before I deal with the man. He'll call back at that time."

"Excellent," said Holmes. "Tell him that the company has decided to pay, but you'll go no higher than fifty thousand dollars."

"What if he rejects my offer?" Richards asked.

"He won't. He's in a hurry. Tell him it's fifty thousand dollars in cash or wait several days for a bank draft. And tell him that you'll meet him tomorrow night at 8:00 p.m. in Dempsey's Restaurant."

"And I am supposed to give him fifty thousand dollars?" Richards asked, his voice rising.

"No, I'll package up the money for you. We'll need seven thousand dollars in hundred dollar bills, but we're only going to risk two thousand dollars. We'll fill the money bundles with newsprint appropriately sized to match the currency."

"You think of everything, Mr. Holmes," said Richards, much relieved.

"One final thing. Tell Parkinson that you'll be joined by Mr. Corbin and Corbin's personal assistant and notary, Simon Watters. I will be Watters. If Parkinson starts asking questions, simply explain to him that the company cannot

MISS ABIGAIL MAYFAIR

spend that kind of money without the approval of the Board of Directors and that will take several days to acquire. Tell him that Corbin is providing the cash for the transaction as a loan to the company, and finish the conversation strongly by telling him to 'take it or we'll see you in court.'"

Our business at Water Power completed, Holmes and I stopped in the Stockholm Saloon and enjoyed a glass of

EDWARD MCNAY

beer before returning to the hotel, changing our clothes, and donning disguises to change our appearance so that we could follow Barlow throughout the evening. Holmes was certain that he would contact McNay.

Barlow departed the hotel at 6:45 p.m. I followed him from the lobby where I had been reading the newspapers. Holmes was out on the street. Barlow walked east with a relaxed, slow pace, drinking in the content of the storefronts that he passed, finally turning into Davenport's Restaurant.

Holmes was across the street and I waited for him to enter the café before me. I followed him a few minutes later and took up residence in the front corner of the establishment, where I unfolded the paper and used it to screen my surveillance of the room. The restaurant was not busy. Barlow had taken a table in the middle of the room. Holmes was at an adjacent table on Barlow's left. We waited for McNay to arrive, but he did not. Instead, we were graced by the lovely presence of Miss Abigail Mayfair, Richards' secretary at Water Power. She breezed through the door, spotted Barlow and embraced him in greeting, and joined him at his table.

I know it's foolishness on my part, having encountered several female villains in the course of chronicling Holmes' work, but I am always taken aback by the discovery that a member of the fair sex is a criminal. Holmes overheard most of their conversation which he reported as such.

Barlow said, "Edward came to my room this morning quite worried."

"What about?" asked Miss Mayfair.

"He was visited by two detectives this morning. They said they were from the Pinkerton Agency and working for Maynes, but Ed is certain it was that famous English detective Sherlock Holmes and his associate—probably working for Water Power."

"I am not aware of Richards hiring any detectives," Mayfair replied. "There have been a couple of men from Westinghouse, but they don't look like detectives to me."

"Ed is getting nervous, too nervous. He wants me to finish the deal so we can get out of town."

"What are you going to do?"

"I called Richards this afternoon, as you know."

"Yes."

"He offered fifty thousand dollars in cash or we go to court. We can't run that risk, so I took the deal."

Mayfair paused for a moment. "Edward will be angry. It cuts each of our shares from thirty-three to seventeen thousand."

"Unless—" Barlow paused before continuing. "Unless we shrink the partnership by one and the remaining members each get twenty-five thousand, which is still a lot of money."

"You're not suggesting—" Mayfair said.

"Yes. Edward is skittish. I am afraid that if the law starts putting pressure on him, he'll sell us out to save his own neck."

"You've thought about this?"

"I have, and I have a plan. I am going to meet Richards and Corbin tomorrow night at Dempsey's Restaurant. After I get the money, we'll all meet at Edward's house and divvy things up," Barlow answered.

"Should I meet you there?" Mayfair asked.

"That would be the easiest. Go in the back door. It's always open and that way the nosy old biddy on the corner won't see you."

The next morning Holmes advised me that he was meeting Corbin to prepare the money satchel for the evening meeting with Barlow. I had little to do so I spent some time making notes of the case and then took a long walk through the city's business district. Spokane was a lively and clean town which I estimated to be about three-quarters of the size of Butte. It was a mercantile center providing goods and services to the surrounding farms and the mining areas in northern Idaho. It was also a study in contrasts with Butte, an industrial city. Where Butte was raw, Spokane was refined. Where Butte was a city of men; Spokane was a family town. Where overalls clad most of the men of Butte; Spokane was a community of suits and ties. I admired Spokane, but I was enraptured by Butte.

I met Holmes at six o'clock. He outfitted me in another disguise and sent me to Dempsey's Restaurant where I was to take a table near the front door to act as sentry. If the transaction soured I was to obstruct Barlow's escape, if need be.

I was seated in the restaurant about fifteen minutes when Holmes, playing the part of Simon Watters, entered with Richards and Corbin. Holmes took a stool at the bar while our clients took a table nearby. Barlow, dressed as Parkinson, entered moments later. He joined Richards and Corbin at their table. After shaking hands and exchanging a few pleasantries, Barlow produced a document from his breast pocket which he presented to Richards. The document was the deed transferring Parkinson's claim to the Post Street property to Water Power. Richards read it carefully as did Corbin. When that was done, Corbin called Holmes to the table where he was introduced as Corbin's notary, Simon Watters. Holmes read through the deed and indicated that it was in order. He then set the satchel containing the cash on the table, reached in and withdrew a bundle of cash and thumbed through it in front of Barlow. "It's all there, ten bundles of five thousand dollars each, a total of fifty thousand dollars as agreed."

Holmes returned the bundle he was holding to the satchel and Corbin said, "If you wish to count it, Mr. Parkinson, go ahead."

"That won't be necessary, gentlemen. Let's get to the paperwork and I'll take my leave." Barlow withdrew a pen from his suit coat and signed the deed, which was then notarized by Holmes. Then Barlow stood up, took the satchel, nodded to the three men at the table, and walked out the front door.

I headed over to the table in time to hear Corbin say, "When do we have him arrested, Mr. Holmes?"

"Within the hour, I think," answered Holmes. "Gentlemen, if you'll excuse me, Watson and I must now spring the trap." A carriage awaited us outside the restaurant, courtesy of Mr. Corbin, and we traveled quickly to McNay's neighborhood. Barlow was taking the streetcar, shadowed by the real Simon Watters to insure that he went to McNay's home.

At the appointed place, about a block south of McNay's residence, Holmes and I met with a band of Spokane city policemen led by Captain James Coverly. Holmes gave them their instructions and then departed for McNay's back door. I was to stay hidden until after Barlow entered the home, at which point I was to take position on the front porch with my trusted Webley revolver in hand.

The wait began. Fifteen minutes went by and Barlow had failed to appear. I was convinced he had run, but my fears proved groundless. I heard the streetcar pass the intersection a block to the west and a few moments later Barlow came into view, carrying the satchel. He entered McNay's house and I climbed on to the porch and listened at the door. In fact, I took a chance that the attention of the three people inside would be focused on one another and I quietly opened the door an inch or so hoping that I could hear their conversation.

"You've got the money?" McNay asked.

"Just fifty thousand dollars. I told Abby the terms of the deal last night and I assume that she told you," answered Barlow.

"She has," responded McNay, "but that doesn't mean you told her the truth."

"You have a telephone, Edward. Call Mr. Corbin or Mr. Richards if you wish. Tell them you're concerned that your partner is defrauding you of half of the money he received from them."

"Shut up you two," Miss Mayfair said. "Let's get on with it and get out of town tonight."

"I'm not going anywhere," McNay said.

"That's true Ed," Barlow responded. "It's time to sever our partnership."

"What do you mean by that?" asked McNay.

I looked through the wooden door and saw that Holmes had surreptitiously entered through the back entrance and was listening to the proceedings from the kitchen door.

"It means you've become expendable, Edward," Barlow said. "You're going to have an accident tonight. That happens from time to time with people on crutches. They fall."

Barlow stepped toward McNay.

"Stop it, Henry," said Miss Mayfair.

"What do you mean, stop it? We agreed last night that there was one too many in the partnership."

"You are correct," Mayfair said. She withdrew a pistol from her handbag and pointed it at Barlow. "You've been an attentive and gallant boyfriend, Henry, but blood is thicker than water. You're not killing my brother."

"What?" shouted Barlow. "You and him are family?"

"Wait, Abby, let's make sure he brought the money," McNay said. "Put that satchel on the floor, Henry. Gently. Now push it over here. Slowly."

"You don't have to worry about the money, Mr. McNay. It's not there." It was Holmes' voice as he stepped into the dining room and walked toward the parlor. I quickly opened the front door without drawing the others' attention and quietly stepped into the front foyer about six feet behind Miss Mayfair.

On seeing Holmes, Barlow said, "Watters!" and Miss Mayfair exclaimed, "Mr. Danforth!"

"Wrong on both counts. My name is Holmes, Sherlock Holmes, as deduced by your associate Mr. McNay. Fortunately for me, you discounted his warnings and I can now put an end to your criminal enterprise. Put the gun down, Miss Mayfair," Holmes continued.

I inched closer to Mayfair and then Holmes said, "Watson, disarm her."

Suddenly, she turned and threw the firearm at me, hitting me in the chest. She fled into the adjoining bedroom and locked the door behind her. Holmes blew his police whistle and in a matter of seconds a force of Spokane policemen were in the home arresting both Barlow and McNay. When the bedroom door was forced open, Miss Mayfair was not there. She had climbed out the window and fled through the neighbor's shrubbery.

Following their arrest, Barlow and McNay were taken to police headquarters where they were questioned by Holmes and Captain Coverly.

Sobered by the attempted double-double cross by his two partners, Barlow made a clean breast of things and fully explained the fraudulent scheme, the salient features of which included:

> *1. Find a property owner who had no family or close friends, and who had recently sold a property to someone who needed the property badly, and therefore was susceptible to fraudulent demands.*
>
> *2. Falsify a new deed giving title to the property to one of the characters portrayed by Barlow. McNay, in turn, would record the false deed and testify to its legitimacy.*
>
> *3. Barlow would then contact the legitimate owners of the property, advise them of his deed, and demand payment in exchange for surrendering his claim to the property.*

Neither Barlow nor McNay would admit to anything related to the death of Maynard Rhinehart or the disappearances of William Sparrow and W. H. Kotter. Both implicitly understood that to implicate the other in murder would subject both to a murder indictment, one for the actual crime and the other for being an accessory.

The next morning Holmes and I met with Richards and Corbin to tell them that the affair was over. Holmes explained the scheme as it was explained to us by Barlow, at which point Richards asked, "What was Miss Mayfair's role in a scheme that only needed two men?"

"She had two roles. First, she was the love interest," explained Holmes nonchalantly. "McNay understood that Barlow might double-cross him and abscond with the money. His sister was there to protect his interest in the partnership, and it worked out as planned the minute Barlow got the idea of terminating McNay's role. She reported it to her brother and they decided to turn the tables on Barlow. Our intervention is the only thing that saved his life."

"What was her other role?" asked Corbin.

"I didn't know it officially until this morning when you allowed me to examine a sample of her writing," Holmes answered. "She forged the deeds that McNay recorded. As I explained to Watson, she has a very distinct way of writing her o's and t's. It's her handwriting, all right."

"I still don't understand how McNay was able to insert a fraudulent deed into a record which is organized in chronological order," Richards said.

"Actually it was very simple, although it took me several hours of looking through the deed registers to see it. Whoever set up the registers years ago skipped the first line on each page of the register books and began the record on the second line. McNay noticed that and whenever he wanted to record a fraudulent deed, he recorded it on the first line on a page that was earlier than the deed they intended to duplicate, thereby giving it precedence over the valid deed. Then he filed the fraudulent deed prepared by Miss Mayfair and the fraud was ready to implement."

"I can see how that scheme would work with certain purchasers, but didn't they understand that trying the scheme with a major commercial enterprise would lead to trouble?"

"I am sure they assessed that risk, but please realize, they had a man or, more accurately, a woman on the inside who could report back to them what you gentlemen were thinking about or planning to do. It was by the sheerest of good fortune that Mr. Corbin contacted me outside the corporation's channels of communication. Had Miss Mayfair discovered that you had contacted us, it's highly likely that Barlow would have disappeared and the matter of the duplicate deed would have had to be handled in the court."

"So, Miss Mayfair came into our employ seeking to defraud us," Richards added.

"No, I don't believe so," Holmes answered. "When the trio relocated to Spokane, she simply needed a job and you, Mr. Richards, hired her to be your secretary. Of course, she learned about the various title problems the company had with some of the parcels along the river, and that gave the trio an idea. This was a case of a major enterprise holding a very valuable property and the thieves were willing to take the risk for a big payday."

"Until Miss Mayfair is found, we'll never know for sure, but I for one accept your explanation," Corbin said.

"I agree, it's most plausible," added Richards. "Washington Water Power owes you a debt of gratitude. A financial challenge of the magnitude created by Barlow and McNay might have created real problems for the company."[40]

In his understated way Holmes acknowledged their thanks and we departed.

A woman answering Miss Mayfair's description was reported two days later in Cheney, Washington, a small farm town about a dozen miles west of Spokane, but she was not apprehended. McNay and Barlow were convicted of fraud and sent to the state penitentiary.

---

40 Editor's note: Washington Water Power not only survived the threat created by "The Case of the Dastardly Deed," but went on to buy out other electric generating companies in the region and become a major public utility servicing Spokane, eastern Washington, and northern Idaho. It prospers today under the name of Avista Corporation.

The Case of the Purloined Papers

Holmes and I had just finished breakfast in the Manhattan Café in downtown Spokane, Washington, the city where Holmes had successfully concluded a little matter which I described to the reading public as "The Case of the Dastardly Deed." Our remaining chores for the day were to stop at the stationers to buy some reading material for our return trip to Montana, pick up our luggage at the hotel, take a cab to the railroad depot, and enjoy a relaxing ride back to Butte where we were to supper that evening with our friend Marcus Daly, President of the Anaconda Copper Mining Company, and some of his associates. I doubted it was truly a social occasion. Daly had a stream of problems for Holmes to deal with, but that was for later. Now, I was interested in finding a book or two by Bret Harte, who wrote extensively about the American West.

As we entered the lobby of the Nagel House Hotel, James, the front desk clerk, called out, "Mr. Holmes, I have just received a telegram for you."

Holmes went to the desk while I fished a cigar from the interior breast pocket of my suitcoat and was about to set it to fire when Holmes announced, "It's from Phoebe Apperson Hearst, Watson."

"Ah, yes, the benefactor of Anaconda's Public Library."

"Among others, Watson. Shall we see what she has to say?"

Holmes was toying with me. He knew it would be another commission, and he knew full well that I wanted to get back to Montana and go fishing with my compatriots in the medical profession, Felix and Leo St. Jean, who had taught me the joy of stalking the wily trout and arctic grayling. "Pray, please continue, old boy. What does she have to say?" I asked, fearful of what I was about to hear.

"It's quite succinct," Holmes answered.

> *Please come to San Francisco. Matter most delicate and urgent.*
>
> *Phoebe Apperson Hearst*[41]

---

41 Editor's note: Phoebe Apperson Hearst was the wife and then widow of George Hearst, a man who made his fortune investing in mines starting with the Comstock Lode in Nevada, the Anaconda Copper Mining Company in Butte, Montana, and the Homestake Gold Mine in Lead, South Dakota, the largest gold producer in the history of the United States. George Hearst was elected to the United States Senate from California in 1887 and served four years before his death in 1891. Mrs. Hearst was also the mother of William Randolph Hearst, who founded the Hearst chain of newspapers and constructed San Simeon, the Hearst Castle north of Cambria, California, now a state park.

In her own right, Mrs. Hearst was an active philanthropist endowing public libraries and educational institutions, including the Golden Gate Kindergarten Association, the Lowie Museum of Anthropology at the University of California, and the all-girls National Cathedral School in Washington, D.C. She was the first woman to serve on the Board of Regents for the University of California.

"Are we going directly to San Francisco?" I asked. "Or are you planning on calling her via the telephone to get more details before you commit yourself to her matter?"

"My predilection," Holmes replied, "is to simply go to San Francisco. I doubt that a woman of Mrs. Hearst's standing would seek my counsel on a trivial matter. She is the American equivalent of a Duchess and certainly has the resources to deal with smaller issues. I sense that her problem will be a matter of interest."

"I will leave the travel details to you, old friend," I said in reply to Holmes, "while I retire to the stationers to find some new reading material. I suspect that we are looking at a journey of several days."

Holmes took his leave and proceeded toward the railroad depot, and I wandered down to the stationers where I purchased newspapers from Spokane, Seattle, San Francisco and New York, the latter several days old, and a few books including *The Handbook of Applied Mathematics* for Holmes. I know he'll read it earnestly and search for errors or questionable suppositions so that he can mail a critique to the author at some future date.

I believe Isaac Newton missed out on a lively exchange of letters with Holmes simply by being born about 210 years before my friend.

We rode the Northern Pacific from Spokane to Seattle, and spent the night in the Grand Pacific Hotel before transferring to the Western Pacific for the two-night ordeal in one of its coaches. It rained heavily in southern Oregon during the night and water leaked in through a faulty window seal and drenched my suitcoat while I intermittently dozed to the rhythm of the car as we rolled south. During

LA HACIENDA DEL POZO DE VERONA

the day I alternated between reading Harte's short stories, reminiscing with Holmes about his past cases, and enjoying the scenery that passed by our windows.

We took rooms in the Baldwin Hotel before proceeding on to Mrs. Hearst's hacienda in Pleasanton, about twenty-five miles east of Oakland, meeting her just after lunch. The butler showed us into a room which must have functioned as the late Senator's office.

Two windows separated by a fireplace looked out over the grounds. Floor to ceiling bookcases covered the two interior walls. The door to the hallway and a bar in the corner finished the fourth wall. An oak desk that must have measured eight feet in length stood before one of the bookcases. It was topped with a red leather writing surface. A sofa and a chair covered in the same leather stood before the desk. A second chair in black leather was to the left of the desk. The bookcases were largely occupied by mementos of the Senator's life, including a picture of him posed with Seth Bullock, the former sheriff in Deadwood, South Dakota. It no doubt was taken when Hearst got in-

HEARST FAMILY: LEFT TO RIGHT, GEORGE HEARST, PHOEBE APPERSON HEARST, AND WILLIAM RANDOLPH HEARST

volved in the development of the Homestake Mine in the middle 1870s.

While I quietly waited in the red leather chair, Holmes padded around the room drinking in everything with his eyes and processing it through his mind.

Mrs. Hearst joined us after a few minutes and took a place on the sofa and motioned to Holmes to join her there. She was more slender than I had pictured her in my mind and quite robust in her mannerisms. Holmes and I were soon to learn that she had a constitution of iron, a woman ordained to command.

After the introductions, I thanked her for donating the library to the citizens of Anaconda, Montana. She responded by telling me that she's also seen to the construction of a library in Lead, South Dakota as well.

That launched her on a talk about the Black Hills and how her famous husband seemed to have a nose for valuable ore and was very successful in finding good properties. She then said, "Mr. Daly recommended that I consult with you."

"You've brought us here, Madam, I assume to help you solve the burglary," Holmes said.

"My goodness, however did you know? Only two people, me and my son, William Randolph, who is back in New York, know about it," Mrs. Hearst replied.

"A small matter really," Holmes replied. "Before you entered the room I walked around it admiring the mementos and photographs commemorating your husband's life. I noticed some scratch marks on the lock of your husband's desk and surmised that someone surreptitiously entered the same, removing, most likely, some valuable papers."

"You astound me, Mr. Holmes," the matron replied. "You've accurately described the problem."

"Pray, please tell us about the documents," Holmes said.

"They belong to my son, William Randolph," Mrs. Hearst replied. "He sent them here for safekeeping. There was a burglary attempt at his home in New York about five weeks ago. The burglar damaged William's safe but never got inside."

"Why didn't he find another place to secure them in New York, perhaps in a bank?" I asked.

"I don't know, Doctor. I didn't ask," Mrs. Hearst said. "They simply showed up here one day with a note from William asking me to keep them safe. William is engaged in a ferocious fight for control of the New York newspaper market with Joseph Pulitzer, his rival. William believes Pulitzer was behind the break-in and I am sure he wanted the papers moved to an area outside of Mr. Pulitzer's sphere of influence."

"And they deal with a delicate matter?" Holmes suggested softly.

"Yes," Mrs. Hearst said tersely, then paused to gather her thoughts. "My son has an altogether much too robust life as a bachelor. He has a penchant for actresses and showgirls."

"And the papers pertain to one or more of the young ladies who have been favored with his company?"

"Correct. Fortunately, it's just one girl, a Mary Jane Donaldson. The missing papers specify the terms for the termination of the relationship."

"I admit to being completely baffled, Madam, as to why your son drafted an agreement for terminating a romance. They fail all the time with hurt feelings and emotional devastation, but that doesn't merit a contract," I said.

"Indeed, Dr. Watson," Mrs. Hearst answered and then drew in a deep breath, "but in this case a child is involved."

"William's child," I blurted out.

"The child is named William," she said.

"You wish to shield the child?" I replied.

"No, I wish to shield my son from the public disclosure of this unhappy turn of events. William—my William, not Miss Donaldson's William—plans to seek political office in the near future, and the public release of this information would be devastating to his chances for a political career. I need not say it but I will, Mr. Pulitzer would be overjoyed to smear my son's reputation with such information."

Mrs. Hearst then turned from me to Holmes and said, "My charge to you, Mr. Holmes, is to recover these papers and return them to my possession."

"A very tall order, Mrs. Hearst," said Holmes as he felt his coat pocket for his pipe. "With no idea as to the identity of the perpetrator and the fact that he has several days head start, I would—"

Mrs. Hearst interrupted, "I know the name of the thief."

"Why then did you not call the police?" Holmes asked.

"I did that as well," the matron replied, "but they have been totally unsuccessful in locating him. He seems to have disappeared into thin air."

"Who is this individual?"

"His name is Walter Webber," answered Mrs. Hearst. "He has worked here in my home periodically doing maintenance. He's a very fine painter and carpenter."

"Why do you suspect him?" I asked.

"One of the housemaids, Greta Ueland, saw him in the hallway the morning of the burglary. He had no reason for being in there at that time since he was not engaged in any repair. Greta asked Mrs. Fogelstad, the head housekeeper, why Webber was in the house. Mrs. Fogelstad had no answer for the girl, but she advised me about Greta's observation. We never discovered that the papers were missing from the desk until several hours later."

"I trust that the police have visited his home and the places he habitually visits?" Holmes asked.

"That's my understanding, Mr. Holmes, and as I said before, totally without success."

"And no one has any idea about his possible whereabouts?"

"Not that I know of. I personally did not know the man. David Chapman, my butler, arranged for his services. He may have more to tell you."

Holmes and I subsequently met with Mr. Chapman, but he added little of substance to what we had learned from Mrs. Hearst. He told us that he had met Webber several years prior while in the employ of another family, and that whenever he needed Webber's services he sent a message to a saloon in the Potrero Hill section of San Francisco. Chapman also claimed that he did not know where Webber lived and, further, after the robbery was discovered he had left a message for him at the saloon with the promise of more work but Webber never replied, a situation which had never occurred before.

After Chapman, Holmes and I met with the housemaid, Greta Ueland. Holmes asked, "Miss Ueland, are you quite certain that the man you saw in the hallway was Mr. Webber?"

"Oh, yes sir," came her quick reply." "I know Mr. Webber very well, all of us girls do."

"Why is that?" Holmes asked.

"He is a very nice man and very funny. When he works here he always eats with us in the kitchen and tells us stories of the places where he has been."

"Such as?" I asked.

"Well, he worked on the railroad for a time in Utah, the town was called Ogden, I believe. He also did some mining near Virginia City in Nevada. Before that, he was a logger, I think in Minnesota, Montana, and Oregon."

Miss Ueland seemed to flush a little as she talked about Webber. Holmes saw it as well and asked, "Miss Ueland, have you ever kept company with Mr. Webber outside of work?"

She hesitated for a moment and then said, "Yes. He asked me to a dance at one of the fraternal halls in Oakland. Another time he took me to a park where we had a picnic."

"When was the last time you saw him socially before the burglary?" Holmes asked.

"Oh, let me think," she replied cautiously. "It's been a

considerable time, over a year, I think."

"Were you romantically involved with Mr. Webber?"

She flushed. "No sir, I was not." She lowered her head and continued, "I wanted to be. I had more interest in him than he had in me."

"Did you talk with him the morning you saw him in the hallway, Miss Ueland?"

"No."

"Did he see you?"

"I don't think so. He was at the head of the stairs going down to the back door with his back to me. I had just come out of the parlor."

"You didn't see his face?" Holmes asked.

"Just from the side."

"And you're sure it was Webber?"

"Certainly, I saw enough of the face and he was wearing his little blue hat. He always wears a blue stocking hat, even in the summer. He's lost a lot of his hair."

"What do you know about him?" Holmes asked.

Greta replied, "Not very much. We talked a lot, but not about him. Once, he told me that he had lived in San Francisco for about six years."

"How old is he?" I asked, injecting myself in the conversation again.

"I don't know," Greta replied. "Late thirties maybe, early forties I would think."

"Please describe him," Holmes asked.

"He has dark brown hair with some gray on the sides of his head. His moustache is more gray."

"Eyes? Any scars, moles or birthmarks on his face?" Holmes asked.

"His eyes are brown. No moles on his face, but there is a scar on his left cheek below his ear about two inches long."

"Do you know where he lived before coming to San Francisco?"

"Not really. He talked a lot about mining so he must have come from Nevada or somewhere around Sacramento."

Aside from a decent description of Webber, our conversation with Miss Ueland didn't provide Holmes with much useful information. After departing her company we visited the San Francisco police and talked with the sergeant who had responsibility for the case where we received Webber's address. He lived in an apartment building in the Potrero District on the south side of the city, which we visited that afternoon.

The landlady was a heavyset woman with black eyes deeply set in her face, a large mole on the right side of her nose, and a permanent scowl on her face. I subsequently noticed that her demeanor improved when the young man in her custody squeaked or called out to her. I judged the young master to be a year and a half to two years of age, likely her grandson. She met Holmes' greeting at the door with a surly "What?" and showed little inclination to talk until Holmes produced a five dollar gold piece from his vest pocket, at which point she became the very soul of equanimity and said that she was Bertha Nelsen. She then showed us Webber's room. It was simply furnished with a single bed, table, two wooden chairs, and a small dresser with a water pitcher and porcelain basin for shaving. There was a small mirror about twelve inches square above the dresser. None of Webber's clothing or personal effects were present.

"When did Mr. Webber depart?" Holmes asked.

"A week ago," answered the landlady.

"Where are his carpentry tools?"

"Sold them to some feller from the next block a few days before he left."

"Did he say where he was going?"

"Said he was going home."

"Where is that?"

"I don't know. He never said. I never asked. All he said to me was, 'Bertha, I need a rest. I'm going home.' Then he walked out the front door with his carpetbag and I ain't seen him since."

"How long did he live here?" I asked.

"Little over four years," answered the landlady.

"Think about it for a moment, Mrs. Nelsen. Did Webber ever mention the names of places he'd been?" Holmes pulled a second five dollar gold piece out of his vest and rolled it around in his fingers.

"He talked about lots of places where he worked—Virginia City, Deadwood, some town in northern Wisconsin, Wausau I think it was, a place called Bonner in Montana. I dunna know, lots of places."

"Any place in particular? A place that he seemed to especially like?"

The landlady paused, grimaced her face, scratched her nose and rubbed her hand across her lips before saying, "Yes, some little town east of the Sierras over by Reno, but still in California. Was called a burg or a ville, some girl's name."

Holmes waited, but all Mrs. Nelsen could do was shake her head.

"Marysville?" Holmes suggested.

"No, that's not it. Marysville ain't that far east."

"Susanville, perhaps?" Holmes offered.

"That's it," Mrs. Nelson said. "Susanville."

Holmes flipped her the second gold piece, offered her our thanks, and we departed.

At the corner several streets away, we waited for the streetcar to return us to our hotel. There, I asked Holmes, "I assume you have a plan for dealing with this matter, my friend?"

"Yes, but not a good one, Watson. We know so little about Webber. He's a man without a history who is going home wherever that happens to be, although he supposedly liked Susanville if Mrs. Nelsen is to be believed."

"I take it that's where we are going," I said.

"It's the only lead we have, Watson. Maybe someone there can tell us more."

The next afternoon we boarded the Central Pacific for travel to Reno, Nevada. It took us sixteen hours to cover a distance of 245 miles, climbing and then descending the Sierras. I was impressed by the richness of the farmland in the great valley surrounding Sacramento. I have no doubt that with the use of the ice box car, California will soon be sending fresh fruits and vegetables throughout the western United States.[42] We saw little of the mountains whose passage we accomplished at night through a series of slow climbs interrupted by fits and starts as the train stopped frequently at small hamlets like Gold Rush, Dutch Elm, Alta, and Shady Run to take on water, coal and passengers, or to exchange packets of mail.

---

42 Editor's note: Watson's reference to an ice box car referred to the first type of refrigerator railcar which used blocks of ice for cooling prior to the invention of mechanical refrigeration. The use of refrigerated cars allowed California growers to ship their produce long distances without spoiling.

I awoke fully when the first rays of the sun climbed over the eastern horizon and told me it was dawn. I looked across the foot space which separated our seats to see Holmes, pipe clenched in his teeth, staring out the window seeing everything, yet completely unconscious of what his eyes were drinking in, so engrossed in the problem that was before him.

After making my morning ablutions, I returned to my seat and was greeted by Holmes saying, "Good of you to return, Watson. I have been mulling over the little problem we face in finding Mr. Walter Webber in Susanville, assuming that he is even in Susanville at all."

"Surely you jest, Holmes. How hard will it be to find one man in a village of 600 to 800 people, half of whom will be women or children?" I asked in reply.

"Oh, to the contrary, my friend, if Mr. Webber does not wish to be found it will be exceedingly difficult to locate him. The minute two strangers with British accents and wearing suits start asking about his whereabouts, he'll hear of it and then go underground until he can determine whether we constitute a threat. None of the local residents will admit to knowing him."

"So," I countered, "we need a disguise and a story explaining why we want to find him. How about dusting off that little ruse where we pretend we are lawyers representing an estate—"

"No," Holmes said, quickly interrupting my train of thought. "For that ploy to work, the subject must have relatives who might plausibly include him in a will. We have no such information about Webber. He may not have any living relatives."

I wasn't about to surrender so easily. "Why don't we pretend that we are English investors planning to set up shop in Susanville looking for mining properties and we need a skilled carpenter to construct or remodel an office for us?"

"I admire your pluck, Watson," Holmes answered, "but we haven't much time and it might be better to have the object of our search simply reveal himself to us."

"How do you propose to do that?"

"Mrs. Hearst believes that Webber is in the employ of Mr. Joseph Pulitzer who is a resident of New York. Pulitzer couldn't employ a man like Webber from afar. He would need a local agent in San Francisco, a man who would be able to earn Webber's trust so that he would commit himself to a risky endeavor."

"I can appreciate that," I said.

"So, I think the way to expose Mr. Webber and bring him out into the open is to have him receive a telegram from his associate in San Francisco telling Webber to contact him."

"And we'll be there to greet him at the telegraph office."

"Correct. Quite elementary, don't you think, Watson?"

At Reno, Holmes went to the telegraph office to forward instructions to the Pinkerton Agency in San Francisco on how to try and contact Webber. I looked to our bags before we boarded a second train, the Nevada, California, and Oregon, or NCO as the locals called it, for a trip north in the vicinity of Susanville.

Aboard the NCO coach, where Holmes and I were joined by only six other passengers, Holmes showed me the telegram he was having sent to Webber. It read:

Major problem has developed. Great danger. Contact client immediately.

*STEWARD HOUSE HOTEL,
SUSANVILLE, CALIFORNIA*

The terrain from Reno north to Susanville was vastly different than lands on the west side of the Sierras, much dryer and the land seemed more suited to cattle raising than field crops. In that sense, it reminded me of Montana.

We disembarked in Hot Springs, California, and took the stage to Susanville arriving at approximately five o'clock p.m. We were both weary and were delighted that the stage deposited us right in front of the Steward House Hotel where we found suitable lodging.

After securing our baggage in the hotel room and washing the dust from the stagecoach ride from our faces, hands and hair, Holmes and I sauntered over to the Pioneer Saloon in search of a glass of beer. One beer was soon three, followed by a dinner of fried beef steak, fried potatoes, bread and butter. I kept thinking of all that produce I had seen in the fields across the mountain and I got a hankering for fresh fruit, but there was none to be had so I settled for a glass of brandy, two steps removed from being grapes.

The longer we stayed, the more interest the barkeeper took in us. Holmes was right, the local folk had their antennae on high alert, carefully monitoring the strangers in their midst. Finally, he came over to our table and said, "English, eh? Here to look at the timber?"

"No," Holmes replied with a disinterested look on his face. "Mines. We're headed to Diamond Mountain."

"Who'd you say you come to see?" the barkeep asked.

"I didn't say," Holmes replied as he shifted his look, subtly telling the bartender that the conversation was over. Soon thereafter we departed the bar and went in search of the Western Union office which we found on a corner not far from our hotel. It was not an easy place to unobtrusively observe, so we planned to "walk the cross" the next day where we would successively keep our eyes on the office in the hope that Webber would arrive.

The next morning I started the surveillance a block from the Western Union office by walking toward it. At the corner I turned right and walked away from it. At that point Holmes started walking toward the structure keeping it in view as I walked away. At the next corner, I turned back toward the office and Holmes turned away from it. Each block we alternated who served as the observer.[43]

I was concerned that "walking the cross" might be too

---

43 Editor's note: Watson walks toward Western Union on Side 1, Holmes waits. When Watson turns away on Side 2, Holmes walks Side 8 watching the office. Then Watson turns back toward the office on Side 3 while Holmes turns away on Side 7. The pattern repeats itself until both men have walked eight blocks, four observing the office and four walking away from it while the other observes.

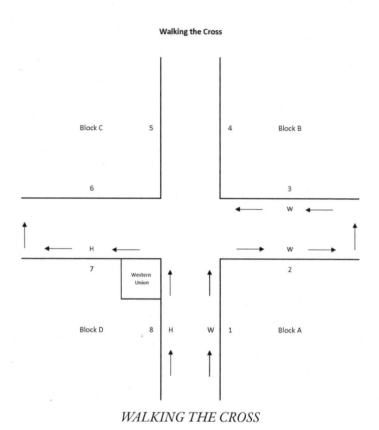

WALKING THE CROSS

obtrusive for a small town like Susanville. It works effective-ly on the crowded streets of London where two men taking a stroll would hardly be observable. But in Susanville, there was no one but Holmes and I on the streets and our repeat-ed passages by a home or store might become the object of curiosity or concern.

My fears proved groundless. We "walked the cross" sev-eral times without anyone seemingly noticing us on the street. Finally, I saw a man matching Webber's description striding toward the Western Union office.

Webber reached the front door of the office before I did, so I turned the corner to the side of the building so my presence wasn't so obvious and signaled to Holmes that Webber was inside. Holmes came at a gallop, stopping before the door to catch a breath and smooth down his hair before entering. Webber was standing at the counter with his return message in hand, the telegrapher still busy at his telegraph seat in the back of the room.

Holmes said, "Mr. Webber, Sherlock Holmes." He then flashed Webber his Pinkerton badge.

Webber didn't look at the shield very carefully and simply said, "The law."

Holmes replied, "I wish a word with you. Perhaps we could do that outside."

Webber shrugged his shoulders and walked past me to the door. His breathing was labored and I could hear a crackle when he inhaled.

Outside on the boardwalk, Holmes introduced me as his associate, John Watson. Then Holmes explained. "Mrs. Phoebe Apperson Hearst has filed a report indicating that her home was robbed of some valuable materials. Furthermore, there is a witness who saw you in the Hearst home the morning of the theft, even though you had no valid reason for being there. What do you have to say on your own behalf, Mr. Webber?"

"I was—" Webber started to reply but his sentence was broken off by a violent fit of coughing. So strong was the cough that Webber bent over at the waist. He then reached for his handkerchief and expelled a copious amount of phlegm. After he righted himself, I saw blood on his lips in the corner of his mouth. I immediately suspected tuberculosis.

SHERLOCK HOLMES: ADVENTURES IN THE WILD WEST

"Excuse me, gentlemen," Webber said. "It's not consumption that I suffer from but cancer. It won't be long before I am bedridden. Perhaps we might go into that café and finish our conversation there. I haven't yet had breakfast."

Holmes readily agreed and together we walked to the eatery. Webber moved slowly and I again heard the crackle in his breathing.

After being seated and served coffee all around, Webber turned to Holmes and said, "I am not a thief, Mr. Holmes."

"Then what were you doing in the Hearst residence that morning?" Holmes asked.

"Saying goodbye to some old friends," Webber replied.

"Don't play me for a laughing stock," Holmes protested. "That stratagem is as dead as a doornail."

I love it when Holmes quotes Shakespeare.[44]

"We interviewed all the staff and you didn't stop by to offer your salutations. Now do you wish to tell me the truth, or do you want me to make arrangements for you to spend your remaining days in the county jail?"

I was surprised by Holmes' aggressiveness. Webber looked as if he'd been hit on the head with a plank.

"No, I wouldn't want to do that," Webber said as he dropped his head. "I came back here to die. I think of Susanville as home, even though I was born and reared near Kansas City. I came here when I was eighteen."

"Then the truth!" Holmes said strongly.

"I told you that I am no thief," Webber said, stifling another cough. "I was hired to carry a parcel away from the

---

44 Editor's note: The phrase "laughing stock" was coined by Shakespeare in *The Merry Wives of Windsor* while "dead as a doornail" appears in *Henry VI*.

Hearst home and bring it here where another man would pick it up from me. I was paid one hundred dollars for getting the parcel and was to be paid another nine hundred dollars when I turned it over to the second courier."

Holmes remarked, "You said 'was to be paid another nine hundred dollars.'"

"Yes," Webber responded. "I was to get another nine hundred dollars, but I won't be getting anything now."

"Why is that?" I asked.

"Because last night I went over to the Pioneer Saloon to play some cards. I saw you two men there but I didn't think anything of it. When I got back to my cabin the place had been ransacked and the parcel was missing. I had hidden it inside the wood bin."

"The parcel you stole from the Hearsts?" Holmes queried.

"I told you before. I am not a thief. I was given the parcel," Webber answered strongly.

"Who gave the parcel to you?" Holmes demanded.

"I don't know the person's name, but I was told that it was needed to protect a young woman's life."

"Can you describe him?" I asked.

"Not well," answered Webber. "A little shorter than me, maybe five feet five inches, I would guess, with light brown hair, no beard or moustache. Not big and kind of delicate features. Certainly not a working man."

Continued conversation with Webber yielded very little. We walked him back to his cabin on South Lassen Street. He had spoken the truth when he said that his cabin had been ransacked. Webber was out of breath so Holmes and I stayed to help him right the cabin.

We departed with Holmes leaving one last admonishment. "Stay here, Mr. Webber. Don't try to flee Susanville. If you do, I'll have you jailed."

"Yes, Mr. Holmes," Webber responded. "I'll not be going anywhere. I came here to die."

As we walked back toward our hotel, I asked Holmes, "How do you propose to find the man who ransacked Webber's cabin?"

He replied, "First we'll visit each of the livery stables and ask if a stranger left town in the past twelve to sixteen hours. Then we'll talk with the stagecoach operator to see if anyone left this morning. If both of these inquiries fail, then we will visit all of the hotels and rooming houses in town and find out what strangers are in town, aside from ourselves."

"You're certain it's a stranger?"

"Indeed, Watson. This exercise has been orchestrated from San Francisco. First, they lure Webber into carrying the goods outside the city on the promise of a thousand dollar fee, and then they cheat him out of ninety percent of the money by having a second man steal it from him."

"Do you think Webber has told the truth?"

"I do, Watson. I hardly believe that he ransacked his home in anticipation of two detectives catching up with him in Susanville and him needing a plausible alibi for why he didn't have the purloined papers."

"Well spoken," I agreed.

"You go back to the hotel and get a list of livery stables," Holmes said. "I will return to Western Union to make sure that if Webber tries to communicate with someone in San Francisco, we'll get a copy of that telegram."

"I thought telegrams were confidential," I said.

"They're supposed to be, Doctor, but if you really want to

see one, I've found that a five dollar gold piece in the hands of an underpaid telegrapher is usually all that is necessary to allow one to look through copies of the transmissions."

Later that afternoon, Holmes and I visited each of the town's livery stables without success. Each of the persons who saddled up a horse of their own or rented one from a livery were local residents, well known to the stable owners.

Our talk with stage line owner Fred Bagin was more productive. He reported that a man had missed the morning stage and was rather upset about it. Bagin said, "The feller seemed rather keen to get out of town, but I told him the next stage wasn't till morning. We'd be leaving at eight o'clock a.m. so he might as well get comfortable for the night."

Holmes asked, "Can you describe him?"

"Yes," Bagin replied. "A big, robust fellow about the Doctor's size. Black hair, clean shaven. Had on a brown suit, wearing a derby. I took him for a lawyer."

"Do you recall when he came to Susanville?" I asked.

"Day before yesterday. He asked me to recommend a boardinghouse so I told him about Agnes Twichell's. It's over on South Lassen Street."

Not far from Walter Webber's cabin, I thought to myself.

Holmes and I found the man in question. Mrs. Twichell also became quite talkative when presented the option of earning an alm when Holmes tossed a gold piece in the air before her. He was registered under the name of Cecil Yarrow and was in the last room on the second floor of the boardinghouse.

After thanking Mrs. Twichell for her assistance, we departed through the front door only to look out back where we found a set of steps leading to the second floor. Holmes left me to monitor the comings and goings from the building while he went to Western Union.

Holmes returned in fifteen minutes, and five minutes behind him came a Western Union delivery boy. A few minutes later, Yarrow departed the building and Holmes and I re-entered using the back steps. Holmes easily picked the lock to Yarrow's room while I stood sentry.

In a few minutes, Holmes was back in the hall simply saying, "I have it." We retreated down the back steps and headed toward our hotel in time to see Yarrow walking back from Western Union.

At the hotel, Holmes opened the package. To our surprise it contained nothing but newsprint cut the size of typing paper.

Holmes slammed down the papers. "Watson, we've been duped. This entire trip to Susanville was a diversion set up to beguile the police, I am sure, but it ensnared me as well. At least now I know who did it. We've got to get back to the telegraph office."

For the fourth time that day, Holmes led us back to Western Union, this time to cable Mrs. Hearst. Holmes' message said:

> *Returning from Susanville tomorrow. Detain Miss Ueland. Use police if necessary.*

The next morning as we prepared to depart the hotel, Holmes received a reply cable from Mrs. Hearst. It said:

> *Greta Ueland departed my employ three days ago. Whereabouts unknown.*

We shared the stagecoach from Susanville to the railhead at Hot Springs with Cecil Yarrow. He wasn't particularly communicative, but he did admit to being from San Francisco where he owned a saloon. I didn't relish spending twenty hours in a railway coach on another nocturnal trip over the Sierras, but I was apparently overcome with exhaustion, falling asleep near Truckee and remaining in repose until we reached Sacramento.

On our return to San Francisco, we immediately re-

MISS GRETA UELAND

turned to Mrs. Hearst's hacienda in Pleasanton. Holmes didn't even offer a greeting but said instead, "Watson and I have just spent five days on a wild goose chase, chasing a packet of old newspapers. If this matter has been propagated by Mr. Pulitzer, he's been very cunning indeed."

"You believe that Greta Ueland is involved?" Mrs. Hearst asked.

"I do," said Holmes between biting through a piece of toast and swallowing a drink of coffee. "In fact, I believe she was the thief, and the bundle of so-called documents she passed on to Webber was simply a diversion, expecting that the police would become involved sooner or later."

"How do you propose to find her?" Mrs. Hearst asked.

"I believe I know where she is. Do you want the police involved now?"

"No," answered Mrs. Hearst.

"Then I'll need the services of four reliable men," Holmes answered.

Mrs. Hearst departed our company and Holmes and I reveled in what was the finest breakfast we'd eaten since departing Montana three weeks previous. Mrs. Hearst returned with her gardeners—four brothers, appropriately named Matthew, Mark, Luke, and John.

That afternoon, Holmes and I returned to Bertha Nelsen's boardinghouse where Webber had lived. Holmes sent Matthew and Mark around to the rear entrance with instructions not to let anyone escape—man, woman, or child.

Holmes posted Luke and John at the front door with the same instructions and the two of us went in search of the landlady's apartment.

The sounds of movement could be heard behind the

door after Holmes soundly rapped on its exterior. Mrs. Nelsen opened it about two inches wide and peered out into Holmes' implacable face, saying nothing.

Holmes said, "I want to see Greta now."

Mrs. Nelsen replied, "I don't know any Greta."

"And I say that you do," Holmes responded. "Produce her now, or my men will batter down every door in the building until we find her."

So much for implacability, I thought to myself. "What is it, Mother?" came a voice from the back in the room.

Holmes immediately pushed the door open and stepped past the landlady. "Good afternoon, Miss Ueland, I've come to retrieve the papers you stole from Mr. Hearst's desk."

"I don't have them," Greta Ueland replied. "I sold them to—"

Holmes cut her off. "No, you didn't." He continued, "You need those papers to protect your son."

"I have no son!"

"Yes, you do. I saw the lad when I visited your mother several days ago. He has your nose and eyes and William Randolph's jaw."

I was dumbfounded by Holmes' allegation that one of the captains of American enterprise had fathered a child with a housemaid working in his mother's home.

Greta paused, uncertain what to do. Holmes continued, "If you return the papers to me, I will intervene with Mrs. Hearst on your behalf to both protect you from jail and to provide for the care of your child."

"Very well, Mr. Holmes," Greta answered, "you've found me out. Mr. Hearst is father to my Philip. I overheard Mrs. Hearst tell you that her son had a penchant for actresses and showgirls. I can tell you that he has a penchant for any-thing in a skirt—waitresses, housemaids, nurses and school marms—it makes no difference. He came to me three years ago with promises that would dazzle the eyes of any girl and I made the mistake of submitting to his will."

Greta Ueland paused her story at that point, I think ex-pecting Holmes to defend the honor of William Randolph Hearst, but Holmes said nothing. Greta continued, "Once I was with child, he would have nothing to do with me. I knew that if I accused him of fathering my child I would be dismissed from my post, so I asked Mrs. Hearst for a few months leave, telling her that I needed to care for an invalid mother. She allowed me to do that and I returned here to have the baby. Mother has taken care of him ever since, but I pay most of Philip's expenses from my earnings."

"Mr. Hearst visited his mother about four months ago and told her about his affair with the actress and how he had entered into an agreement with her pledging to pay to care for the child in return for her silence about the matter. I have no money to hire a lawyer, and no way, other than my word, to prove that my Philip is his son."[45]

"Then I saw the papers on the elder Mr. Hearst's desk after they had arrived. Mrs. Hearst must have been inter-rupted while reading them and I saw the details of William Randolph's agreement with the actress."

"Eavesdropping and spying on one's employer is not a

_____

45 Editor's note: There was no scientific way of proving paternity in the 1890s. The mother's testimony was the chief evidence but, of course, it could be discredited. Blood typing was not discovered until 1900 and not widely used until the 1920s. It wasn't until the 1960s that highly accurate genetic paternity testing became available.

becoming character trait," Holmes lectured.

"I never eavesdropped, Mr. Holmes. Rich people act like their servants are just another piece of furniture. They forget that we can see, hear, speak, feel, and think. I was in the office dusting the bookcase when Mr. Hearst told his mother about his problem back in New York City and how he handled it. When I read those documents I learned that he was willing to pay that woman one thousand dollars per month for mothering his child, and yet he left me with nothing. I made a resolution then and there that he was going to help me raise Philip, not as a parent, but financially like he was doing with that other woman. When that arrangement is put in writing, I will return the papers I took from Mrs. Hearst's home and not before."

Holmes said, "Miss Ueland, I believe that I can accomplish that goal for you, but if you persist in denying me access to the documents, I will have no other choice than to tear this building down board by board, brick by brick, until I find them."

"You'll not find them, Mr. Holmes," Greta answered. "I took precautions. The papers are a long way from here, in an envelope addressed to Mr. Joseph Pulitzer. Anything happens to me, Mrs. Hearst's concern for her son's welfare and political career will end up being a tragic nightmare."

"Checkmate," I said to myself. The woman has pluck and may be the most worthy adversary Holmes has faced since Irene Adler in a little affair I titled "A Scandal in Bohemia."[46]

Holmes, ever the gentleman, simply instructed Miss Ueland to get her sweater. We were all going to return to

---

46 Editor's note: *The Strand* Magazine, July 1891.

the hacienda for a conference with Mrs. Hearst.

Back at the hacienda, Miss Ueland poured out her story for a second time.

Mrs. Hearst said very little, but her body bespoke her mind very clearly. She was disgusted with her son for consorting with a woman that she could only consider a trollop. Nevertheless, after Miss Ueland had said her piece, Mrs. Hearst called her secretary and a settlement was negotiated on the spot. She never contested Miss Ueland's claim of the child's paternity. Instead, Miss Ueland received an immediate payment of one thousand dollars for past privations and an agreement to pay her one hundred fifty dollars per month henceforth until Philip reached the age of twenty-one. In turn, Miss Ueland pledged to keep the matter confidential.

After we departed the hacienda on our way back to San Francisco and our hotel, I asked Holmes how he figured out that it was Miss Ueland.

"I didn't do nearly as well as I should have, Watson," he replied. "I violated my own rule regarding the obvious fact.[47] I accepted the Pulitzer theory and acted on it without considering that it could be another person with another motive altogether."

"Yes, but what caused you to see the error of your ways?" I asked.

"Our conversation with Webber in Susanville started my thinking."

"What did he say?"

---

47 Editor's note: "There is nothing more deceptive than an obvious fact." First uttered by Holmes in "The Bascombe Valley Mystery."

"It was the description of the person from whom he received the packet of papers. He described that individual as a 'person,' not a man or woman. I, and I am sure that you as well, automatically assumed that it was a man. Webber then described the individual as having light brown hair, shorter than he, with delicate features. He didn't have the wits about him to make up a false description, and instead described Miss Ueland. Unfortunately, I never recognized it until the next day when I opened the package Yarrow had removed from Webber's cabin and discovered that we were chasing a stack of old newspapers."

"And Yarrow?" I asked.

"Just a friend of Mrs. Nelsen who was hired by Miss Ueland to stage a burglary to insure that the parcel disappeared in the event the police were successful in tracking down Webber."

"She never bargained on Mrs. Hearst bringing in the most brilliant of investigators," I answered.

"No, she didn't. But, as we both discovered, Miss Ueland was brilliant in her own right. She crafted a plan that would have stymied every law enforcement agency in the world including Scotland Yard and the Surete."

"But Holmes, the important thing is that Miss Ueland was not able to carry out her plan in a way that would harm Mr. Hearst. William Randolph is now free to pursue his political career,[48] and Miss Ueland will have more than

---

48 Editor's note: William Randolph Hearst was elected twice to the U.S. House of Representatives as a Democrat from New York's 11th Congressional District, serving from March 1903 to March 1907. He ran unsuccessfully for Mayor of New York City in 1905 and 1909 and for Governor of the State of New York in 1909.

sufficient financial resources to support her child."

"All's well that ends well, eh Watson?"

I could see immediately that Holmes did not mean what he had just said, but I agreed for once, too tired from all the traveling to protest. I looked forward to a good meal, reading some more of Mr. Harte's short stories, and a long night's sleep.[49]

---

49 Editor's note: According to Watson's papers, Holmes was never satisfied with the outcome of "The Case of the Purloined Papers." While the Hearst family accepted Miss Ueland's claim regarding the paternity of her child and paid handsomely to quietly settle the matter, Holmes was more skeptical and the uncertainty followed him until his final days. He always wondered if the real father had, in fact, been Webber all along and that the Hearsts had been taken in by a sophisticated swindle orchestrated by Miss Ueland.

Although more accurate methods of determining paternity became available later on, Philip Ueland was never tested. He died in 1918 on a battlefield in northern France at the age of twenty-four. His remains were never recovered.

The Case of the Missing Marchese

I t was a beautiful afternoon in early October. The sky was a deep blue, for me reminiscent of the North Atlantic which Sherlock Holmes and I had crossed several months ago to venture to Montana. Here, Holmes had solved several mysteries to his satisfaction and we were enjoying a few carefree days before contemplating our travel back to the British Isles. Holmes had departed earlier in the day with Dr. Spelman, with whom he had forged an intellectual bond, to examine some Indian habitation sites the Doctor had discovered in the nearby Deer Lodge Valley.

I, in turn, had spent the morning updating my journals which documented Holmes' activities in Montana. Following lunch I had enjoyed a brisk walk to the Anaconda Race Track on the western end of town and now, having returned, was sitting in the lobby of the Montana Hotel enjoying a cup of coffee while I watched the clouds race overhead through the front window.

I observed two gentlemen climb the front stairs of the ho-

SHERLOCK HOLMES: ADVENTURES IN THE WILD WEST

tel. Both were immaculately dressed, one in a blue suit, the other gray. Both wore derby hats and carried canes. They looked as if they had just stepped out of a cab in Trafalgar Square. After walking in the door they surveyed the lobby, finally turning in my direction and commenced walking toward me.

"Dr. Watson," said the man in gray, his English accent quite pronounced. I guessed he was from the English Midlands. They obviously weren't from Trafalgar Square, but perhaps accustomed to Albert Square in Manchester.

"Yes, I am Dr. Watson," I replied. "Which fellow Englishmen do I have the pleasure of meeting?"

"My name is Thomas Bellingham," answered the gentleman in the gray suit. "And this is my business associate, Stephan Coopersmith. As you've already surmised, we share your birthright in the United Kingdom."

"Please, sit down and join me. I trust you've recently arrived from England. I would love to hear some news from the motherland."

"Indeed," Coopersmith answered. "We departed a little over six weeks ago. It's most astounding how the steamship and steam locomotive have shrunk the size of the globe we inhabit."

"I had a similar conversation just the other day with my compatriot, Mr. Sherlock Holmes, who predicted, and I quote, 'While I won't live to see it, Watson, the world will soon see transoceanic liners making the trip from Southampton to New York in less than four days, and soon some other technology, perhaps through the air, will make that speed seem slow by comparison.'"[50]

"Mr. Holmes, is he about?" Bellingham inquired.

"Out for the day, but I expect that he will return for dinner," I answered.

"We would very much appreciate an audience with Mr. Holmes, if you could arrange the same, Doctor," Bellingham countered. "It's a matter of some importance and urgency."

"Could you give me some snippet of information that I might use to entice Holmes' interest? He's quite selective about the type of cases he undertakes."

"Certainly, Doctor. Please advise him that we have been defrauded of twenty-five thousand American dollars."

"That should be sufficient to hold Holmes' attention," I replied. "Should we say seven o'clock this evening in the hotel's dining room?"

Holmes returned just before six o'clock and I explained the circumstance of my meeting with Bellingham and Coopersmith. I could tell by the way his eyes danced about that he was already mentally engaged. It was a matter of absorbing the details of the case.

Our fellow countrymen were already seated in the dining room when we arrived. After introductions, Holmes got right down to business. "So you gentlemen came over on the *RMS Campania*?"

Bellingham looked at Coopersmith. They looked at me.

---

50 Editor's note: Holmes was very conversant with technology and he correctly assessed that transatlantic voyages would get significantly faster, ultimately culminating in the *SS United States* setting a speed record of three days, ten hours and forty minutes in 1952. Holmes also correctly assessed that some form of air travel would supplant the steamship as the fastest means across the Atlantic. Holmes was no doubt aware that in 1895 Count Ferdinand Von Zeppelin had patented a design for a rigid frame airship, now known as a Zeppelin or dirigible, in Germany.

MESSRS. THOMAS BELLINGHAM (L)
AND STEPHAN COOPERSMITH (R)

I shrugged my shoulders to indicate that I knew nothing. Of course, Holmes was just dazzling them with his deductive brilliance.

Bellingham asked, "How, Mr. Holmes, could you possibly know which liner we sailed on to America? Neither of us mentioned it to Dr. Watson."

"Just a little trifle, Mr. Bellingham. Your associate Mr. Coopersmith is wearing a Cunard Line pin on his lapel."

"Why, yes, yes I am," replied Coopersmith. "I found it one morning on the floor in the passageway outside our stateroom and kept it as a memento of our voyage."

"So, if you were on a Cunard liner, the only one that could have possibly brought you to the United States a little over six weeks ago was the *Campania*. It docked in New York on September 28th. Knowledge of train and steamship schedules is an important tool for a consulting detective," Holmes explained.[51]

"Very impressive, Mr. Holmes," replied Bellingham. "You are definitely the right man to help us with our problem, an opinion shared by Sheriff Fitzpatrick who recommended that we see you. The sheriff said you enjoyed a difficult puzzle, but that if you were not interested in our matter we should return to him."

"An excellent man, the sheriff," Holmes replied. "We

---

51 Editor's note: Watson's original manuscript contained an interesting revelation on Holmes' powers of detection. It said, "The next morning at breakfast I chided Holmes for telling the two Englishmen that knowledge of train and steamship schedules is an important tool for a consulting detective." In fact, Holmes paid little attention to such matters. He frequently said to me, and I thus reported in a case entitled "The Five Orange Pips" (1891), that "a man should keep his little brain attic stocked with all the furniture he is likely to use, and the rest he can put away in the lumber-room of his library where he can get it if he wants." Holmes knew about the sailing schedule of the *Campania* because, a few days previous, we had discussed arrangements for returning to England and had examined the steamship schedules of the Cunard, White Star and Inman Lines.

have worked together successfully on several endeavors since Watson and I came to Montana. Pray, please tell me now the nature of your problem."

"I don't know where to begin," answered Bellingham.

"Please start in England. You two gentlemen appear to be successful businessmen. The fact that you are here in Montana's most prosperous mining region indicates to me that you have been engaged in mining back home and have come to Montana in quest of other opportunities."

"Quite correct again, Mr. Holmes," answered Bellingham. "You seem to have the uncanny ability to read both a man's character and his mind from the cut of his clothes."

"Not really, sir. Again, it is simply a matter of seeing the obvious. It's long been an axiom of mine that the little things are infinitely the most important to a detective," Holmes answered.[52]

"Stephan is from Manchester and I, Sheffield. We met at the Royal School of Mines in London."

"Yes," Holmes responded. "I am quite familiar with the institution."

Bellingham continued. "We are both from families who have successfully engaged in commerce for several generations, and we both received a share of our inheritance from our fathers so that we might establish successful careers."

"Outside the family business," I observed.

"Yes, Dr. Watson," Bellingham answered. "While my father is a successful merchant, the business will not support all seven of his sons. My older brothers John and Eugene are

---

52 Editor's note: Holmes first articulated this principle of detection in the case Watson chronicled as "A Case of Identity" published in 1891.

following in my father's footsteps. The rest of us must find our own way, and I chose mining."

"And you, Mr. Coopersmith?" Holmes asked.

"My family is in dry goods, a subject with which I am intimately familiar and totally disinterested. I had an uncle who told me about mining in South Africa, both diamonds and gold. It piqued my curiosity and now it's become a passion."

Coopersmith continued. "After graduating from the School of Mines we both took positions working in the collieries[53] near Barnsley. We put several small investments together, all of which were successful, and the earnings from them allowed us to acquire a major share of Hoyland Silkstone Coal and Coke."

"You've done very well indeed, gentlemen," Holmes replied. "I understand it to be an exceedingly well-managed and prosperous company."

"It is," replied Bellingham. "So well managed, in fact, that it requires little of our time. So we started looking for additional opportunities."

"Which led you to Montana," I interjected.

"Not immediately," Bellingham replied. "Our inquiries took us all over England and Wales and then, about two months ago, we stopped in Manchester and met Stephan's father for drinks and dinner at the Manchester Reform Club."

"So you're a liberal by descent, Mr. Coopersmith," Holmes said as he turned away from Bellingham.

"In the matter of politics, Mr. Holmes, this acorn fell a long ways from that tree. Liberalism is my father's fancy, I

---

53 Editor's note: The British term for a coal mine and associated buildings and equipment on the surface.

am afraid," answered Coopersmith.

Holmes and I both chuckled. "Pray, please continue, Mr. Bellingham," Holmes said.

"During the course of the evening we met Major Archibald Lewis, formerly with the Royal Engineers, now retired."

"Did you say Archibald Lewis?" I asked, uncertain of what I had heard. "Short man, bald head, but with a massive moustache?"

"Exactly," replied Bellingham. "You must know him, Doctor."

"Indeed, I am an old military man myself. But we can discuss that later. Please, go on with your story."

"Major Lewis is the one who told us about the opportunities in the U.S., in both Colorado and Montana. Ultimately, it was he who told us about the Mohawk Mining Company," Coopersmith said.

"What is the Mohawk Mining Company?" Holmes interjected.

"A small mineral exploration venture located about five miles west of Anaconda," Coopersmith continued. "Thomas and I came over to look at the property and perhaps acquire some shares, but things have gone awry. That's why we are here to see you, Mr. Holmes."

At that point our meeting was interrupted by the wait staff bringing us our meal. For the next forty-five minutes all thought of business was waylaid while we enjoyed roast beef so succulent that it seemed to melt in one's mouth and an assortment of roasted vegetables including potatoes, carrots, parsnips, turnips, and rutabagas. There was fresh sourdough bread with copious amounts of butter and jam. For dessert

THE CASE OF THE MISSING MARCHESE

we enjoyed tea with a thick slice of Black Forest cake baked that afternoon by Assistant Chef Heinz Reinhold, a native of Bavaria who had possession of his grandmother's recipe for the cake, the perfect combination of chocolate, whipped cream, and cherry liquor filling, a confection the likes of which I have never enjoyed since those days in Montana.

When the dishes had been cleared away, Holmes turned to Coopersmith and asked that he continue their story.

"As I said previously, Major Lewis is the one who told us about the Mohawk Mining Company and we discussed our interest in securing new investments."

"Did the Major strongly recommend that particular investment?" Holmes asked.

"No. He simply mentioned it as a potential opportunity should we be looking for investments in the States. He did say that he regretted not being able to participate himself because the group planning to bring the Mohawk into production as an operating silver mine had made him a small fortune in Colorado with a return of over four hundred percent."

"Astounding!" Holmes remarked quite forcefully.

"Indeed," continued Coopersmith, "but Major Lewis seemed rather nonchalant about it. In fact, the Major excused himself and wandered off to talk with some other gentlemen at the bar. After visiting about it with Thomas and getting the opinion of my father, we agreed to get further information about the company. Later that evening, we again talked with the Major and he kindly gave us the name and address of Mr. Frank Botterbusch, the General Manager of the Mohawk Mining Company."

Coopersmith continued. "That led to an exchange of

cables between the parties. Ultimately it was decided that we would come to Montana and tour the mine. The tour was scheduled for a week ago this past Monday." At this point, Coopersmith paused his narrative and suggested that we retire to the bar where we might enjoy a libation and good cigar.

I heartily endorsed his suggestion and we were soon situated at a corner table in the Tammany Bar. There, Holmes and I took brandy while our English clients opted for scotch and water.

"Pray, please continue," Holmes said. I could see that he had absorbed more than enough background material. He wanted to get to the facts of the case.

"When we arrived at the mine just after noon, there were four people in the room. Mr. Botterbusch stepped forward to introduce himself and his foreman, Mr. Don Kelly. Botterbusch was a very big man, over six feet with powerful arms and a thick scar across his chin. He was clean shaven and wore round spectacles which looked out of place on a man so robust. Kelly was much smaller, with a physique similar to yours, Mr. Holmes, but at least four inches shorter. Kelly seemed to have recently arrived from Ireland. His Irish brogue was quite pronounced. Botterbusch then introduced us to Mr. Alberto Visconti, the Marchese of Pisa and Iglesiente. Pisa we knew about. We subsequently learned that Iglesiente is a mining region in Sardinia where the Visconti family had holdings."

"Anyone else?" Holmes asked.

"Yes, but we weren't formally introduced to him. Mr. Botterbusch said that he was an interpreter because the marchese did not speak English. Later on I heard Mr. Kelly call him Rinaldo and the marchese called him Mr. Capelli."

"Please describe these latter two men," Holmes asked.

"I had better defer to Thomas. He's the more affable of us and pays more attention to people than I," Coopersmith responded.

MR. RINALDO CAPELLI

"Certainly, Mr. Holmes," said Bellingham. "First, the interpreter. He had a more distinctive look. He was a small fellow, perhaps five feet four inches tall with a wiry build, perhaps nine stone in weight.[54] He had black hair with very husky brown eyebrows and his eyes were sunken back in his face, which was narrow and sharply angled. It's not a face that I would have associated with an Italian."

"Complexion?" Holmes asked.

"Very dark," Bellingham replied. "More Arab in look than Italian, and he talked like an Arab as well, with a high-pitched staccato voice. If I were to summarize his face, I would say he looked like a ferret."

"And the marchese?" Holmes questioned.

"He was definitely Italian. The skin was a light olive brown, very Mediterranean. Not a big man either, but taller than the translator by two or three inches and heavier as well, maybe two stone heavier."

"Hair, eyes, distinguishing characteristics?" Holmes asked.

"Medium brown hair, sideburns, small moustache, no scars or anything unique about his look that I remember. Oh yes, there was something," Bellingham said. "His hands were rough. More the hands of a workingman than a gentle-man, but I—we never questioned his authenticity. He knew a great deal about mine finance, certainly a subject well beyond the educational level of the working class."

"You talked to him then?" Holmes asked. "I thought he needed a translator."

---

54 Editor's note: A stone is equal to 14 pounds. The interpreter weighed about 125 pounds; the Marchese about 155 pounds.

Mr. Botterbusch thought so, but the marchese later told us that he liked to feign ignorance of the English language so that he can hear what others say about him."

"A man of some cleverness," Holmes observed. "Now, if you may, please go back and describe the events."

"Mr. Botterbusch led us into the mine portal. The marchese, Mr. Kelly, and the translator were behind us. We followed the track into the hillside for several hundred feet. At the end of the drift there was a solid wall of argentiferous galena.[55] Mr. Botterbusch showed us the width of the vein and explained how it ran laterally into the hillside for an unknown length toward the old Blue Eyed Nellie Mine. The Blue Eyed Nellie was a high grade silver mine that operated in the 1870s. Botterbusch explained that the vein they had discovered on the Mohawk claim was an extension of the Blue Eyed Nellie vein that had been offset to the east by faulting."

Holmes and I were getting a lesson in geology which was beyond my comprehension, but I knew that my companion understood every word of it.

Coopersmith paused briefly to take a drink of his scotch and said, "Then Mr. Botterbusch brought out a sheet of paper and showed us the assays from ten samples they had taken from the vein. It averaged six hundred thirteen ounces of silver per ton, twenty-one percent lead, and three percent zinc. The silver alone, Mr. Holmes, made that rock worth $306 per ton.

"After Botterbusch finished his explanation, the transla-

---

55 Editor's note: An ore which contains the minerals argentite, a silver sulphide (Ag_2S), and galena, a lead sulphide (PbS).

tor explained it all over again in Italian to the marchese."

"The marchese got excited, didn't he, Stephan?" interjected Bellingham.

"His hands were flying about and he began speaking quite rapidly. Then he went back over to the rock face again and picked up some of the ore laying in a pile below it. He put a rock in his pocket, then handed one to me and through the translator told me to get it assayed and see for ourselves," Coopersmith explained.

"Then Botterbusch told us we could 'get in on the ground floor,' to use his terminology, and he went on to explain that he expected the marchese to take a fifteen percent stake in the property. The translator quickly translated what Botterbusch had said to the marchese. The marchese shook his head no and told Botterbusch he wanted twenty-five percent."

"After that," Coopersmith continued, "we followed the translator out to the surface and then met with Botterbusch in his office. The marchese was waiting for a private audience with Botterbusch after we left."

"We spoke with Botterbusch for about thirty minutes. He started the discussion by offering us ten percent of the company for $50,000. Thomas and I then questioned him at length about what the money was going to be used for, how soon before the mine would go into production, and things of that type. We were both satisfied that he knew what he was doing, but $50,000 was a lot more than we had planned to invest so Thomas told him that we would think about it, confer with our partners in the U.K., and get back to him."

"You have partners?" Holmes asked.

"No," responded Bellingham this time. "It was just a little ruse on my part to give us more time to talk things over. We left the mine about three o'clock and got back to the hotel near four o'clock. About an hour later the front desk sent up a boy with a note from the marchese asking us to meet him for a drink and dinner that evening at seven-thirty. We met at this very table, the marchese sitting where Dr. Watson is at rest. When we entered the room the marchese was alone, and when we reached the table I said, 'Hello, Marchese.'"

"'Please sit down, gentlemen,' the marchese replied in English with a clear Italian accent."

"Needless to say, we were surprised by his speech, and I said, 'Excuse me, Marchese, we were expecting your interpreter to be here as well, but you seem to speak English.'

"'Indeed, I do,' answered the marchese, 'but only when it pleases me, Mr. Bellingham.' Stephan and I were, admittedly, somewhat confused by this statement so the marchese elaborated. He said, 'When I was just a young boy, I accompanied my father and grandfather on a trip to the mining regions of the Harz Mountains in Germany. My father and grandfather both spoke excellent German, the whole family does, but throughout the trip both pretended to be ignorant of the language. It was truly astounding what our hosts said in front of us, believing that we didn't understand them. I've adopted that policy myself whenever I'm outside Italy, with similar positive results. And so, Mr. Frank Botterbusch and his associates think I speak only Italian and were kind enough to provide a translator, Mr. Capelli.'"

"Frankly, Mr. Holmes, Dr. Watson, I thought the marchese's explanation was simply brilliant and we moved forward with our conversation," Bellingham explained.

"Stephan then asked him, 'Did you learn something of interest from Mr. Botterbusch that we might wish to know? I mean, I trust that's why you invited us to join you for dinner.'

"'You're very perceptive, Mr. Coopersmith,' answered the marchese. 'I learned that Mr. Botterbusch is, to use the American expression, playing you for a sucker.'

"We were both astounded by the marchese's remarks," Coopersmith said. "So I asked the marchese, 'How is that so?'

"'By offering to sell you stock in the Mohawk Company at a much higher rate than it is being offered to other investors,' the marchese said. 'Did Botterbusch not offer to sell you a ten percent stake in the company for $50,000, with the proceeds to be used to build a mill?'

"I told him that was correct," Coopersmith said. "The marchese took a small sip from his whiskey and said, 'Gentlemen, Mr. Botterbusch offered me fifteen percent for $15,000.'

"We were thunderstruck by that revelation, Mr. Holmes. I am afraid the tenor of my voice caught the attention of two gentlemen across the room."

"'Go easy, Mr. Bellingham,' the marchese counseled. 'The whole world doesn't need to know your business.'

"I apologized to the marchese," said Bellingham, and then he continued.

"'There are two things going on here, gentlemen,' the marchese said. 'First, Botterbusch knows that both of you are largely ignorant of silver mining. You're both from the English Midlands and I suspect that you've made your money either in coal or iron, maybe the steel business.'

"'That's correct,' I told him," said Coopersmith. "'Coal.'"

"'Well, coal is a much different business than mining

precious metals like silver,' the marchese explained. 'Botter-busch is counting on you two thinking they're basically the same. Second, he needs me a lot more than he needs you. The Visconti family has been associated with some of the most successful silver mines in the world. On my mother's side, we go back 400 years. Her family was originally from Bohemia and owned mines in Joachimistal. Since then, the family has been involved in mining in Germany and Sardinia, which is where our most important holdings are today. My father even acquired a small piece of the famous Comstock Lode, but he got there late so it didn't turn out to be as successful as he'd hoped. Now, it's my turn to tour the world looking for investment opportunities.'

"'An impressive history, Marchese, of that there is no doubt. But why are you worth so much more to Botter-busch than us?' I asked," said Bellingham.

"'That's easy,' the marchese answered. 'Botterbusch wants me on his board of directors. The Visconti family has close ties to the Rothschilds, and they with financiers the world over. With me on the board Botterbusch assumes, correctly I might add, that he can attract investment capital in whatever quantity he needs. But he has a problem.'

"'What's that?' I asked in reply.

"'He needs an operating mine,' the marchese said. 'You won't see the Rothschilds investing in properties that are unproven. Botterbusch needs your capital to build a small mill. Once he's producing silver he'll be able to get the money he needs to turn the Mohawk into a world class operation.'

"I asked him if he thought the mine had that potential," Bellingham said.

"The marchese said he did. Specifically, he said, 'You saw

that vein. I am certain it connects with the workings of the Blue Eyed Nellie up the hill, and only God knows how far it strikes to the south. I am certain Mr. Botterbusch is on the cusp of a bonanza.'

"'So what does that have to do with us?' I asked him," Coopersmith said.

"'I am interested in forming a business association with you two gentlemen, assuming that you are interested in investing in the Mohawk,' came the marchese's reply.

"'That's already been decided,' we told him. 'We are.'

"'Excellent, then it's simply a matter of getting the best possible deal for our money,' the marchese answered.

"'This is my proposal: I will be meeting with Botterbusch the day after tomorrow, on Wednesday, and I can negotiate a much better price for the shares than can you gentlemen. In exchange you, Mr. Coopersmith, will act as our family's agent for our investment in the Mohawk. I believe that I heard you tell Botterbusch that you were moving to the United States.'

"'That's correct,' I told him," said Coopersmith. "'Thomas and I have also made an investment in a company called Colorado Fuel and Iron, and I will be moving to Denver so I can look after that holding.'

"Then the marchese asked me if I would be willing to oversee the Viscontis' share of the Mohawk. I told him that I would be pleased to do so as well.

"The marchese answered by saying, 'Excellent. It appears that we have an agreement in principle.'

"At that point I asked the marchese, 'How are we to manage this situation with Mr. Botterbusch?'" Bellingham said. "Then the marchese advised us to stall him until at least Friday. 'Tell Botterbusch that you need to cable England for further instructions.'

"The marchese then said, 'If I'm to get anything done with him it will be this Wednesday, Thursday at the latest. Should I not be able to close the deal on terms I find acceptable, I will tell you, and you gentlemen can proceed on your own.'

"'Very considerate of you, Marchese,' we told him," Coopersmith said.

"On Wednesday afternoon we received a note from the marchese asking us to meet him for dinner at Whatley's Café. He asked us about our discussion with Botterbusch. There wasn't much to tell. We told him that our associates in England had not yet approved the transaction but we expected an answer by Friday. Mr. Botterbusch was not happy," explained Bellingham. "The marchese then told us about his meeting with Botterbusch and he gave us two options. We could purchase 25,000 shares from the marchese for $25,000, or we could go back to Botterbusch and see what kind of a deal we could put together on our own. Suffice it to say, we wanted the marchese's shares and we agreed to meet him the next morning at the Daly Bank to close the transaction."

"The marchese then advised us not to talk to Botterbusch until the following Monday," Coopersmith said. "He said Botterbusch was feeling 'a bit abused' by the marchese's hardened negotiating stance, but would cool down once he realized that he had sufficient funds to build an ore processing mill plus do additional underground work.

"As scheduled, we met the marchese at the bank the next morning," confirmed Coopersmith. "The marchese deposited our bank draft in the Visconti account and provided us with a stock certificate for 25,000 shares in the Mohawk Mining and Improvement Company. He also gave me a letter designating me as the agent for the Visconti family on all matters pertaining to the operation of the Mohawk Mine. Soon after, the marchese excused himself saying that he had a meeting at the offices of Anaconda Copper.

"As planned, we met Mr. Botterbusch at his office on Monday morning, whereupon I showed him the letter authorizing me to represent the Visconti family. While he was reading the letter, I also expressed our disappointment in him for trying to hold us up for such an exaggerated price while being willing to sell stock to the marchese for $1.00 per share.

"Botterbusch put down the letter and said, 'Gentlemen, there is some confusion here. Marchese Visconti did not purchase any shares in the Mohawk Company so you, Mr. Coopersmith, represent nothing unless, of course, you wish to purchase shares at the price I quoted you last Monday.'

"I started to laugh, Mr. Holmes, and said, 'Why would I do that when we've already purchased 25,000 shares through the marchese?' and showed him our stock certificate."

"Then I entered the conversation," Bellingham interjected. "I said, 'Look, we have a stock certificate with his signature on it, a signature that matches one on a letter received from him prior to our departure from England.' I demanded that Botterbusch explain himself.

"He said, 'The certificate is a forgery.'

"From there, Mr. Holmes, Dr. Watson, the conversation deteriorated into an argument with Botterbusch denouncing us as frauds and denying us our rights as shareholders.

"We went directly to the sheriff at that point. He talked to Mr. Botterbusch to no avail and then went in search of the marchese, who apparently checked out of the hotel last Thursday afternoon and hasn't been seen since that time."

Holmes then asked Coopersmith and Bellingham a series of questions, many of which they could not answer. At the conclusion of his examination Holmes said, "I generally don't involve myself in cases of fraud simply because they are usually straightforward instances of one being victimized by his own greed." Holmes paused to let his admonishment take root. Then he continued, "But your case involving Mr. Botterbusch and the marchese offers several points of interest, so Watson and I will look into the matter."

Our countrymen were delighted and soon made their goodbyes. Holmes and I tarried over another glass of brandy. I could see from his furrowed brow that Holmes' mind was already racing. I asked him, "So what is your theory about the case, old boy?"

"You know better than that, Watson. It is a capital mistake to theorize before you have all the evidence. It biases judgment.[56] I think you do this simply to rile me, Watson."

"Nothing could be further from the truth," I said, hiding a smile. "I myself see several possible explanations, but the fact that Major Lewis appears to be involved indicates that his mentor, Colonel Sebastian Moran, will be nearby, and if Moran is involved there likely will be a trail back to that archvillain, Professor James Moriarity. Am I not correct, old chap?"

---

56 Editor's note: A Holmes maxim first reported by Watson in *A Study in Scarlet* published in 1887.

"My thoughts exactly, Watson," replied Holmes. "Had our English friends not mentioned Major Lewis, I would not have taken their case. But, before I can decipher it I need more information, so, now please let me hear your views, Watson."

"I see several possibilities. First, is that Lewis, Botterbusch, and the marchese are in league with one another to defraud Messrs. Coopersmith and Bellingham. Second, Botterbusch may be acting on his own without Lewis, but with the marchese. Third, the marchese could be working with Lewis to defraud both our English friends and Botterbusch. It sounds as if Botterbusch went into a rage when he found out that they had already purchased stock in the company. If so, Mr. Botterbusch was putting an act on for them, or he was angry and that would most likely occur if he had been betrayed."

"Very good, Watson," Holmes said. "How about option number four?"

"What's that?" I asked.

"The marchese was acting alone."

"I thought of that as well, but I dismissed it. Unless the marchese were in league with Botterbusch, how would he know the Englishmen would be here? Also, where would he obtain a stock certificate to give to our countrymen?"

"Very thoughtful, Watson. We'll discuss this issue more on the morrow. I need to go to the telegraph office and send a cable to Mycroft. There are seven hours of time difference. He'll have it by the time he reaches the office."

With that, Holmes disappeared, leaving me to finish my brandy in a contemplative mood.

The next morning Holmes and I walked over to the Mohawk Mining office on East Commercial Street about two blocks from the hotel. It was open and the front office occupied by a man I assumed was mine foreman Dan Kelly. Holmes explained that we were investigating an apparent case of fraud involving the marchese and the two Englishmen. Kelly abruptly told us to "go away, I know nothing about it."

Holmes persisted until Kelly loudly ordered us to leave the office, at which point Holmes threatened to call the sheriff and said we could do the interview at the county jail. That settled Kelly and he perfunctorily answered Holmes' questions but refused to meet the detective's gaze. Instead, he talked to me which gave Holmes the opportunity to survey the room. I noticed his eyes fixed on a bookcase to my left and behind me.

Kelly confirmed the details of the mine inspection the week before and the name of the translator, Rinaldo Capelli, who he claimed he met for the first time on the day of the tour. He also said that he had never seen either the marchese or the Englishmen before or since.

When Holmes asked him questions about the mine's finances, its development plans, or anything to do with stock or investment, Kelly maintained he knew nothing about those subjects and that if Holmes wanted that information, he should "talk to Frank" (i.e., Botterbusch).

I offered my opinion to Holmes after we had departed the Mohawk offices that the interview had been a waste of time.

"To the contrary, Watson," Holmes replied. "We know two things we didn't know before. First, we know that Kelly is distancing himself from Botterbusch and the more light that is shed on these events, the more likely he will be to abandon his associate."

"And the second?" I asked.

"We know exactly where the Mohawk Mining Company keeps its financial and corporate records. They are right there in the bookcase, and tonight we'll have the chance to examine them in more detail."

We returned to the Mohawk office about nine-thirty that evening. Holmes is a masterful locksmith and quickly picked the lock to the outside door of the building and then the interior door leading into the Mohawk sanctuary. Once inside, Holmes detailed me to act as the lookout while he systematically went through each folio. There must not have been many records to review because he closed the final folio after about fifteen minutes' time and said, "Our work here is done, Watson." He did not reveal what he had learned, but whatever it was, it prompted a thoughtful look on his face. He never said another word to me until he bade me goodnight in the hotel corridor as we returned to our respective rooms.

Following breakfast Holmes asked that I arrange for transportation to the Mohawk Mine while he visited with Sheriff Fitzpatrick. We reached the mine near one o'clock. Botterbusch was in the back room of the little office building. He greeted us warmly, and it was clear that he had been briefed by Kelly about the nature of Holmes' investigation.

Botterbusch explained how he came into contact with both the Englishmen and the marchese. He sounded like a man with nothing to hide.

He tensed slightly when Holmes asked him if he knew Major Archibald Lewis, and I was surprised when Botterbusch said, "Yes. I would call him an acquaintance." He went on to say that he had met Lewis in South Africa several years ago when he (Botterbusch) had been there to study mineral processing technology. He also confirmed that Lewis had been an investor in small mining ventures in Colorado that were successful.

Holmes then asked, "What role did Lewis play in bringing the Englishmen to your attention?"

Botterbusch answered, "Very little. I had sent the Major a prospectus on the Mohawk but received no reply. Instead, Mr. Coopersmith cabled me, as he reported it, 'on the Major's advice.'"

"And the marchese?" Holmes asked.

"Very similar circumstance. Lewis knew someone in the Visconti organization and told them about the property. The next thing you know, I get a cable from the marchese's secretary saying that the marchese was going to be in the United States and wanted to visit the mine, and I readily agreed."

"I understand," Holmes said, "that after the tour a week ago Monday both the Englishmen and the marchese came back and visited with you about investing in the company."

"Not so," replied Botterbusch quickly. "Coopersmith called on me at the office to say they needed more time to get their affairs together and then they both came back last Monday with that fake stock certificate. I never saw the marchese after the mine inspection, nor did he send any kind of message."

"Interesting," said Holmes.

"Interesting is not the right word, Mr. Holmes. It's outrageous. The marchese flummoxed Coopersmith and Bellingham out of their money and I've been victimized myself.

I have to start all over trying to find new investors."

"If it's as good of a property as you say it is, why not talk to Marcus Daly?" I interjected.

"I have no interest in being swallowed whole by the Anaconda Company," Botterbusch replied heatedly. "Little guys like me don't partner with the likes of Anaconda. They want the whole thing and they run it their way. This is my project. I carried it this far and I plan to see it go into production on my terms. I have an excellent, maybe world class orebody and I'll find other investors."

Holmes closed the conversation soon thereafter by offering Botterbusch the best of luck with his future endeavors.

In the buggy back to town I asked Holmes, "Why didn't you ask to see the mine?"

"Because we'll see it tonight, when we'll have time to make a thorough investigation," Holmes answered.

I was disappointed by Holmes' answer. I was hoping to spend the evening in the relaxing company of a good book followed by an early retirement to bed. As much as I liked being involved in Holmes' adventures, I found these nocturnal forays exhausting.

After a light dinner I met Holmes in the hotel lobby. It was only seven o'clock, but it was already coal black outside, the enveloping darkness pushed back by Anaconda's electric street light system, a comfort that we'd lose in less than a mile's distance. To my surprise, Holmes was talking with Coopersmith and Bellingham as I arrived on the floor.

"I hope you don't mind, Watson, but I've invited our clients to join us. That way, if we are discovered we'll be in the company of one of the property owners and the good sheriff would have scant reason to arrest us for trespass."

Holmes' comment was for the Englishmen. He never worried for a second the night before when we surreptitiously entered the Mohawk Mining Company offices after hours.

An hour after departing the hotel we entered the Mohawk Mine tunnel. Holmes had a supply of candles and we each lit one. From there Bellingham led us back into the mine. I saw Holmes pick up and carry a steel scaling bar used by miners to pry loose rock off the ribs (i.e., sidewalls) and back (i.e., roof) of the mine opening after blasting.

When we got to the face (i.e., working surface where the rock is excavated) it was a mesmerizing sight. The light from our candles danced off the silver ore in a manner reminiscent of fireworks. I picked up a small sample from the pile at the base of the face. It was heavy, ungodly heavy, for such a small rock.

"Beautiful, isn't it, Dr. Watson? Botterbusch called it argentiferous galena," Bellingham said to me with a smile as wide as his face. "This ore is north of $300 to $350 per ton and it's just a question of how much there is. Silver ore of this quality hasn't been seen since the heydays of the old Comstock Lode."

"I suspect you're right," said Holmes in reply to Bellingham, "but for all the wrong reasons." Then Holmes plunged the scaling bar into a crack between two protruding chunks of ore and pried them loose. The rock behind the silver ore was no longer silver, but whitish gray. Holmes picked up the two rocks which he had loosened from the wall and handed Bellingham one of the rocks. "There is no orebody here, my friend," he continued. "This material has been cemented in place with mortar."

Coopersmith wanted to see for himself, so Holmes handed him the other rock. Both men were visibly shaken by Holmes' news.

"One thing is certain, gentlemen," Holmes said. "Mr. Botterbusch and his associates have salted the mine with the explicit purpose of selling you a 'pig-in-a-poke.' A ten percent share in this hole isn't worth ten American cents, much less the $50,000 share offered to you. In one sense, gentlemen, you were lucky. The marchese sold you a worthless twenty-five percent interest for $25,000, cutting your potential loss in half."

"What about the marchese?" Bellingham shouted in rage.

"His role is unclear," Holmes replied. "He may be in league with Botterbusch. The whole thing may have been set up to have the marchese relieve you of your cash while Botterbusch remains behind and keeps his hands clean, so to speak. Or, the marchese could be acting independently or with an unknown third party and simply stepped in when he saw your eagerness and vulnerability."

We turned around and started our trek back to the portal when suddenly a light flashed on the left side of the tunnel. Something had been lit on fire. Then the process was quickly repeated on the right side. "What is it, Holmes?" I cried out.

"Someone has just lit two fuses to blow the tunnel entrance," Holmes calmly explained.

"We must get out of here now!" Bellingham shouted.

"No!" Holmes yelled in return. "You run up there you will be blown apart. Quickly now, lay down on the floor and cover your ears."

I didn't need to be convinced. I was fully aware of the

concussion caused by artillery rounds going off. Here in a narrow tunnel, those effects would be magnified. Ten seconds later three explosions went off in rapid succession and we were enveloped in a cloud of thick acrid smoke. We were sealed in our tomb, quite alive for now but not for long, I said to myself.

After the last echoes of the explosion died away, Holmes slowly pulled himself to his feet, relit his candle and said, "Let's go about finding a way out of here."

Holmes is always unflappable, but even I, who have been with him in some harrowing places, was impressed by his nonchalance. After inspecting the rubble pile that blocked our way to safety, Holmes said, "I visited with Mr. Reno Sales, Anaconda's chief geologist, about this property yesterday and he told me that it holes through into the Blue Eyed Nellie Mine up the hill. That means we'll have to go deeper into the mine and look for a bulkhead or something that leads us into the other mine."

We found the other tunnel behind the back of an equipment bay where the Mohawk ore cars and explosives were stored, not far from the face where the silver ore had been cemented in place.

At that point Holmes said, "I'll go. It's several hundred feet to the surface up the Nellie's shaft and the ladders may not be in good condition. I suggest that you three go back to the portal and start digging. I advised Sheriff Fitzpatrick of our plans tonight. He is to call on me at eight o'clock tomorrow morning. If I am not in the hotel, he is to come looking for us here."

Then he slipped into the darkness and we could hear his footsteps recede. The three of us did as Holmes instructed and took turns shoveling rock away from the pile in the tunnel. It was exhausting work and notwithstanding almost twelve hours of effort on our part, we had moved only about four feet of the material. The exertion had caused us to sweat, heightening our thirst.

About 10 a.m. I heard sounds on the other side of the tunnel and digging in earnest began from that direction. A little past noon, a hole was punched through the top of the pile big enough for the three of us to crawl through. I was delighted to see the sheriff's smiling face and beside him Holmes, who had thoughtfully arranged for coffee, food, and a change of clothes for me. Behind him was a squad of several workmen and deputies who had rescued us from our would-be grave.

We left Coopersmith and Bellingham at the hotel. As much as I wanted to sleep, I wanted the satisfaction of seeing the sheriff arrest Botterbusch for attempted murder.

The three of us rode to the Mohawk office where we met two deputies outside the building. We were informed that Botterbusch was inside. Once in the office, the sheriff confiscated Mohawk's financial records from the bookcase in the outer office and then led us into the back room which served as Botterbusch's lair. He was defiant from the beginning. When informed why we were there he shouted, "I didn't have anything to do with blowing up the mine! Kelly and I were in the Union Beer Hall last night playing cards until after eleven o'clock."

"Where was the interpreter?" the sheriff asked.

"I don't know," Botterbusch answered somewhat less loudly. "He lives in Butte."

"What's his name?" the sheriff followed up.

"Vincente Carparelli, and I haven't seen him since the day of the tour. If someone blew up the mine, it was the marchese," Botterbusch answered.

Botterbusch called him Carparelli. The Englishmen said his name was Capelli. Someone is lying, I thought to myself.

"Now why would he do that?" the sheriff asked.

"To kill the Englishmen he stole from and put the blame on me," answered Botterbusch.

"But you salted the mine. You cemented the silver ore onto the face specifically for the purposes of defrauding the Englishmen, and perhaps the marchese as well."

"That is not true," Botterbusch answered, his defiance once again at the fore.

"A court may see it differently," the sheriff replied.

Botterbusch quickly answered, "You have no evidence whatsoever to make that claim, but more importantly, I never took a dime from the Englishmen. The criminal in this case is the marchese."

"Who you are working with? A masterful plan, I admit, Mr. Botterbusch," the sheriff said, "but attempted fraud is every bit as much of a crime as attempted murder. You've also got a problem explaining how the Englishmen came into possession of a genuine Mohawk Mining stock certificate signed by you."

"Can't you see?" Botterbusch said with a voice that was more of a plea than a comment. "The marchese is not just a swindler but a master forger as well."

"You can make your case in court," the sheriff said. "Get up."

"Sheriff, if I could have a word with you privately?" Holmes interjected. The three of us retreated to the hallway leaving Botterbusch behind his desk to ruminate about his future.

Outside, Holmes spoke. "Sheriff, this is your jurisdiction and you are free to do your job in any manner that you feel advisable. I won't interfere, but I would like to suggest another course of action."

"And what would that be?" asked Sheriff Fitzpatrick.

"Let Mr. Botterbusch go for the time being. Alert the railroad ticket agents and stable operators to watch for him trying to leave town. We'll have him secretly observed to insure that he stays put and see if anything of interest develops," Holmes explained.

"What do you suspect?"

"I am unsure of that myself, Sheriff," Holmes answered. "There are two facts in doubt. We don't know what role the marchese plays in this matter. Is he allied with Botterbusch in the scheme to hoodwink my countrymen, or is he acting independently as Botterbusch continues to insist? Also, we don't know whether Botterbusch, or even the marchese for that matter, has a partner outside the local area. When Coopersmith and Bellingham came to seek my counsel and assistance, they explained that they had been led to the Mohawk Mining Company by Major Archibald Lewis. That name means nothing to you, but Lewis is a scoundrel of the first order and he keeps company with one of Britain's most notorious villains, Colonel Sebastian Moran. If Moran is involved, then it is highly likely that Professor James Moriarity is as well."

"Yes, I recall you speaking of both the colonel and the professor, who you called the 'Napoleon of crime,'" replied Sheriff Fitzpatrick.

"It is also possible that the marchese is in league with Lewis or one of his confederates. Simply put, there are many possibilities here and we need some time to see what connections might be drawn. It would be infinitely easier to do that if Mr. Botterbusch is not sleeping in the county's bastille."

"I get your point, Mr. Holmes, and it makes sense, so I'll accept your reasoning."

"Capital, Sheriff, and would your sons still be about town?"

"No, school has started and they are back on the ranch, but if you need a group of lads I can round up several to serve as your—what did you call them?"

"Irregulars," answered Holmes. "We'll need six to eight so that we can monitor both Botterbusch and Kelly, and perhaps the interpreter should he grace us with his presence."

The sheriff departed to round us up a party of diminutive undercover agents. Holmes and I returned to Botterbusch's office where Holmes advised him that the sheriff had gone to see the county attorney and that we were to keep Botterbusch company until the sheriff returned. A half dozen boys were waiting outside the building as we exited the front door and Holmes gave them their orders and slipped each of them a quarter as an advance on their salary.

The sheriff invited Holmes and me to dinner, but Holmes begged off, protesting that he had another engagement. I was more than happy to join the sheriff, and we ate at the Commercial Hotel where the sheriff keeps his room. Afterward, we found a friendly game of pinochle and played companionably until past nine.

I didn't see Holmes until breakfast. "How was your engagement last night?" I queried.

"Excellent, Watson. The plot thickens."

He told me that he had donned one of his many disguises and posted himself across the street from the Mohawk offices. He saw Kelly enter the building just after five and then he and Botterbusch departed together around six. The boys followed both. The two men parted company on the corner of Oak Street and Park Avenue with Botterbusch appearing to be going home. Holmes followed Kelly into Schutty's Saloon.

"I took a seat at the table next to Kelly and about ten minutes later the interpreter arrived. Kelly called him Rinaldo and invited him to have a beer. Once settled, Kelly didn't waste time reprimanding the little Italian. He said, 'Your efforts to blow the mine's tunnel fell short, Rinaldo, seriously short. They escaped. The sheriff showed up on site and dug them out. We've got a bigger problem now than Coopersmith and Bellingham. That limey detective Holmes and his sidekick were with the two Englishmen in the mine. Now he's investigating and the boss is not happy. We have to fix things and the Englishmen have to go.'"

"They plan to kill Coopersmith and Bellingham?" I asked Holmes.

"Perhaps, but you and I fall under the definition of Englishmen as well, so for the sake of prudence I will assume that they mean all four of us."

I was momentarily staggered. Murder is comparatively rare in England, but not so on the American frontier. I made a mental note to go back upstairs and get my Webley revolver.

"How and when do they plan to do this, Holmes?"

"That wasn't discussed, Watson. The Rinaldo fellow simply nodded in agreement and smiled. I also don't know who the boss is. I infer that Kelly meant Botterbusch, but again being prudent, it might be someone else."

"Someone else with no compunction about murder like Lewis or Moran!" I exclaimed.

"A prospect I shudder to consider, Watson, and particularly so given the information I received from brother Mycroft in a cable this morning."

"What did he tell you?"

"That the marchese is a fraud. The Visconti family swears it did not have anyone in the United States looking for mining investments. More importantly, Major Lewis departed Britain three weeks ago headed for America. Unfortunately, we don't know where he's going once he arrives, but I fear we'll find out in the next few days."

"What is to be done with our two young friends from the Midlands?" I asked Holmes, referring to Coopersmith's and Bellingham's place of birth.

"We need to safeguard them in some way, Watson, but I am not sure how to accomplish that."

"Surely, Mr. Daly can provide us with a place where we can temporarily sequester them for their own safety."

"No doubt, Watson. Our problem isn't finding them a place to stay, it's getting them to agree. I've had my irregulars shadow Coopersmith and Bellingham along with Kelly and Botterbusch, and to put this as delicately as possible, our young friends have discovered a paradise of sinful companionship over on Front Street."

I was mortified. "Two gentlemen, with their breeding, are consorting with whores in the brothels?"

"It would seem so, Watson. That and enjoying a drink or two more than is good for them. But surely you're not surprised. Not an old military man of your experience."

"No, I guess not, Holmes," I decried. "I've seen it many times. When a young man from a good family leaves home, the restraint which has characterized his life is thrown to the winds and he engages in every imaginable debauchery, at least for a time."

The next afternoon we met Coopersmith and Bellingham for coffee, whereupon Holmes explained the threat to the young men's lives, but it was as Holmes envisioned. They would not agree to being sequestered. As Thomas Bellingham put it so succinctly, "We came here looking for investment opportunities, not to take a vow of monasticism. We're enjoying the pleasures of life down on Front Street for a fraction of the cost for similar entertainment in Manchester or Liverpool."

The next two days were quiet. Per Holmes' instructions, I avoided the hotel lobby and other public places lest I accidently encounter Major Lewis, whom Holmes was certain would arrive. In the meantime, Holmes sequestered himself in the offices of the Anaconda Copper Mining Company across the street, doing what I did not know. In the afternoon of the third day I received a note from him telling me to meet him at the Collins Cafe for dinner.

Holmes was waiting for me when I arrived. I had no sooner sat down when he said, "It starts tonight, Watson. A man answering to Archibald Lewis' description got off the train this afternoon and he has taken a room in the Montana Hotel, room 326, in fact. We're moving over to the Commercial Hotel with Sheriff Fitzpatrick until we see this matter through. The staff will collect your belongings."

"Good thinking, Holmes. I have little desire to answer my door thinking it's you, only to discover Lewis with a knife," I answered, relieved by Holmes' caution in the matter.

"I am certain Lewis will meet Botterbusch soon, probably tonight, where he no doubt will be told that you and I are in town. Once he hears that, Lewis will act quickly. Of that I am sure, and I am equally certain that he will act against Coopersmith and Bellingham."

"What do you want me to do?" I asked.

"I want you to accompany our young friends in their upcoming night of debauchery," Holmes replied.

"No!"

"I didn't say I wanted you to partake in the pleasures of the flesh. Simply accompany them. Tell them you are acting on my orders as a bodyguard. I want to know everywhere they go and the routes they take to get there. In the meantime, I will attend to Major Lewis."

It was an exceedingly long evening. A night of reverie passes quickly when you are the celebrant, and quite slowly when you are its observer. Per Holmes' instructions, I met him in his room following my night on the town and gave him a full report.

"Ah, Watson, how good of you to come. I myself finished hours ago with Major Lewis and his associates here in Anaconda and have been waiting to hear your report so I can formalize my counterattack."

"As you wish, Holmes," I said through a big yawn. "First, our gentlemen friends had no objection to me accompanying them. In fact, they appreciated the idea of a bodyguard.

We started with a drink in the Union Saloon on East Park around seven o'clock. We then proceeded down Park Street to Cedar Street where we turned toward Front. There we had dinner in the International Restaurant, and I must admit Holmes, the food was much better than the first time I ate there. After dinner, by which time it was near nine, we walked up to the Metropolitan Hotel and climbed the back stairs up to the third floor. The boys were heartily greeted by the Madam, whom they referred to as Miss Clara. She recognized me from our photo in the Anaconda Standard several weeks back and bade me welcome. When I told her that I would not be participating in the boys' evening romp she surprised me by saying, 'Better yet. I hope you will at least join me in a glass of sherry and some pleasant conversation.' I was happy to oblige her and we spent a companionable hour while the lads dissipated their manhood. She was quite interested in your cases, Holmes, and I regaled her with some of your earlier exploits.

"When the boys finished, we went up the street to the Nevada House for what I assumed was another round of carnal joy. I was incorrect on that point, however. Coopersmith and Bellingham, after several rounds of drinks with the 'ladies,' retired to a back room where they played whist of all things, with a group of Cousin Jacks[57] who moved here to work at the smelter. From there we walked back to the hotel. They told me this was their usual route for a night on the town. Although they only play cards one or two

---

57 Editor's note: Cousin Jack is the nickname for people from Cornwall in Southwestern England. Cornwall was the center of English copper and tin mining in the 19th Century. Mine owners in Montana recruited miners and smeltermen from this district to work their holdings in the state.

nights per week, they are very regular of habit, I would say."

"Indeed, and I am sure that Mr. Capelli, who appears to be Botterbusch's and Lewis's assassin, knows it by heart," Holmes replied. "Are they likely to be playing cards again tonight?"

"No," I answered. "Assassin," I said out loud, more to myself than Holmes. "You learned something as well."

"Yes, I followed Lewis. He went to Mohn's Saloon on Park Street just after nine where he met Botterbusch, Kelly, and Capelli. The bar was quite crowded and I was unable to get a seat at an adjoining table, so I had to read Lewis's lips. He was quite angry to learn that you and I were in town. He said, 'It complicates things, but the boss wants his money back and he wants those coal mines. Coopersmith and Bellingham have to go.' Then he looked directly at Capelli and said 'tomorrow,' and Capelli nodded yes in reply."

Holmes continued. "He won't strike during the day. There would be too many witnesses, which means he either goes after them in the hotel, in one of the brothels, or on the street."

The next morning Holmes roused the boys from their beds and over coffee inquired into their financial affairs. He asked, "I need some information about your financial circumstances, gentlemen. I understand that your investment in Hoyland Silkstone pays you a good living, but I don't understand how you can invest in Colorado Fuel and Iron and mining properties in Montana at the same time."

Neither Coopersmith nor Bellingham responded, but I noticed a reddening on the side of Bellingham's neck. Some embarrassment, I presumed.

"Please, gentlemen, I believe there will be an attempt on your lives in the near future and I am trying to ascertain who might be involved in this rot."

Again, no response from either man.

"Well, let me offer an opinion," Holmes said. "I believe your appetite for investment exceeds your means and that you've borrowed money to finance your venture in Montana. Am I correct?"

"Yes," Bellingham said cautiously.

"And you borrowed these funds from Colonel Sebastian Moran."

"Yes again," Bellingham replied. "And we pledged our share of Hoyland Silkstone as collateral. If you're not successful in finding the marchese so we can get our money back, we will be wiped out."

"At this point, that's the least of your problems," said

100 BLOCK OF MAIN STREET,
ANACONDA, MONTANA

Holmes in retort. "Moran has sent one of his henchmen, your acquaintance from the Reform Club, Major Archibald Lewis, to see that you are murdered. He met with Botterbusch, Kelly, and the interpreter last night."

Bellingham and Coopersmith were shattered by Holmes' remark. The confident nonchalance of last evening which bordered on arrogance gave way to profound fear. "Murder?" Coopersmith croaked.

"Indeed," replied Holmes casually. His demeanor was in sharp contrast to our fellow countrymen. Coopersmith began to sweat while Bellingham began tapping the floor with his right foot. "It's why I wanted to sequester you in safety last night. Now that we know their true intentions, we can move forward with plans to protect both of you and foil their plans."

Holmes went on to explain the situation to the young men in greater detail until Sheriff Fitzpatrick arrived. Together they devised a plan to both protect the young Englishmen and take their would-be assassin into custody.

Coopersmith and Bellingham departed the hotel about six o'clock to partake in their night's pleasure, but with the threat of death hovering over them, they did so solemnly.

Holmes was certain that the attack would take place on the 100 block of Main Street when the Englishmen returned to the hotel. He explained that there was substantially less foot traffic on that part of the street than next to the fleshpots on Front Street, and several more routes of escape for a man on horseback. Sheriff Fitzpatrick would help to point the assassin toward Main Street by putting several deputies on foot along Front Street.

About eight o'clock Holmes and I took up station in a

second floor window of the Petritz Building in the middle of the 100 block of Main. An hour later, a man rode up the street on a big roan filly, tied it to a hitching post, and disappeared into the shadow of a darkened doorway across the street from our station.

"Capelli," Holmes said. "Right on schedule." He then departed the room and went down the back stairs of the building to circle around to get into position behind Capelli. I also left our observation post and went down the front stairs, posting myself inside the exterior door where a small window allowed me to monitor the west side of the street where Capelli had hidden himself.

Time passed slowly. It was only twenty minutes, but it felt like an hour. I couldn't see either Coopersmith or Bellingham, but I saw Capelli step out of the doorway and start to slowly shuffle to the north in the direction from which Coopersmith and Bellingham would walk back to the hotel. Suddenly Holmes was behind Capelli, moving swiftly like a jungle cat toward his quarry. I saw his right hand come up and then swing down as he used his police sap to knock Capelli cold. That was my signal. I departed the doorway and ran toward Coopersmith and Bellingham, who were stopped in the street about seventy-five feet from the prone Capelli.

Holmes reached into Capelli's coat, pulled out a revolver, and quickly fired three shots, two into the air, and one into the moulding of a door near the young lads, and they fell to the sidewalk in front of Lossee and Maxwell's clothing store.

I was on them in seconds and quickly emptied a small vial of cow's blood on each of their shirts. Then, I began rendering first aid.

The pistol shots attracted the attention of men in the nearby saloons and they spilled into the street. Within a couple of minutes Sheriff Fitzpatrick arrived and took custody of would-be assassin Capelli, who was revived from his comatose state by a bucket of water thrown over his face. A wagon was secured to function as an ambulance, and I accompanied Coopersmith and Bellingham to Saint Anne's Hospital where they were safely secured in a second floor room behind a locked door.

I pronounced them dead and filled out two death certificates listing the cause of death as gunshot wounds to the abdomen.

Capelli was taken to the Deer Lodge County jail where he spent the night in an isolation cell. The next morning the sheriff questioned Capelli, who maintained that he had done nothing wrong. The sheriff explained that he was apprehended by none other than Sherlock Holmes who was out for a walk with his friend, Dr. Watson. "Both men saw you kill Mr. Coopersmith and Mr. Bellingham, and both will testify against you in court. This cock-and-bull story that you're trying to peddle to me about being knocked out and someone else doing the shooting isn't going to sell with a jury. I have two witnesses who saw you shoot the English gentlemen, we have your gun, and we have a slug of the same caliber as your pistol. You're going to hang."

The sheriff left him at that point but returned in the afternoon accompanied by the county attorney, Holmes, and myself. Capelli was pacing around his cell, muttering to himself, his agitation readily apparent.

The sheriff said, "I've discussed your situation with Mr. Trippett, our county attorney, Mr. Holmes and Dr. Watson.

Mr. Holmes tells me that you are in the employ of a British criminal by the name of Major Archibald Lewis. Now, if you want to tell us all you know about Lewis, Botterbusch and Kelly, Mr. Trippett will not ask for the death penalty. Instead, you'll serve a long sentence in the state penitentiary."

Capelli was quite happy to talk and explained how he, Botterbusch, and Kelly got together in Colorado. Botterbusch had known Lewis for some time and brought Lewis into the scheme to steer European investors to the group for a fleecing. The plan was very simple. They would acquire a mine, salt it to boost the assays, and then fool investors to put their money into the property. Once they had the cash, they would spend the company into bankruptcy by ordering mining supplies and equipment and then turn around and sell the material to other mine operators at a discount, keep the money, and fail to pay the equipment supplier. They had run the scheme successfully in Colorado, New Mexico, and Nevada before coming to Montana.

"So what did you do here?" Holmes asked.

"Same thing," Capelli replied. "Frank thought we could up the ante if we could show the investors a real orebody. He got the idea to buy good silver ore from another mine and then mortar it in place in the mine to make it look like a bonanza had been discovered. We needed a couple of miners so he hired the big Swede and a dago. Neither one of them could speak English. They were perfect. The Swede was a good miner, and the dago, Guido, was a mason. He cemented the ore in the back of the tunnel up at the Mohawk."

"Where does the marchese fit into this?" Holmes continued.

"Frank thought of it. We'd use the dago to pretend he was Marchese Visconti. I bought him a suit of clothes, cleaned him up, and told him what to say when the Englishmen were with us in the mine. He played it like a pro. He acted excited, told Frank he wanted a big piece of the mine, and the Englishmen were sold."

"What was this Italian fellow's name?" Holmes asked.

"Frank called him Guido."

"Last name?

"I don't know."

"Then what happened?"

"Something went wrong. I don't know what, but somehow Guido got ahold of the two Englishmen and talked them into buying stock from him instead of Frank. He grabs $25,000 and disappears. I traced him back to Pozega's Boarding House on Cedar Street where he lived with a bunch of Croats. He ain't there now."

"The marchese gave Coopersmith and Bellingham a stock certificate. Where did he get that?" Holmes asked.

"Don't know," Capelli said. "Frank can't figure it out either. All the stock records were in the office and the place wasn't burglarized."

"Maybe Botterbusch gave him the certificate," the sheriff said. "Then he and the marchese split the money later on."

"Frank ain't that stupid. The Major gets to thinking that's what's up, Frank gets a bullet in his head. The Major has friends in high places in England, maybe America too. I never seen the guy, but the major said the two Englishmen had borrowed money from somebody named Sebastian and he wants his money back."

Late that afternoon Botterbusch and Kelly were arrested, but Major Lewis was nowhere to be found. Holmes was convinced that he left earlier in the morning, most likely heading for Canada and a return to Britain. Miraculously, Coopersmith and Bellingham came back to life and returned to their rooms in the Montana Hotel and renewed their visits to the entertainment center of Front Street.

With that part of the crime solved, Holmes turned his attention to the missing marchese. The sheriff had distributed a description of the marchese to other sheriffs' departments in Montana and adjoining states but no one seemed to have seen him.

Holmes believed that if the marchese was a local man as Capelli had described, he was more than likely still in the area, probably with a changed appearance, but nearby. On the other hand, if he was in league with Major Lewis, it would be unlikely that we would find him.

The next day Holmes and I traveled to Butte. Late in the day we went into Thomas Hobba's Barber Shop on West Galena Street. He remembered the marchese. "Came in here and got a shave and haircut, two or three weeks ago. I remember because he was carrying two suitcases," Hobba remarked. Further effort on our part led us to the Southern Hotel where the afternoon clerk checked him in but never saw him again.

Holmes and I divided up a list of hotels, boarding houses, barber shops and haberdasheries, and we started making the rounds to these businesses. I stopped for supper at Quinlan's Restaurant on West Quartz Street. There I observed a bald-headed man wearing spectacles and reading the newspaper as he ate. I tried to envision him with head and facial hair and decided he was a decent match for the marchese. Unfortunately, I stared a bit too much and he saw me. Minutes later he paid his bill, talked briefly with the cook who was also acting as the cashier, and stepped out into the street.

I went to do the same thing but the cook-cashier dropped my money, then miscounted my change, and by the time I got to the street the bald-headed man had disappeared.

I told Holmes of my discovery and failure to apprehend the man. The next evening Holmes went to Quinlan's while I checked the boarding houses in nearby Meaderville which was home to a large Italian population.

Holmes told me that his visit to Quinlan's was unproductive. The cook claimed that the bald-headed man was not one of his regular customers and didn't recall seeing him before. We returned to Anaconda the next morning without the marchese, and Holmes had to tell Coopersmith and Bellingham that he was unable to recover their money and the case was concluded. They departed two days later, intending to travel to Denver, Colorado.

It was quite unlike Holmes to not completely solve a problem that he was entrusted with. I expected him to be downcast, but his equanimity was unaffected. I did tell him that successfully thwarting two murders was a job well done, even if it wasn't possible to recover the money the marchese had swindled.

I completed my journal entries and put the folder in my steamer trunk, not to look at it again until we reached England several weeks later. Holmes asked that I not publish anything about the episode, saying that he wanted the sheriff to have more time to see if he could find the marchese and bring the matter to a more satisfactory conclusion.

In truth, I had no intention of sharing "The Case of the Missing Marchese" with the public. It was one of so few cases where Holmes had not enjoyed complete success that I had no desire to tarnish, however slightly, his reputation with the reading public.

After we returned to England, Holmes received a cable from Sheriff Fitzpatrick which said that Botterbusch, Capelli, and Kelly were all sentenced to long terms in the state penitentiary at Deer Lodge for attempted fraud and murder. Botterbusch only lived eleven days behind bars. He was stabbed by an unknown inmate. The Warden thought that he had been done in by Capelli, but there was no evidence against him. I wondered if Lewis had another confederate in the lockup who did the deed. Moran and Moriarity are tough taskmasters. Failing them leads to certain punishment, and Botterbusch had failed.

One afternoon almost five years later, I heard the afternoon post arrive. Holmes was completely preoccupied with one of his chemical experiments at the table in our sitting room, so I retrieved the mail which consisted of a single letter to me. It was postmarked from Butte, Montana. I was quite puzzled. Who in the world would be writing me from Butte?

I opened the letter and was greeted by a handwritten letterhead which said *Mr. Alberto Visconti, Marchese of Pisa and Iglesiente.* The missive stated:

> *At the request of Mr. Sherlock Holmes, I am writing to inform you that I have repaid $25,000 to Messrs. Coopersmith and Bellingham. This payment represents a full accounting of the money I liberated from them in Anaconda, Montana, nearly five years*

*ago when I sold them 25,000 shares of stock in the
Mohawk Mining and Improvement Company which
I did not own. If you or Mr. Holmes wish to verify
the veracity of my claim, you may contact former
Sheriff Fitzpatrick at his ranch near Finn, Montana,
or by going directly to Messrs. Coopersmith and
Bellingham at their offices on Larimer Street in
Denver, Colorado.*

"Holmes!" I shouted.

"Yes, Watson," he replied in a low and disinterested voice
without taking his eyes off the test tube he was heating in
the flame of a Bunsen burner.

"I just received a letter from the Marchese of Pisa and
Iglesiente informing me that he has repaid the $25,000 he
stole from Coopersmith and Bellingham in Montana, and
moreover, that he wrote this letter on instructions from you."

"Indeed," answered Holmes.

"As I recall, you distinctly told me that you never found
the marchese when we were in America."

"True, Watson, but he made such a compelling case. I
thought the interests of justice were better served by not
having him arrested. Don't you agree?"

"You haven't read the letter fully, have you, Watson?"

"Only the first page," I admitted. Holmes bent toward
the Bunsen burner and I knew he would say no more until I
fully read the lengthy letter. So, I began:

*I met Mr. Holmes in my cabin in the back yard of
Quinlan's Café and Boarding House. He told me that
Botterbusch, Capelli, and Kelly were in police custody
and asked me to make a full accounting of my role in
the entire affair. I had to tell him my life's story.*

The name I was given at birth was Giovanni Larosa. Since leaving Anaconda with the Englishmen's money I have answered to the name of Guido Battaglia for reasons explained in the story I am about to tell you.

I was born in the village of Canolo Vecchio in Calabria, the province that makes up the toe of Italy across the Strait of Messina from Sicily. My father was a "Caposquadra" or overseer in one of the stone quarries near the village. When I was fourteen I graduated from primary school and went to work for my uncle on his fishing boat, but I was no sailor, done in by seasickness. My father secured me an apprenticeship with a stone cutter by the name of Enzo Fillipone. My older brother Giorgio was already working for him.

Fillipone was a kindly man and an excellent stone cutter, and business was very good for a while. Fillipone received a contract to supply a large number of pieces of cut white limestone for the reconstruction of a church in Naples. For the first time in his life, he had a little extra money and was able to both enlarge his house and buy some land, a milk cow, and several goats. Fillipone's success did not go unnoticed. Soon one of the local Mafioso chieftans showed up at Fillipone's door and told him how much he had to pay them every month, for protection they said.

Fillipone was a brave man and told them to go to hell. The chief came back the next day with four men. They didn't touch Fillipone. He was a master stone carver and without him, the church contract would disappear. So the Mafioso beat his two youngest sons, Carlo and Tomas, to within an inch of their lives.

Fillipone started making the required payoffs and after that was done, there was nothing left for himself.

He was making a fortune by Italian standards and yet Fillipone struggled to feed his family, which included four sons, and his two apprentices.

One day in early August my father came to the stone cutting shed and told Giorgio and me that we were being sent to America along with Carlo and Tomas Fillipone. Three days later we started for Naples to get a ship to New York, where we arrived on September the 3rd. Fillipone's cousin Vincenzo, also a stone cutter, met the ship and took us to his home in Little Italy, just off Mulberry Street. The next day, the four of us started work as part of his crew, not cutting stone mind you, but as laborers on a masonry crew. It was tough work and the living conditions were terrible. There were nine people crowded into Vincenzo's two room apartment, where there was hardly space to sit down. The Fillipone boys, Giorgio and I spent most of the fall out in the street. We got to know lots of people and I learned to speak English quickly, helped by Vincenzo's second son, Paolo, who taught me how to read English. It was perhaps the most wonderful gift I ever received, although I didn't realize it at the time, all from the efforts of a twelve year old boy wanting to help his "cousin" Giovanni.

A year quickly passed. It was early September, around the 10th, I think, and I was sitting on the stoop outside the building when Giorgio came home. He was real agitated. He'd been down at the saloon on the corner when Lupo the Wolf, the local mobster, came through the door with three of his guys and they beat some fellow who owed Lupo money. Giorgio told me that we couldn't stay in New York any longer. "It's just like Calabria, and the Mafioso." Several days later we moved to Toronto and went to work with some masons, and everything was going fine until winter struck and we damn near died from the cold.

Once it got cold, all the bricklaying stopped and Giorgio and I got laid off. Six or seven weeks later Giorgio got a job at the St. Lawrence foundry. He was a master stone carver but he could carve wood real good too, and he got hired in the pattern shop making patterns for ornamental iron work. This old Irishman named McKenzie was the chief pattern maker and he took to Giorgio right away, and Georgio talked McKenzie into giving me a job too, but just as a laborer. My job was to stoke the furnaces. It was a hard, dirty job but I didn't complain. At least it was warm and I was inside, out of the snow.

I was working with this guy named Ferguson. He was a good looking guy, and quite a few years older than me. Ferguson liked the ladies and so did I, and we had a good time going to the dances and socials around town. About April, I don't remember exactly, Ferguson tells me that he knows a guy, who knows a guy, who's got a cousin who's a big shot at a smelter in Trail, British Columbia, and he'll get us a job there. We can make a dollar a day more than we are making at the foundry. So, I went along.

When Ferguson and I got to Trail, there was no big shot who could get us a job at the smelter. Fact is, we couldn't find a job anywhere—in the mines, on the railroad, in the woods—times were tough. We'd been in town about ten days, late May, I think, when I saw this drayman unloading a wagon at one of the stores. You could tell he's got a bum leg, and is really struggling to get the crates off the wagon. I offered to help him and when we were done, he bought me a beer and we started talking. I tell him my tale of woe about not being able to find a job and he tells me that he's going to the States at the end of the week to another mining town called Butte. He says there's "lots of work, the mines are always hiring," and I asked him if I can tag along and he says "sure," so on the next Friday I take off with Ceplak, the drayman. He was a Slovenian and we both spoke enough English to get along. Ferguson was invited to come with us, but he said he was going to stay in Trail a while longer.

I've got to tell you, Butte was a bustling place. Over 20,000 miners were working on the hill. There were five smelters, a red light district as big as the one in Naples, and that's saying something, and more bars than you could count. After shift, the miners would line up three deep at the bar and pour down the whiskey and beer like there was no tomorrow.

The third day we were there I got a job at the Moose Mine, working on the surface crew. I'd been working at the Moose for about a month when I found out that they were looking for masons in Anaconda, a little town about twenty-five miles west of Butte. I figured it was a good place to go and get away from the bad air in Butte.

I spent the better part of the summer laying brick on various jobs around the smelter. In late August, a storm front blew through and reminded me that winter wasn't too far away, so I started thinking about getting a job inside before the snow started to fly. That evening over dinner at the boarding house where I was living, several of the fellows were talking about an advertisement in the newspaper looking for miners. I'd never thought of mining as an inside job, but I guess it was in a way—you're definitely out of the weather.

I went and found the newspaper and sure enough, the Mohawk Mining and Improvement Company was hiring. I'd never heard of the company, but it had an office on Commercial Street and would be hiring on the forthcoming Saturday.

There was a long line of fellows ahead of me, and any hope I had about getting a job underground for the coming winter was fading fast. I was getting ready to leave when one of the Italian fellows from the boarding house came down the stairs shaking his head back and forth while muttering to himself.

He saw me at the foot of the stairs and spoke to me in Italian saying, "Giovanni, I don't understand these Americans. All the time they want to know if you speak in English and we're all trying to learn the English. Then I come here today and the man in the suit say, 'sit down,' and I sit down. Next he say, 'Can you speak English?' and I say, 'Yes, sir, I read the newspaper all the time. That's how I know about your job.' Then he say, 'thank you,' and yells into the front office, 'next!' and they show me out through the side door. It's crazy. It's like he don't want to hire people who can speak English."

When I finally got into the office, a man in a dark suit pointed at a chair, indicating that I should sit there while he escorted the guy who was in front of me in line into another room. I gazed about the room. There was a small table next to the wall containing a man's hat and ring of keys. Opposite me, also along the wall, was a bookcase containing a series of files labeled Mohawk Stock, Board Minutes, Correspondence, and the like. It didn't look like the Mohawk Company had much in the way of records. I waited less than five minutes before the man in the dark suit returned and took me into the back office.

The man in the suit told me to "sit down," but I just

stood there pretending that I didn't know what he had said.

Then, he asks me if I speak English. I try to look dumbfounded and respond by saying, "No English, Italiano, me."

I thought I saw a small smile cross his face and then he asked, "What kind of work do you do?" I answered him haltingly, saying "Good worker, me," two or three times. Then he asks me if I was a miner and I respond by saying, "Miner, miner, me miner. Mason too, good worker, me."

Both men nodded in agreement and the man in the suit showed me through the door into a third, much smaller room. There was a big blonde-headed fellow sitting in there on a wooden chair. The man in the suit again pointed toward one of the empty chairs and said, "You wait here, capeesh?"

So I nodded yes and sat down.

The walls between these two rooms must have been made of paper. I could hear everything being said next door and heard the man in the suit interview another dozen men, all of whom spoke English, and none of them were brought back to the room where I was sitting with the big Swede.

Finally, I heard a deep voice that I hadn't heard before say, "What do you think, Frank?"

Then, I heard the man in the suit reply by saying, "Not as good as I had hoped. I think the dago, what's his name, Guido, will do fine. I got my doubts about the Swede. He may be too dumb. But if that Guido is actually a mason, well, it gives me an idea."

All my life I've been Giovanni—Giovanni Larosa.

Now, all of a sudden, a man I've known for less than ten minutes tags me with the name Guido and I become Guido.

Monday morning found me walking into the portal of the Mohawk Mine a few miles west of Anaconda. I was joined by the Swede who was introduced to me as Ole, and I to him as Guido. Our guide that morning was the big guy who sat at the end of the table during the interview. He introduced himself as Dan Kelly, and he was foreman at the Mohawk.

We walked in several hundred feet to the face. Then Dan pulled out a piece of chalk and started making three rows of x's on the rock where he wanted us to drill. The Swede was a good miner, thankfully very accurate when he swung the sledgehammer. Since I was holding the drill, I was very appreciative of his skill. The rock was limestone and not too hard. We made pretty good progress.

Drill, blast, muck. The process was repeated each day for a week. Then Kelly showed up in the mine with Frank, the guy from the office. I later learned that Frank's last name was Botterbusch. They talked for a few minutes and then Kelly told us to "Go home, come back Monday."

On Monday morning, we found five wagons parked on the waste dump next to the track just outside the mine portal. One wagon had a half load of sand, several barrels of mortar, and a canvas bag full of masonry tools. The other four wagons were covered by tarps but we soon discovered what was inside. Each contained about a ton of silver glance, a high grade silver ore whose proper name, as I learned later, was argentite. Kelly had us shovel the ore from the wagons into the ore carts and push them back into the mine.

I never knew where the ore came from but it was beautiful. Back in the drift, the light from our candles reflected off the rock in such a way that it looked like flickering stars.

After lunch Kelly showed up with a small, ferret-faced fellow who introduced himself to me in Italian. His name was Rinaldo Capelli, and he told me that he was to act as a translator between Kelly, Botterbusch, and me. I knew instantly that I couldn't trust Capelli for a second, Italian or not. The Swede was put to work mixing mortar and hauling buckets of the ore up to the face. Capelli told me to line the face of the drift with the silver glance, cementing each piece in place with mortar. It took almost a week to finish the job, but when I was done it looked as if the drift had intersected a high-grade vein of silver about seven feet wide.

About a week later, Rinaldo was waiting for me outside the boarding house where I was living in Anaconda. He took me to a saloon where he handed me the bundle that he had been carrying and said, "There's a suit of clothes inside and some shoes. Tomorrow afternoon go over to the Mohawk office. There's a toilet down the hall in the back. Put on the suit, walk over to the Montana Hotel, and check in using the name of Alberto Visconti. Understand?"

I nodded yes in reply. To be honest, I was speechless. The Visconti family was one of the most prominent in all of Italy. They had estates in Pisa and on Sardinia. Even a humble peasant boy like myself knew about the Viscontis. I had no idea what was in store for me, but I didn't think I'd fool anyone by pretending to be a Visconti.

If Rinaldo noticed my surprise, he ignored it and continued, "After you check in, stay the night and have breakfast. A carriage will pick you up in front of the hotel at eight and take you to the mine."

I asked Rinaldo, "What's this all about?"

"I don't know," he replied. "Frank will tell us more the day after tomorrow. You keep this to yourself and you'll be handsomely rewarded. You talk and—" Then Rinaldo drew his finger across his throat. I got the message. At that point Rinaldo drained the last of his beer and bade me a good evening.

I hated to board the carriage the next morning. It didn't help that Rinaldo was the coachman and he talked all the way to the Mohawk. Botterbusch met us in the yard and hauled the two of us into the office. There, he gave Rinaldo my orders and Rinaldo translated them into Italian. I was told that I was to accompany two other men on a tour of the mine. Underground we'd look at the silver vein I had installed and whenever Rinaldo talked to me, I was to speak rapidly and act excited.

I had no sooner received my instructions when Botterbusch looked out the window and said, "Our English guests have arrived." A few minutes later I was introduced to Thomas Bellingham and Stephan Coopersmith, and I to them as Alberto Visconti, the Marchese of Pisa and Iglesiente. I also knew that the minute I opened my mouth and revealed my south Italian dialect, these Englishmen would know I was neither a Sardinian nor a Tuscan but was, in fact, a fraud. But, it never happened.

Botterbusch led the Englishmen into the mine portal and showed them the face which glimmered with the silver ore I had cemented in place. He then told them that the ore had over six hundred ounces of silver per ton. The two Englishmen gasped in surprise. Then

Rinaldo talked with me in Italian for a few minutes, did some arm waving of his own, and I responded on cue, acting thrilled to be there and very excited about what I was seeing.

Botterbusch then told the Englishmen they could be part of the Mohawk Mining Company and further commented that he expected the marchese—me— to take at least a fifteen percent ownership interest in the company as well. Rinaldo quickly translated Botterbusch's words to me and I shook my head no. Then I told Rinaldo to tell Botterbusch I wanted twenty-five percent. Botterbusch just beamed when he heard Rinaldo's translation. I knew then that I was a natural actor.

Back at the office, I was shown a chair in the outer office and given a cup of coffee. Botterbusch and the Englishmen went into the back office and Rinaldo stepped outside to have a smoke. The walls were thin and even though the door was closed, I could hear virtually every word that was being spoken. They talked for about fifteen minutes with Botterbusch finally getting to the point that he wanted $50,000 for a ten percent share of the company. That prompted a series of questions from the Englishmen.

The conversation started to lag, I got bored, stood up and started walking around the office. On the wall behind the desk that the foreman Kelly used was a framed copy of a Mohawk Mining and Improvement Company stock certificate. That triggered a memory of my visit to the company's office in downtown Anaconda where I recalled seeing several folios on a shelf and it gave me an idea. I realized this was opportunity knocking at my door. All I needed was the courage to let it in.

I looked inside the desk drawer, found some paper, and checked to see if Rinaldo was around. He was nowhere to be seen so I quietly slipped outside the front door, scooped up two handfuls of muddy clay from a puddle next to the building, wrapped the clay patties in the sheet of paper, put them in my coat pocket, and returned to the office.

A few minutes later the Englishmen and Botterbusch stepped out of his office. They shook hands and Botterbusch told them that he would see them tomorrow and hoped that their stay at the Montana Hotel was comfortable. As if on cue, Rinaldo poked his head through the front door, whereupon Botterbusch instructed him to "look after the marchese's comfort while I see our English guests off."

Rinaldo and I visited for a couple of minutes until Botterbusch returned and signaled that it was time for us to go. I excused myself with the claim that I needed to use the privy. Once behind the office, I slipped in the back door of the building, found Botterbusch's keys on the desk just where I expected to find them, and pressed each key into one of the blocks of clay I held in my pocket, making a mould of each.

After Rinaldo drove me back to Anaconda I entered the hotel lobby, went straight to the desk, and gave the clerk a note addressed to the two Englishmen asking them to join me for dinner in the hotel dining room. I then returned to my room, changed into my own clothes, slipped out the side door of the building, and went in search of my friend Francisco, a moulder at the foundry located on the far east end of town near the railroad yards. I found him at Schutty's Bar and gave him five dollars and the two moulds and asked that he make me a set of keys which I needed by suppertime the next day. After receiving Francisco's nod of assent, I excused myself and went back to the hotel. There, I put on the fancy suit Rinaldo had provided me, found an inconspicuous table in a corner of the Tammany Bar, ordered an Irish whiskey, and waited for the Englishmen to appear.

Mr. Holmes told me that the Englishmen related to you the substance of our conversation that night and two days later when I met them at Whatley's Café and made a deal to get them 25,000 shares of Mohawk stock for $25,000. You are also wondering, I am sure, how an ignorant Italian immigrant could negotiate a deal to buy a major share of a mine. Well, the answer is easy. I was very fortunate in my past association with Ferguson and Ceplak. Ferguson grew up in Glasgow, Scotland, and had some education. For a short while he worked in the shipyards and then moved south to England where he got jobs in both the coal and iron mines. Somehow he became acquainted with the Overseer. I think they're called Deputies in England, and he got a job in the office as a clerk and secretary to the Deputy. He told me that he sat in on a bunch of meetings where he took notes and learned a lot about boards of directors, shares of stock and bank drafts, all of which he shared with me during our travels. He had a good job. I never did understand why he quit and moved to Canada.

My friend Ceplak, who was much older than I, maybe in his early fifties, was also a fountain of information. Before coming to the U.S. he worked around Europe. He was the one who told me all about the mines in Bohemia, Germany, and even Italy. I knew very little about the Visconti family, only that they were rich and powerful, until I met Ceplak. When Capelli told me to check into the Montana Hotel as the Marchese

SHERLOCK HOLMES: ADVENTURES IN THE WILD WEST

Visconti, I couldn't believe my ears.

After I got the keys from Francisco I went back to the Mohawk office after dark. Just as I expected, one key was for the outer door, the other for the office. Inside, I went through the folders I had previously seen on the shelves. I found a stack of blank stock certificates and a register of all of the stock owners. In Botterbusch's desk I found a fountain pen and bottle of ink, and I registered both of the Englishmen and Alberto Visconti, the Marchese of Pisa and Iglesiente as stockholders. I then filled out a certificate for the Englishmen and went home. On Thursday I met them at the bank as scheduled, took their money, and gave them their stock certificate.

After a cheerful round of goodbyes I departed the bank, only to return just after noon to withdraw the funds in cash and catch the 2:10 p.m. express to Butte.

Upon arriving in Butte, I took a cab uptown from the station, made my way to Thomas Hobba's Barber Shop on West Galena Street, and had my hair cut very short. From there it was about a three-block walk to the Southern Hotel on East Broadway. In my room, I took out my straight razor and shaved off my moustache and sideburns. I then departed the hotel using its back entrance and checked in at the McNamara House on West Copper Street, whereupon I shaved all the remaining hair from my head, excepting only my eyebrows, completely altering my appearance.

The next day I rented the cabin behind Quinlan's Café. When asked my name, I told Mrs. Quinlan it was Guido Battaglia. Frank Botterbusch gave me the name Guido, and I adopted Battaglia on the spot but have used it ever since. A few days later I saw you watching me in the café and made arrangements with Mr.

Quinlan to delay you long enough to make my escape.

Mr. Holmes found me in the cabin the next evening, and we entered into an arrangement with the consent of Sheriff Fitzpatrick, guaranteeing me freedom in exchange for paying back the Englishmen within five years as I have now done. Mr. Holmes also instructed that I should write this account of my role in the affair so that your record of Mr. Holmes' exploits would be complete.

Very truly yours,

Guido Battaglia

"Fascinating story, I am sure you agree, Watson," said Holmes as he turned off the Bunsen burner and turned to face me.

"So, you found him," I replied.

"Yes, your surveillance was impeccable, old boy. Battaglia was living not sixty feet from where you saw him in the restaurant."

"I am still puzzled why you didn't bring him to justice."

"I decided that justice would be better served if he remained free. As you have undoubtedly noticed, Mr. Battaglia is quite an intelligent and resourceful individual. In a matter of a few minutes' time he devised a plan to frustrate Botterbusch's fraudulent scheme while securing $25,000 for his own account with which to launch a new life for himself in the United States."

"Nevertheless, Holmes," I said in reply, "the man committed fraud."

"Indeed he did, Watson, which is why the sheriff and I agreed that he had to repay the money. But seen another

SHERLOCK HOLMES: ADVENTURES IN THE WILD WEST

way, it was a most beneficial swindle. If Battaglia had not relieved Coopersmith and Bellingham of their money, they would have bought Mohawk Mining stock from Botterbusch, and then later been killed so that Colonel Moran could claim their shares of Hoyland Silkstone Coal and Coke as repayment for the money they had borrowed from him. Battaglia's swindle saved Coopersmith's and Bellingham's lives."

"I can see that," I said.

"Moreover," continued Holmes, "if our two English friends had not brought us the case, the role of Lewis and Moran would have never been revealed. Through the good offices of brother Mycroft, a reputable buyer was found for Coopersmith's and Bellingham's share of Hoyland Silkstone. They were able to pay off Moran and have some additional cash for their ventures in Colorado that have worked out handsomely for the both of them."

"If they were dependent on their earnings from the Hoyland mines to support their lifestyle, how did you ever get them to sell their shares in the company?" I asked.

"I didn't," Holmes answered. "Both men gave their fathers power of attorney to manage their affairs in England while they were in America. Mycroft visited the fathers, explained the peril their sons faced from Moran, and both gentlemen saw the wisdom of selling their sons' interest in the coal company and repaying Moran his due. Fearing that Moran might not have extracted all that he would from young Coopersmith and Bellingham, Mycroft advised the families that it would be wise for their sons to stay in the United States indefinitely. That advice was also accepted, which accounts for the company of Parker, Cassidy, Coopersmith and Bellingham being established in Denver, Colorado. In addition, Mr. Battaglia had used the nest egg he received from them to acquire the ownership of several eating and drinking establishments, a confectionary, and bakery in Butte. According to our good friend Sheriff Fitzpatrick, he's become a pillar of society there."

"Holmes, I am puzzled as to why you would give this Battaglia fellow five years to repay Coopersmith and Bellingham. In the little time before you found him, certainly he hadn't spent all of the money."

"He hadn't spent any of it, Watson. I could have chosen to force repayment then and there, but I decided for several reasons to wait, primarily to teach our young victims a lesson or two about life. Coopersmith and Bellingham, while not noble by birth, have lived a life of nobility because their fathers and grandfathers before them were highly successful merchants. Neither man had ever known any want in his life, nor had they ever truly earned their way in society by their own means. Both were anxious to be independent, and both asked for and received their inheritance early so they could establish their own careers. They wisely invested in the Hoyland Silkstone Company on the advice of Bellingham's father, but since then have lived the life of wastrels from the dividends paid by the mines."

"A final question, if I may, Holmes. How could you be sure that the marchese, pardon me, Battaglia, would pay the money he owed after five years? Nothing would have prevented him from absconding at the last minute."

"It's a fair question, Watson, and I have to admit I was more trusting than Sheriff Fitzpatrick. He suggested and Battaglia agreed to the establishment of an escrow account at the bank in Anaconda. He put funds into the account periodically to repay Coopersmith and Bellingham. The account was set up so that he couldn't withdraw the money without the sheriff's permission. It was a matter of trust, but established in such a way that the sheriff and I were able to verify that our trust was wisely given."

"So, a home run, as the American baseball aficionados say, eh Holmes?"

"Not quite, Watson. We freed the world of Botterbusch, Capelli, and Kelly, but they were just small cogs in the wheel. Lewis, Moran, and most of all, Moriarity remain free. It has been a case with a happy but inconclusive end, but no doubt, old friend, there will be other opportunities to deal them another blow."

Holmes wandered over to the settee, picked up his violin, and began playing Mozart's Violin Concerto No. 5 in A, Second Movement, while I drifted back to my memories of Montana, its sapphire blue skies, the verdant hillsides carpeted in conifers, its industrious, welcoming people, and the most exquisite beef steak known to man. My stomach growled in reminiscence as well.

The Case of
the Lost Herd

I was beginning to wonder if we'd ever leave America and get back to England. Our departure had been cancelled several times and I thought that perhaps it would be better to wait until spring. Crossing the North Atlantic in winter held no attraction to me and Holmes certainly had no shortage of things to do. Each week seemed to bring him another matter of interest and, truthfully, I had never seen him so mentally engaged and his health so robust. Any thought I had about staying in Montana through winter, however, quickly fled when I stepped outside the warm security of the Montana Hotel, our home away from home, to be whipped by a cold wind from the west.

After two days of merriment, saying goodbye to the many friends we'd made in Anaconda, Holmes and I boarded the BA&P[58] train to Butte. We'd overnight there and catch the

---

58 Editor's note: BA&P stands for Butte, Anaconda and Pacific Railroad, a short line owned by the Anaconda Copper Mining Company. It extended from Butte on the east to Southern Cross west of Anaconda, a distance of about 40 miles. Its principal mission was to haul ore from the mines in Butte to the smelter in Anaconda but it also provided passenger railway service between the two cities.

Northern Pacific east to Minneapolis-St. Paul and then proceed to Boston. We had just settled into our rooms in the McDermott Hotel in Butte when came a knock on Holmes' door across the hall and I heard the familiar voice of Reno Sales, chief geologist for the Anaconda Copper Mining Company, greet my friend heartily. A shudder of dismay coursed through my veins. No doubt Sales had a "little problem" that merited Holmes' attention and we'd be stuck in Butte for several days, a prospect I found dismal indeed as the snow pelted my room's window.

My apprehension was for naught. Sales was making a social call and took us out to dinner, followed by a drink at the Silver Bow Club where a small faux pas on my part, involving a glass of brandy, led us to being introduced to Mr. W. A. Clark, another of Butte's Copper Kings and Mr. Daly's chief rival for control of Butte. I was taken aback by his look, a man of average height and build with a full head of brown hair and a thick goatee and broad moustache of the same color, no mean feat in a man approaching his sixtieth birthday. While I offered my profound apologies and a clean linen handkerchief to Mr. Clark, he stared a hole through my forehead, his eyes ablaze with anger. I judged him to be a man of choleric character expressed through imperious condescension to we mere mortals. My apology seemed unheard and it finally dawned on me that Clark was looking at Holmes who was standing behind me. Sales stepped into the breach, introduced us to Clark, and then steered us to a table nearer the fireplace. Clark remained speechless although his countenance was clear. Sales made light of the encounter by suggesting that Clark's normal temperament was extremely taciturn, particularly toward the friends and associates of Daly. I wasn't convinced and resolved to question Holmes about it later.[59]

The next morning we departed on schedule. My seat faced toward the rear of the train and I was treated to one last view of Butte as our train slowly worked its way to the crest of Homestake Pass over 6,300 feet above sea level. The air was still, the sky clear, and the industrial might and energy of the world's greatest metal mining metropolis, evident in its headframes, powerhouses, and smelters, receded into the background.

We reached Livingston, site of the railroad's main repair shop in Montana, and after a brief stop to replenish the coal tender and change train crews our journey east continued pushed by a warm Chinook wind.[60] We reached the City of Billings in the late afternoon and took lodgings overnight in the Grand Hotel. Holmes had some last-minute business to transact for Daly and I was somewhat apprehensive that this "little task" would somehow mushroom into a larger project and further delay our travels.

The next morning Holmes' mood was quite expansive and we conversed at great length on all manner of subjects, including several matters Holmes expected to take up upon

---

59 Editor's note: What Watson may have discussed with Holmes remains unknown, although Watson left another reference to Clark in a set of materials unconnected with a specific case which noted "Clark's penchant for bribery."

60 Editor's note: A chinook is a warm wind from the west which can quickly elevate winter temperatures causing snow to melt. Temperature changes of 30-40° Fahrenheit in a matter of a few hours are not uncommon.

MR. MICK DEVLIN

our return to London.[61] Holmes had completely disengaged from Montana.

At four o'clock that afternoon we pulled into the station at Glendive, Montana, where the train would be idled for approximately thirty minutes. The sun was diminishing in the west but the day was still warm and I suggested a short walkabout and quick stop to quench our thirst.

We had no sooner stepped inside the front door of Dion's Saloon when the bartender greeted us heartily.

"Mr. Holmes, Dr. Watson. I was wondering if I would see you again."

I recognized the face and immediately fished my memory for a name, but Holmes rescued the day.

"Mr. Devlin, Mick Devlin, if I remember correctly. A pleasure to see you as well. I'm surprised that you would have remembered us. There must have been several thousand people through those doors since we had last partaken of your hospitality."

"Aye, sir, that would be true," replied Devlin with a broad grin across his face, "but none so important as to grace the front page of the newspaper."

With that, Devlin reached under the bar and brought out an old copy of the *Anaconda Standard* which featured Holmes' portrait in conjunction with his successful con-

---

61 Editor's note: Watson's notes do not contain any references regarding the matters that Holmes discussed following their return to England. Holmes was involved in three cases which Watson chronicled as "The Adventure of the Missing Three-Quarter," "The Adventure of the Abbey Grange," and "The Adventure of the Devil's Foot." Watson's narratives indicate that each of these cases began rather suddenly and would thus not appear to be matters brought to Holmes' attention when he was in Montana.

clusion of the Tammany Affair.[62]

Devlin continued, "Several months ago a gentleman departed the 4:40 to wet his whistle with a short beer, just like you're a doin', and he left it on the bar."

Devlin paused momentarily to rearrange the paper so I could see it better and then continued, "I was going to throw the paper away, not being much of a reader myself, but then I told myself, you know that fellow," as he pointed to Holmes' picture. "So, I saved the paper hoping you'd come back in. And look, you're here just in the nick of time when we're in awfully big need of some detection service."

Holmes looked at his watch and rather uncharacteristically replied cynically, "We've got twenty minutes, Mr. Devlin. I can't believe there could be any matter in Glendive, Montana which would take any more time to solve."

Then he smiled, that small, sardonic little smile he uses from time to time when he doesn't want to be bothered, and said, "How can the good Doctor and I be of assistance?"

Devlin, not knowledgeable of Holmes' moods, failed to take measure of Holmes' cynicism and replied simply, "It's a pretty serious matter. A few nights ago, my friend Stephen Porter lost over 160 head of his breeding cows. Their tracks led up a dry irrigation ditch, then they just disappeared into thin air. Even for a man of your considerable abilities, Mr. Holmes, I think it'll take you more than twenty minutes."

Devlin paused at that point, poured some brown liquid from a glass jar into a chipped porcelain cup, and drained it

---

62 Editor's note: As reported in *Sherlock Holmes: The Montana Chronicles*, edited by John Fitzpatrick. Riverbend Publishing (Helena, MT), 2008.

in a long swig. I learned later that he was drinking cold tea, but at the time thought it was cheap whiskey. I marveled at his capacity to consume six ounces of hard liquor in a single gulp and keep standing, not to mention continuing the conversation. Holmes paused in mid-sip, the corner of his mouth registering a quiver ever so slight when Devlin had said, "they disappeared into thin air."

"I know it's presumptuous of me to ask, Mr. Holmes," continued Devlin after wiping his mouth with the cuff of his sleeve, "but Stephen and his missus are going to be wiped out and lose their ranch if those cattle aren't found. The sheriff is completely baffled by this situation as are we all."

"Regrettably," answered Holmes softly, "we must return to London. Cattle rustling, I believe that's the term you Americans use for it—"

"Aye," interrupted Devlin. "It's rustling. That, or the Almighty himself reached down and snatched those beefs to heaven."

I smiled at the prospect of God running a cattle ranch in the sky over our head.

"As I was saying, Mr. Devlin," continued Holmes, "cattle rustling falls outside the realm of my experience. My agrarian skills are strictly limited to apiaries."

"Apiaries?" questioned Devlin, completely baffled by the term.

"Bees," I injected. "Mr. Holmes is an amateur beekeeper."

The look of puzzlement remained on Devlin's face while Holmes explained. "Watson and I are city folk, used to working in the streets of the city."

"Or the drawing rooms of the English gentry," I added.

Holmes shot me a quick dagger of a look while I quietly snickered. While firmly a member of the English middle class, Holmes is without an iota of pretense, equally comfortable in a tavern filled with coal miners as in the company of Queen Victoria with whom Holmes holds a most cordial, but largely unknown relationship.[63] I wanted to terminate the conversation and reboard the train, and was mystified by Holmes' expressed attitude toward Devlin and the problem he presented. It was so uncharacteristic of him.

Devlin, however, was not about to be put off. "Isn't it true, Mr. Holmes, that you can follow the track of a felon through the busy streets of London?"

"It's been done, Mr. Devlin, I admit a time or two."

"Then you should have no problem out here, Mr. Holmes," asserted Devlin. "There's hardly a soul about in the countryside, mostly it's cows, coyotes, and wolves. You should have no problem picking up the scent of the villain. One day, it's all I ask of you."

"I daresay no, Mr. Devlin," responded Holmes. "For the past several weeks I promised Watson that we would be off to England. It would be grossly unfair on my part to tarry in Montana any longer."

A locomotive steam whistle chimed in with a short blast, indicating the imminent departure of our train, but right then I was struck with a flash of peevishness. In all of

---

63 Editor's note: Uncharacteristic of Watson's writing, at this point the original text contains a long discussion in which Watson describes a private dinner with the Queen and Prime Minister Robert Gascoyne-Cecil, the 3rd Marquess of Salisbury, at Windsor Castle in 1887 following the conclusion of the case entitled "The Naval Treaty" which was published in 1893.

our travels together, I had never seen Holmes use another person, certainly not me, for an excuse and I resolved to not let him pick up a bad habit at this late stage in life.

"Holmes," I interjected, "the case appears to have a point or two of interest. After all this time I'm sure one day more or less won't make any difference."

At that point there was a long, pregnant pause while I mentally conjured an image of Holmes leading me across the plains on horseback in pursuit of a cow thief. Holmes is athletically gifted, a superb swordsman, well acquainted with the manly arts, and a decent rider, but my friend is not fond of the equine. We've discussed the issue on several occasions but he never fully explained his attitude. Frankly, I suspect it's a control issue. Notwithstanding his equestrian

MERRILL AVENUE, GLENDIVE, MONTANA

skills, Holmes can't fully control the mind of a horse and there are times, particularly at full gallop, where your life hangs in the balance, fully dependent on the judgment of a dumb animal.

Holmes' failure to respond prompted me to take another jab. "It might be good for your reputation, old boy. Solving a cattle rustling mystery in the heart of the American frontier will only add to your considerable reputation."

"It's settled then," said Devlin.

"Indeed," I answered quickly, then turning to Holmes added, "Allow me to return to the station to collect our bags. I'll also cable your brother Mycroft to advise him of our temporary delay. You can get the particulars of the case from Mr. Devlin."

"Mick, call me Mick," interrupted Devlin.

I fully expected to find Holmes quite annoyed with me upon my return to the saloon, but instead found him engaged in easy repartee with the genial barkeeper and a Mr. Dion, the owner of the establishment.

Dion was also a violin player and soon he and Holmes were taking turns on the fiddle while Devlin and I cheered them on. We all talked and lingered into the night as if we had just been reunited with old school chums.

We found lodging in a dirty rooming house across the street from the depot. The indignity of the entire experience was summarized in a breakfast of burnt coffee, rancid bacon, and stale bread. It was altogether the worst meal I had eaten on the North American continent. Devlin arrived with the saddle horses just after seven and we settled into our ride to the Porter Ranch about six miles west of town.

Glendive was a small settlement, probably not more

than a thousand souls, built around a rail yard and a short row of business establishments along Merrill Avenue opposite the railroad depot. The railroad had surveyed the townsite laying it out in a grid on both sides of the tracks. Given the size of the survey, the railroad, which owned most of the land in the townsite, obviously expected it to grow into a small metropolis. But that would be in the future.

As the sun arched into its track above us, it seemed as if you could see forever. We were in a landscape of brown earth and blue sky, big sky—immensely big sky—and it was intoxicating.[64]

Regrettably, that feeling was displaced by one of a baser sort. My innards started to rumble in protest to the soiled repast recently consumed. I thought my years in Afghanistan had hardened my entrails to all manner of gastronomic distress and was both surprised and embarrassed by my current plight. Fortunately, it passed quickly and we were able to reach the Porter place in good time.

The ranch consisted of a sprawl of several buildings surrounding a large, white clapboard ranch house at the center. Even at a distance I could make out a chicken coop, pig sty, horse barn, several corrals, and livestock sheds. Across the road to the north was another smaller domicile, most likely the bunkhouse for the hired men.

Devlin introduced us to Stephen Porter. We exchanged pleasantries for a few minutes until Porter mounted his horse to lead us to where his cattle disappeared. Holmes

---

64   Editor's note: This is the earliest known reference to Montana being referred to as "Big Sky." In the 1960s the State began using "Big Sky Country" as its unofficial nickname. The State's official nickname remains The Treasure State.

rode up front with Porter while Devlin and I kept to the back. The path of the cattle was clearly evident in the soft, wet earth. We rode south away from the ranch house toward the Yellowstone River for about a mile until we reached a ditch perpendicular to our line of travel. There, the cattle's tracks disappeared. Holmes dismounted the mare he was riding, walked into the meadow below the ditch, and sank up to his ankles in mud.

"I am sorry, Mr. Holmes," yelled Porter. "The chinook melted all the snow this past couple of days. The mud can be deep."

Holmes gave him a brief wave in response and then walked along the ditch both east and west of where we were standing. He returned quickly, apparently seeing something of interest.

"Mr. Porter, if you might, please tell me what happened. I am particularly interested in why your cattle were at this specific place."

"We moved 'em here a few days ago. In the fall we gather the cattle off the range, sell most of the calves, and winter over the cows close to the house so we can keep watch on 'em. We had the whole herd in a pasture north of the house but I decided to split it up and put some of them down here. There's a spring in that draw down yonder, so they generally stay close by."

"I see," replied Holmes, "and I trust that you've searched the entire area and determined that the cattle didn't just wander off."

"We searched, Mr. Holmes, very carefully. At first I thought the same thing. When I didn't find them here, I rode a big loop all around," said Porter as he waved his arm in a circle. "Then I got Jasper and Josiah, my hired hands, to help and we looked everywhere."

"Perhaps they got mixed in with your neighbor's cattle," I offered.

"No, Doctor," answered Porter quickly. He was exasperated. "We looked into that as well. What makes this all so puzzling is the absence of tracks. When 167 head of cattle move across wet ground, their path is so clear a blind man could follow it. But if you go a hundred yards up or down river from this place, the tracks are gone. I've never seen the likes of it before."

Holmes changed the subject. "What is the significance of this ditch, Mr. Porter?"

"Significance?"

Porter wasn't the only one puzzled by Holmes' question.

"I am not sure I follow you, Mr. Holmes," Porter replied. "It's just an irrigation ditch. There's a diversion dam and head gate upriver near Fallon."

"How far is that?" asked Holmes quickly.

"About twenty miles."

"Where does the water go?" countered Holmes.

"It's used to water all the land on the north bank between the ditch and the river," explained Porter as his arm swept in a large semi-circle pointing south. "The river's just beyond those trees and you can see the railroad line up on the south bank."

Holmes waited. I wasn't sure if this discussion factored into the investigation he was conducting, or if Holmes was merely satisfying his own curiosity.

Porter continued. "Those of us with rights to the water turn it out at various places along the ditch to flood the hay meadows down below for a day or two. Then we shut it off and flood another section. We call it flood irrigation."

"Show me," replied Holmes quickly.

Porter dismounted, turned to the east and walked about fifty feet. "Right here."

A wooden frame was built into the ditch. It looked like a window frame with a slot in the middle where a sliding window would go. "This is one of my gate sites, Mr. Holmes. I have a set of wooden gate panels up at the shop. If I want to turn out water here, I push the gate panel in place and bolt it down. The water backs up behind it and flows over the side of the ditch into the meadow, right here where it's lined with rock."

"To prevent erosion from the water flow," answered Holmes.

"Exactly," said Porter. "My system is a little more elaborate than my neighbors. I've installed gates about every 200 feet."

"Most interesting," said Holmes, his eyes moving across the field to the south. "Excuse me, gentlemen." With that Holmes walked out into the field crisscrossing it from east to west several times, his eyes shifting from side to side as he combed the ground in front of him.

As Holmes searched the field we heard the report of a steam engine and I spied its telltale smoke approaching from the east.

Devlin seemed to read my mind. It's the midday freight, Doctor. Gets into Glendive at 11:30 a.m., changes crews, and departs for points east at noon. The train going west comes through in early evening." I was counting the hours.

When Holmes returned to the party he asked Porter to "accept my apologies and bear with me so that I am certain I understand how you manage your lands. You described this tract as a hay meadow that you irrigate during the summer from this ditch."

"Correct," answered Porter.

"And where is the hay?" countered Holmes.

"We cut it and put it in those stacks over yonder, Mr. Holmes."

At that point Holmes started to laugh and looked up at the three of us aboard our horses and said, "Watson will bear witness that I am world renown for my powers of observation and yet, I either didn't notice those stacks or didn't comprehend what they were. In Europe, hay is generally bound in small sheaves."

"That was my father's practice as well when I was a lad in Ohio, but out here our herds are much bigger, so we put several ton in each of those stacks and then haul it out and feed the cattle through the winter."

"That's got to be a tremendous amount of work," I observed.

"It is," answered Porter, "but it beats having them starve. The winter of '87-'88 almost destroyed the livestock industry in Montana and all the way back to Minnesota. Up to that time a lot of land was open range and the ranchers turned out their cows to fend for themselves. All year a cow can paw through snow and uncover grass to eat, but not that winter."

"What happened?" I asked.

"We got a heavy snow. Then a chinook came through, melted some of the snow, and suddenly it turned bitter, bitter cold. I am talking ten, twenty, thirty degrees below zero. The snow froze hard as ice and the cattle couldn't dig through it. Then the snow kept coming, for months. When spring finally came, most of the cattle were dead, thousands and thousands.[65] After that the smart ranchers, and I think of myself as one of 'em, started putting up hay to feed the cattle through the winter. There's still a few fellas around here that aren't feeding their cattle, but the day of the open range is about done."

"With your indulgence, Mr. Porter," said Holmes, "could you take us down to the river?"

It took us about ten minutes to reach the river bank. Devlin, Porter, and I kept up a companionable conversation while Holmes lagged behind, his inscrutable powers of observation being put to the test as we crossed the meadow.

The river was covered with ice. It reminded me of the River Beauly in Northern Scotland, seen one bitter winter many years ago with pack ice pushed up on the shore and mounded into low lying ridges out on the river. The ice looked to be twelve inches or so thick.

"Is it safe to cross?" asked Holmes of Porter.

"River ice is never safe, Mr. Holmes. The current underneath can erode the ice just as quickly as a steam line. Why do you ask?"

"I want to cross the river."

"Well, it would be best if we left the horses here and crossed over by foot. The warm weather we've had the last few days has probably made it worse. If one of us falls

---

65 Editor's note: Montana artist, Charles Marion Russell, memorialized the hardship of the winter of 1887-88 in a small painting entitled "Waiting for the Chinook," which shows a thin starving cow in a winter storm. The picture is also known as the "Last of the 5000."

through, at least we won't have to deal with a horse thrashing about."

With that we all dismounted and hobbled our horses. Porter then played out the rope he had affixed to his saddle and we each grabbed hold with about ten feet separating us. Porter then led us across a good sixty to seventy yards of river channel to the south bank where we followed a crude pathway up to the railroad line. My nervousness increased with each step, fearful that I would plunge through the ice into the near freezing water below. Fortunately, my apprehension was for naught.

"This is called Colgate siding," announced Porter. "That hut is used by the section crews when they're working on the track."

The siding consisted of a single length of track, perhaps 300 feet long with a switch to the main line at each end. The building was wood frame, painted white, about fifteen feet square. The door was unlocked. Inside we found a wooden table, three benches, a stove, a three-sided box filled with coal, some hooks on the walls for hanging up coats, and a long cabinet along the north wall whose doors were secured by a heavy padlock.

"Tool storage," said Porter as Holmes inspected one of the locks. "They keep their shovels, picks, and the rest of their tools locked up rather than hauling them out from town every day."

The building's interior was filthy. The floor was covered with mud and there were rags, tin cans and other forms of refuse pushed into the corners.

"Is this place used often?" asked Holmes.

"Mostly in the summer," answered Devlin, "but they'll

come out during the winter if there's a problem."

Holmes paced around the room, his left hand rubbing his chin as his eyes combed the room. He stopped in front of the stove, opened its front door, looked inside, and then announced, "I think that's all for today, gentlemen."

With Holmes' announcement we re-crossed the river and departed for Porter's ranch house and, hopefully, a strong cup of coffee. We rode in silence. Even though the day was fairly mild, a strong wind had built from the west and I was chilled.

We stopped outside the stable, dismounted, and I began to remove the saddle from my mount when Porter asked, "Have you come to any conclusion, Mr. Holmes?"

"Conclusion, no. Some ideas, perhaps, but no conclusions. There are, however, a number of points of interest about this case that I did not expect, in all candor, and I feel compelled to see it through to a conclusion."

"Thank you, Mr. Holmes," injected Mick Devlin. "We need a man of your ability."

"It may take several days," replied Holmes. When I heard that I was crestfallen, but tried not to betray my feelings. I had, after all, goaded Holmes into looking into the matter and had no one to blame but myself if I didn't see the British Isles before Christmas.

"If it suits you, Mr. Holmes, you can stay here at the ranch. We've got plenty of room for you and Dr. Watson," Porter said.

"Hmm. It probably would be more convenient than staying in Glendive. What say you, Watson?"

"I trust that Mrs. Porter is a better cook than—"

"An excellent cook, Doctor," interrupted Porter.

"Then it's settled, Holmes," I replied in haste.

"One more thing, Porter, if I may, said Holmes. "It would not be helpful to the investigation if Watson and I were known to be investigating the crime. I propose that you introduce us to your family and others that we meet as Mr. Sherlock and Mr. Johns, two agents from England here to acquire ranch land for a British investment group."

"All right, if that's your desire, Mr. Sherlock, but the only folks hereabouts are my wife, four sons, and two hired men."

"Thank you, Porter, but I am not totally unfamiliar with life in agrarian lands. It's always amazing to me how quickly news passes between people in areas where people live so far apart. I trust Mr. Devlin, from his place behind the bar, will do his part to spread the word that the two English gentlemen are in town to buy land?"

"You can count on my every discretion, Mr. Holmes—I mean Mr. Sherlock," answered Devlin.

"Come, gentlemen. Sarah will have held dinner for us."

Upon entering Porter's home we were introduced to his wife and four sons ranging from two to ten years of age and to the two hired men, Jasper and Josiah Maier, twin brothers. Porter's three older sons were blonde headed with blue eyes; the baby dark haired with dark, almost black eyes. The older boys had their mother's coloring but their father's eyes. With the baby, it was just the opposite.

The hired men were in their fifties, both about five feet six inches tall and of robust build. I would place their weight at about fourteen stone[66] each.

---

66 Editor's note: A stone is a measurement of weight used in Great Britain but not the United States. A stone is equal to 14 pounds. Thus, Watson estimated the weight of each of the Maier twins at approximately 196 pounds.

After being seated around the dining room table, Porter offered a short blessing and Mrs. Porter served us a meal of bean soup, beef steak and fried potatoes with bread, butter and raspberry jam, and hot coffee. It was, in all ways, superior to the fare at the boarding house in Glendive. Porter then commenced to ask the hired men questions about the status of their work, much of which had to do with repairing fence, and concluded by turning to Josiah and asking, "What have we got to look forward to with the weather, Josiah?"

"It's going to get bitter cold again, Stephen. My bones is hurtin' so much it's causing my whole body to twitch."

"You forecast weather with your bones, Mr. Maier?" asked Holmes quietly.

"Indeed, Mr. Sherlock," he replied earnestly. "The bones always tell me when the weather is about to change. Don't know why that's so, but I always know when we're getting a storm, a day or two out."

"It's truly amazing," said Mrs. Porter. "I don't think he's ever been wrong."

"Fascinating," said Holmes.

I expected him to follow this line of inquiry to some further point, but he surprised me by dropping it and the conversation lagged for several seconds until Mrs. Porter asked, "Excuse my impertinence, Mr. Sherlock, but what brings you and Mr. Johns to such a lonely outpost as Glendive, Montana?"

"Pardon me, Mrs. Porter, it is I who am at fault," Holmes answered. "We come as guests to your home and table and fail to declare our purpose. Please forgive me."

Mrs. Porter responded with a smile as her eyes widened and she drew Holmes into her gaze. The old Holmesian magic, I said to myself. The man is almost completely dis-interested in women, yet when he decides to be gracious I daresay there's not a woman on Mother Earth who can resist his charm. I once saw Queen Victoria rise from her chair to pour Holmes a second cup of tea while she called the serving girl to attend to Prime Minister Gladstone, My-croft Holmes, and me.

In reply to Sarah's questions, Holmes said, "Land and cattle, Mrs. Porter. I am acting as agent for a group of Brit-ish investors who wish to establish a large-scale cattle breed-ing and ranching operation in the United States."

"Cattle breeding?" asked Jasper Maier quizzically. "We've got plenty of cattle breeding in this country right now."

"Not this particular breed," answered Holmes firmly.

"What might that be?" injected Porter.

"Aberdeen Angus," replied Holmes. "The breed hails from Scotland. It's very hardy and the investors think it will thrive in the northern climes of the States."

"Angus? I believe I've heard of it," answered Porter.

"Some animals of the breed were imported to your state of Kansas about twenty years ago," continued Holmes.

"Our cattle handle the cold just fine," injected Jasper Maier. "I can't see why anyone would take the risk of bring-ing beef across the ocean. That's got to be hard on 'em."

"You're correct, Mr. Maier," answered Holmes, "but Angus cattle offer several distinct advantages over your American breeds, most importantly they are naturally polled, they gain weight quickly, and the fat distributes itself throughout the muscle tissue making the meat more tender and flavorful."

Yesterday Holmes was turning down the case, telling Devlin and me that he knew nothing about the agrarian arts save beekeeping, and now he's discussing cattle breeding as if he invented the science. Holmes' encyclopedic knowledge of any subject never fails to impress.

Polled?" followed Jasper. "You said these Angus cattle were naturally polled. What does that mean?"

"They don't have horns," answered Holmes, "and because they don't, they don't injure themselves, other animals in the herd, or the human keepers like your American short and longhorns are prone to do."

"This has been a most interesting discussion, Mr. Ho— Sherlock, but my men must get back to work. I would, however, like to discuss this breed further with you, if we may," Porter said as he stood up and put his napkin on the table."

Jasper and Josiah pushed back their chairs. Holmes and I did likewise, and as I rose I thanked Mrs. Porter for a truly excellent meal and noted, "Your bread is without peer, Mrs. Porter. I don't know when I've had finer."

"Thank you, Mr. Johns. I bake it fresh every Sunday afternoon, although I may not this weekend. The children were ill with some type of stomach malady, thankfully now gone, and we didn't go through our victuals as we normally do."

Devlin also thanked Mr. Porter, talked with the hired men briefly, and departed for Glendive. Porter then took Holmes and I on a short tour of his property. We saw the barn, chicken coop, and pig sty where Mrs. Porter was depositing the residue of the day's food preparation, then a large shed where he repaired his equipment, his two wells, and a duck pond now frozen over. When we returned to the house he withdrew a folio from a cabinet, spread it on the dining room table, and showed us a series of surveys which outlined his property boundaries and the location of the various stock ponds and irrigation ditches. Porter was a meticulous record keeper. That concluded, Holmes took out his pipe and went out on the front porch to smoke a bowl as he paced back and forth processing what he had learned today. I took a book from my pack, begged another cup of coffee from Mrs. Porter, and took up residence next to the parlour stove.

I didn't read for long. Adam Porter, the youngest of the tribe, tottered up to me and raised his arms into the air several times before I figured out that he wanted me to pick him up. Once safely ensconced on my lap he proceeded to talk with me, a mixture of childhood gibberish broken up with an occasional word I could understand. His older brother, Joshua, joined us in time and I soon had two Porter boys aboard my knees. Joshua was full of information, mostly about horses, and the three of us spent a companionable hour together until their mother arrived and sent them off to do their chores. The boys' visit caused me to think about Holmes' other cases and I could scarcely remember one where either of us had experienced the company of young children.

Both Holmes and Porter joined me in the late afternoon, and Porter was kind enough to offer us a drink. I yearned for a smooth brandy but happily took the glass of Kentucky bourbon that he offered.

Supper was promptly served at 6 p.m. We were joined by the hired men and Porter children. Once everyone was served, Sarah took up where she left off at lunch and began asking questions, inquiring if Holmes and I shared a business acting as agents for various parties. I cast a furtive glance to Holmes while I struggled to come up with a story properly explaining my role.

"Oh heavens no, Mrs. Porter," answered Holmes once he sensed my predicament. "Johns is a medical man. The good Doctor simply joined me on this foray as a source of recreation—a rare chance to see a part of the world unlike anything we're used to in the United Kingdom."

I coughed and then stammered an answer as well. "Indeed. Sherlock and I have been friends for many years and from time to time I accompany him on his expeditions. In this case I was coming to the U.S. to attend a medical conference in Boston. When Sherlock told me of his travel plans I arranged to join him in New York and have shared the trip with him ever since."

"What was the conference about, Dr. Johns?" Mrs. Porter asked.

I coughed again, excused myself, and blurted out the first word that popped into my head, "Vaccinations."

"What's that?" asked Josiah.

"It's a medical procedure designed to give a person immunity to a disease. Doctor Edward Jenner pioneered the technique over a hundred years ago when he injected a young boy with cowpox serum. The lad came down with a mild case of cowpox. When they tried to infect him with smallpox, he never caught the disease."

"We've heard about that, Josiah," said Jasper. "Remember when we were in St. Louis?"

Josiah gave his brother a quizzical look and shrugged his shoulders.

"I've heard of it as well, Dr. Johns. Is it safe?" asked Mrs. Porter.

"Not completely. It comes with some risk, but it's much safer than getting smallpox. I witnessed an outbreak in Afghanistan when I was with the British Army. It killed about eighty percent of the children who got infected and about half of the adults. It's a devastating disease."

"Could we get our sons vaccinated?" asked Mrs. Porter.

"Yes," I replied, "but it's not commonly done in rural areas. You'd probably have to travel to Butte or Minneapolis to get it done."

"So, pray tell, Doctor, what was discussed at the conference?" asked Holmes. He was testing me, just trying to see how long and how far I could push the charade.

"Certainly, but I doubt our host and hostess care much about arcane medical procedures," I replied, hoping that the subject would get changed.

"To the contrary, Doctor," said Porter involving himself in the discussion for the first time. "Medical progress is of interest to us all, of that I am sure."

Chagrined, I had no choice but to continue my masquerade. "The conference dealt with new opportunities for vaccination. Since Jenner pioneered the technique in 1796, Robert Koch, a German, and Louis Pasteur, a Frenchman, have developed several additional vaccines useful against cholera, anthrax, and rabies. There is considerable belief in the medical community that vaccines can be developed for a number of fatal maladies, potentially eradicating these scourges from both human populations and the animal kingdom."

"I'd want them to find a cure for whooping cough," Mrs. Porter said. "Mark and Arthur both had the disease last winter. It's a miracle they're still with us. If Joshua and Adam had caught the disease, I don't know if they would have survived."

"Yes, whooping cough, called pertussis in the medical world, was one of the diseases discussed at the conference along with tetanus, which most people know as lockjaw."[67]

"That's bad," commented Jasper.

I could tell by Holmes' sardonic little smile that he had enjoyed giving me the sticky wicket, but he then relented, probably concerned that if I kept talking I might divulge our true identities. He changed the subject by asking Josiah and Jasper, "How did you gentlemen get to Montana? Your speech suggests to me that you came from parts of America much farther to the east."

"Very keen of you, Mr. Sherlock," answered Jasper with a broad smile. "We hail from near Lancaster, Pennsylvania, but left there when we were but wee lads. Our father was killed in the Civil War and our mother moved us to Iowa where we lived with her sister and husband."

"A miserable bas—" Josiah stopped in mid-sentence, his face flushed in anger while he caught Sarah's glare. "A miserable man. Jasper and I were glad to go."

"We got jobs with the railroad," continued Jasper, "reached Glendive in '82 and stayed on working in the shops. We bought the ranch in the spring of '88."

---

67 Editor's note: While the Holmes Canon reveals very little about Watson's proficiency as a physician, it was considerable. Watson was well versed on developments taking place in medicine. The case notes indicate that Watson talked about vaccines for a considerable period and listed several maladies which he thought might be eradicated by vaccination including diphtheria, measles, and mumps.

"So you missed the winter from Hades," I said.

"Yes, but that's how we managed to buy the ranch, or at least part of it. Henry Shaw got wiped out. Lost the entire herd and we had enough to buy him out."

Holmes looked at me, then to Porter and back to the hired hands.

"No doubt you're wondering how we came to work for the Porters," said Josiah with a frown.

"It crossed my mind," admitted Holmes.

"Our luck wasn't any better than Shaw's," Josiah said. "But it wasn't winter that took us down. It was disease. By '91 we had a decent herd, then all of a sudden the cattle started aborting. The cattle didn't show any signs of sickness but they couldn't hold a calf to full term. It happened to us again in '92.[68] Our neighbors were having similar problems but we had it the worst. Thinking something might be wrong with the land, we all moved our cattle to the north on some open range."

"That's when things went to Hades, as you observed, Mr. Sherlock," Jasper said, taking over the explanation from Josiah. "The cattle came down with blackleg[69] and we lost everything. Porter bought us out and was kind enough to

---

68 Editor's note: The cattle were likely suffering from brucellosis. British medical officers first identified the disease in the 1850s on the Island of Malta and it was originally called Malta fever or Mediterranean fever. It is highly contagious and spreads by eating contaminated milk, meat, and the exchange of body secretions. In humans, it is often called undulant fever.

69 Editor's note: Blackleg is an infectious bacterial disease which most commonly strikes cattle, sheep and goats. It causes fever and necropsy in the muscle tissue and the onset of death can be sudden. It is caused by bacterial spores in the soil.

keep us on. He even let us stay in our house across the road. We're saving our money and hope to be able to get us another place in a few years. In the meantime, we're here and glad of it. Aren't we, Josiah?"

"Very grateful," answered Josiah, but his tone sounded less than sincere.

"It was a bad time," said Porter. "Several families lost their land. I bought Jasper and Josiah's place and the property to the east. My neighbor, Thomas Mellon, bought the three ranches to the west."

Holmes was watching the hired men very carefully and I wondered what calculus was spinning through his mind. He completely surprised me when he said to Josiah, "I see that you do some cooking, Mr. Maier."

Josiah was taken aback but admitted that he baked biscuits now and again, "to give us something to eat in the evening." He then asked, "What about me could allow you to deduce that, Mr. Sherlock?"

"It's no great deduction, Mr. Maier. You must have scratched your head while preparing your dough. There's a smidgeon of flour in your hair above your right ear. I have also noticed that your brother suffers from rheumatism in his legs."

"You're very observant," answered Jasper. "Was it my limp?"

"No, the wear pattern on the heels of your boots plus the fact that you told me how you can forecast the weather with your bones. A keen sense of observation is very useful to a man who earns his living negotiating commercial transactions. I can watch a man's face and know exactly when I've reached the sale price."

"Is that what you are doing now?" asked Mrs. Porter.

"Forgive me, Mrs. Porter, no. Your husband has already told me no, and I know that he means it. I'll take a day or two more in the area to see if I can find an interested party. If so, perhaps we can come to some arrangement. If not, we'll move on to our next stop, a town called Deer Lodge, near Butte, I am told."

Holmes' answer prompted several more questions from Mrs. Porter, Jasper and Josiah. Porter and I watched, he out of curiosity, me from intrigue. I've known Holmes long enough to know that this was not idle conversation. There was a purpose behind his facile exhibition of his deductive skills and the provocative tone of his conversation.

Immediately after dinner, the hired men returned to their cabin across the road from the main ranch house. Holmes, Porter and I visited amiably in his parlour, periodically interrupted by visits from young Adam with whom I seemed to have developed a special bond.

We all retired to our respective bedrooms about 8:30 p.m. and, after making notes in my journal regarding the day's events, I climbed into bed and pulled the blankets up to my neck. My room was above the front porch and I daresay it was quite cold in the room. I hadn't quite drifted off to sleep when I heard a soft knock on the door, watched it open slowly, and saw Holmes enter quietly.

"Dr. Johns, a few moments of your time, but very quietly. I don't want to wake the others."

"What is it, Holmes?" I asked in a hush.

"I've reached some conclusions about the case and wanted to inform you of my further plans."

"You have a solution?"

"Not fully. I believe I know how the cattle disappeared, but not the perpetrators."

I climbed out from under the covers, wincing as my bare feet hit the cold floor. Holmes, who was still fully dressed, chuckled quietly. He sat down at the foot of the bed.

"Doctor, please give me your impression of the people we've met thus far in this little drama."

"Well, Devlin is a splendid fellow and—"

Holmes cut me off. "I agree, but Devlin wasn't whom I had in mind. How about the Maier twins, and Mr. and Mrs. Porter?"

"If you met the Maiers separately," I said, "you might not take them for twins. They certainly share a strong family resemblance—same body type, hair and eye color, but they are clearly fraternal, not identical twins. Their temperaments are decidedly different. Jasper is as gregarious and light-hearted as Josiah is moody and taciturn. There's a darkness about Josiah. He strikes me as a man who carries around a lot of anger. I hesitate to suggest this because it is purely conjecture on my part, but perhaps Josiah is angry over their loss of the ranch and harbors some resentment toward Porter. Their misfortune was his fortune."

"You're correct, Watson, it is conjecture on your part but certainly reasonable given the circumstances. What about Mrs. Porter?"

"A devoted wife and mother, an excellent cook, and very much a full partner in the ranch."

"Why do you say that?"

"When you were on the front porch smoking your pipe and thinking through what you had learned, I was in the parlour and overheard a long discussion between Porter and Sarah. They were talking about the implications of the cattle theft and what it meant for the family. Porter questioned her thoroughly and wanted her opinion, not just about how it affected the family, but on the business. She had a thorough grasp of their financial circumstances, which I find uncharacteristic of women."

"More so in Britain than in the U.S., Watson. American women, especially out here in the west, are much more their husbands' peers, as we've discussed before."

"Indeed. The Porters also talked about your presence at the ranch. Sarah was quite interested in the prospect that you might wish to purchase it. Porter told her that he didn't want to pull up stakes and start all over again."

"What was her reaction?" Holmes asked.

"She said, 'Husband, think carefully about your decision and I will support you in everything that you wish to do.' When Porter left the room he gave me a knowing glance. I sensed he was discomfited by his lack of forthrightness with his wife."

"Thank you, Watson. That's very helpful." Holmes paused as if to collect his thoughts. "Tomorrow morning after breakfast," Holmes continued, "I am going to ride the perimeter of the ranch and after lunch, ride back into Glendive. I wish to speak with Mr. Devlin again and I need to send a cable to London. I should be back before the dinner hour, but if I am delayed, please tell Mrs. Porter not to wait for me."

With that Holmes rose and as he turned toward the doorway I said, "Pray, Holmes, please indulge me. What is your opinion of the dramatis personae here at the ranch?"

"Certainly, Watson. The Maier twins are not twins, they are not even brothers. I believe their relationship is of an intimate nature, but by claiming they are bachelor brothers are able to live together without arousing suspicion."

"My God, Holmes!" I stuttered, completely shocked. The thought of such a relationship had never entered into my sensibilities. I was about to ask Holmes how he knew these things but deferred. There are just some things a God-fearing man doesn't want to know.

Holmes registered my reaction and said, "Protect that information with your life, Watson. If you don't, it could cost them theirs." He then added, "Porter is not Mrs. Porter's first husband. She was married before."

"When I saw the coloring of those four lads, I had a similar thought, Holmes."

"Mendel's laws of genetics may allow for three blondes and a dark brunette from such a union, but the statistics are against it. Perhaps you can quietly probe that issue with one of them tomorrow. Good night, Watson."

In a count of two, Holmes disappeared like a phantom and I gratefully returned to the warmth of my bed.

Breakfast was uneventful. Porter and the hired men went about their work and Holmes disappeared per plan. Josiah's weather forecast was accurate. The cooling trend which started yesterday in the late afternoon continued un-abated, and by morning it was well below freezing. Fortunately there was no wind, so I took a twenty minute walk down the road to loosen up my legs and then retired to the chair next to the parlour stove. Mrs. Porter had the two older boys at the dining room table doing a school session while the two younger lads played quietly in a corner of the room with a big pile of wooden blocks their father must have made for them.

I read for a few moments but my mind kept flashing back to the previous night's dinner and Holmes' display of his powers of observation and deductive reasoning. It didn't make sense to me, although I long ago learned that when Holmes does something there is a reason for it. Why would he want to impress Jasper or Josiah Maier or the Porters with his skills? Reaching no satisfactory conclusion, I resolved to ask Holmes about it directly at my first opportunity.

At approximately 10 a.m. I heard Mrs. Porter tell her sons, "I want you to finish reading this chapter and then practice your writing. Mama has to do some baking for our company that's coming." Soon the inside of the house was saturated with the fragrance of freshly baked bread and my anticipation grew as the lunch hour neared.

About half past eleven, I stepped outside for a breath of fresh air and observed two horsemen about a quarter mile apart approach the ranch house from the west. I recognized Holmes as the second horseman and wondered if the first was the "company" Mrs. Porter had mentioned. I returned to the house and picked up my book to read when Porter entered the parlour and engaged me in polite conversation. A few moments later we heard footsteps on the front porch and a heavy knock on the front door.

"Thomas!" Porter exclaimed as he opened the door. "Come in."

"Hello, Stephen. I was headed back to my place and hoped I might find some company and a noonday meal."

"You're always welcome at our table," said Porter jovially. "Allow me to introduce you to Dr. Johns, another of our guests. His associate, Mr. Sherlock, should be with us shortly."

Thomas was Thomas Mellon, Porter's neighbor to the west. After a brief exchange of pleasantries Mellon excused himself and went into the kitchen to greet Mrs. Porter, her children, and the hired men who had come in for lunch.

Through the front window I saw Holmes enter the yard and went outdoors to advise him of the presence of Mellon. He listened patiently and then said, "I've had a productive morning, Watson, and will stay with my plan to return to Glendive after our midday repast. I would like you to stay here and keep your eyes and ears open as you've so ably done this morning."

Lunch was cordial but nothing was discussed that seemed related to the case. Afterward Mr. Mellon asked for a few moments of Holmes' time. Porter graciously allowed us some privacy in the parlour and Mellon asked Holmes about his interest in buying land. Holmes continued the charade and over the next hour he and Mellon discussed land, cattle, and water. Holmes asked Mellon why he wanted to sell out.

"The land doesn't have the carrying capacity of states in the Midwest," he replied.

The term "carrying capacity" was certainly new to me, so I injected my one comment of the afternoon by asking what it meant.

"It's how much land is needed to support one cow," Mellon explained. "In Montana, cattle feed on grass; in the Midwest, they eat corn. It takes a lot more land out here to feed a cow than in Iowa. The more land you have, the more expense. Now, it all needs to be fenced. And water's always a problem too."

"True," replied Holmes, "but my investors seem to think

Montana offers opportunities not found farther east. Once you decide on a price, I will cable Britain and get you an answer."

"I'll think about it some this evening, and get you an answer tomorrow or the next day, Mr. Sherlock."

"That is most gracious and businesslike of you, Mr. Mellon. Most of the men I've met thus far claim to be interested in selling me their land but seem to think that I should estimate its value," answered Holmes.

"Sherlock," mused Mellon. "It's a unique name, certainly unheard of in these parts."

"It's quite common in the British Isles. It means 'fair haired' in old English and is both a common first and last name. I suspect that it arose sometime about a thousand years ago following the Viking invasions of Great Britain and Ireland. They left behind their seed and a legacy of blonde hair and blue eyes."

"Seems to me," Mellon answered, "that I heard or saw that name in conjunction with a crime involving a naval treaty a few years back."

"You did," I replied. "There's a policeman by the name of Holmes who lives in London and works with Scotland Yard. He solved a crime involving a stolen treaty document."[70]

"I doubt I could live so dangerously," injected Holmes. "I have enough trouble managing the funds and temperaments of the men who make up my investment group.

---

70 Editor's note: "The Naval Treaty Case" involved the theft of a secret naval treaty. There was considerable fear that the treaty might become public and damage Britain's foreign relations. Holmes solved the case, recovered the missing document, and earned the enduring gratitude of Queen Victoria and her government's ministers.

I can't imagine why anyone would seek a life dealing with ne'er-do-wells."

Holmes rose signaling that the meeting had come to a close, and Mellon quietly departed.

After Mellon had departed Holmes chided me for being too talkative. "My dear Doctor, I believe you said all too much to Mr. Mellon."

"Whatever do you mean, Holmes?"

"Mellon's comment about the name Sherlock was designed to ferret out information and when you expounded, however briefly, on the naval treaty, I believe he had the information he required, that is, our true identities."

"Come now, Holmes. You're a renowned figure throughout the United Kingdom. Say the name Sherlock and the coal miners of Wigan as much as the gentry in Surrey know about England's most famous detective. You're even celebrated in Dublin, which is no small achievement given the contrary nature of the Irish race."

"What you say is true, Watson, in the British Isles, not the U.S. I tried to disarm Mr. Mellon with my exposition on the derivation of my name, but—" Holmes paused. "I may have to change plans. I'll know tomorrow after I've finished my inquiries in Glendive."

I was about to again protest when we heard a knock on the door and Sarah Porter poked her head through the opening.

"Doctor, Mr. Sherlock, I am sorry to intrude, but a few moments ago I saw another rider coming toward the house. I suspect it's another landowner that would like some of your time. If Jasper and Josiah know something the whole county knows, and surprisingly quickly."

"Thank you, Mrs. Porter. If your next guest is indeed interested in talking with me, I will be happy to oblige him."

A few moments later Mrs. Porter introduced us to Mr. Matthew Crowder, a rancher whose property lay to the northeast of Porters' land.

Crowder struck me as a pretentious man, and when Holmes asked him about his property he seemed evasive, telling Holmes that "We can sort that out after I know what you're paying." Holmes demurred, telling Crowder that "My price depends on what you own and its condition, and that requires that I thoroughly examine your property before I put any offer on the table."

Crowder then made the mistake of trying to argue with Holmes, only to be rebuffed a second time. He then suggested that Holmes partner with him and Crowder would manage their collective assets. Holmes dispatched him for the third time by telling Crowder that "my investors will be looking for a ranch manager, of that you can be sure, but that person will have to have demonstrated that he knows the cattle business and how to care for the land. Inasmuch as I've not been able to ascertain those qualities in you, we will not consider any such business arrangement."

Crowder was clearly angry with Holmes' answers and made haste to leave, but not before announcing, "You'll be sorry that you turned down my offer, Mr. Sherlock. I am the most successful rancher in these parts and within a matter of a few years I'll own all of this county."

After Crowder had departed, Holmes simply said, "I am late and best be leaving now."

Following dinner, young Adam again came to me and I put him on my lap and then proceeded to read him Ambrose Bierce's story, *An Occurrence at Owl Creek Bridge,* the tale of a confederate sympathizer condemned to death and ultimately hung at the Owl Creek Bridge. Adam, of course, didn't understand a word of what I was saying, but he seemed to like the timbre of my voice and he cuddled on my chest until Sarah took him to bed. My experiences with the Porter children were quite out of character for me, a man who has spent his entire adult life in the company of men, first in the army, and then as Holmes' companion. My marriage to Mary Morstan was not blessed with children, which was a great sadness to her although given her early and untimely death, perhaps a blessing in disguise. My limited exposure to young Adam, while gratifying, caused me to reflect on how little I knew about the wee creatures and how difficult it would have been for me to raise them properly after Mary's death.

Before retiring, I went out on Porters' front porch for a breath of fresh air and gazed at the immensity of the heavens. The stars wrapped around the earth in a band of luminosity.[71] As I've noted before, in Montana the sky seems to go on forever.

I slept soundly and enjoyed another hearty meal at Sarah Porter's breakfast table. The hired hands were not present and Sarah told me that Josiah cooks breakfast in their cabin on those days when they get up extraordinarily early so as to not disturb the Porter household. She added that Jasper and Josiah were going hunting north of the ranch

---

71 Editor's note: Watson was looking at the edge of our galaxy, the Milky Way, frequently seen on dark, clear nights, although not known as a galaxy until Astronomer Edwin Hubble recognized that the Milky Way was one galaxy among many. Prior to his observations in the 1920s, the Milky Way was thought to be the entire universe.

in the hopes of bagging some venison to supplement the ranch larder. I borrowed a horse and rode west along the irrigation ditch which we had visited two days earlier, scouring the ground with my eyes in the hope that I might find something of interest for Holmes. Mid-morning found me several miles west of the Porter Ranch, but I'd seen nothing of consequence except a small herd of cattle about a mile to the west. I assumed the cattle belonged to Thomas Mellon but encountered nothing to indicate that I was on his land. Apparently neither Porter nor Mellon had yet erected fence to demark their mutual boundary.

I returned to the ranch house just before 11 a.m. and sat at the kitchen table nursing a hot cup of tea. Mrs. Porter said she preferred it to coffee. It was an expensive delicacy, difficult to obtain in nearby towns, but she kept a tin for special occasions. She was busy preparing the noon meal and I thought it an opportune time to talk with her. I opened the conversation by complimenting her on the children and told her how much I enjoyed their company, especially my new friend, young Adam. She was pleased. I then casually mentioned that it was hard to believe that he came from the same family as his older, fairer complexioned brothers.

She quickly replied by remarking that they were Adam's half-brothers. "I was married before, Dr. Johns. My husband was a brakeman on the railroad. He contracted pneumonia three winters ago and coughed himself to death in three days' time."

After receiving my condolences she continued. "The people of Glendive were very good to me. They kept us in food and the railroad supplied us with coal or we would have either starved or frozen to death. The next summer

Jasper introduced me to Stephen. We were married a few months later. He's been very good to us, although the older boys miss their father."

"You knew Jasper previously?" I asked cautiously.

"Actually, my late husband knew them. Jasper and Josiah also worked on the railroad. As a married woman I didn't consort with the bachelors around town."

"Understood," I said, recognizing that the formality which characterized male-female relations in Britain's palaces was little different in America's working men's homes. I then changed the subject and commented that I was surprised that Mr. Mellon and Mr. Crowder had both heard of Sherlock's interest in acquiring land.

"It is surprising," Sarah answered. "We seem to live in an unpopulated land, and yet news travels very quickly from house to house."

"How does that happen?" I asked, trying to sound mystified.

"The cowhands. They're out working the cattle or building fence and they meet up with one of their own from a neighboring place and the word goes across the county like a private telegraph."

It made sense, but given the vastness of the landscape I found it hard to believe that two people meeting would be little more than a chance happening. After lunch I followed the hired hands to the building that Porter used as a repair shop. The wind had come up, blowing briskly from the west, and it was bitter cold. I didn't envy Holmes his return ride from Glendive.

The repair shop was tightly constructed and a fire was burning in a large cast iron stove in the middle of the room.

Josiah stoked the embers and tossed in a shovel of coal from the nearby fuel bin. Then it struck me, coal was a godsend to these people. In western Montana where forests covered the land, people heated their homes with wood. But here on the plains there was very little wood.

"Where does the coal come from?" I asked Josiah.

"Just about everywhere, Doctor," came his swift reply. "You can't go anywhere in eastern Montana without finding coal. Most of it is brown coal, some is just hard peat.[72] If you watch the river banks or the sides of the dry gullies you'll frequently see brown or black stripes of earth."

"Yes, I recall that."

"That's coal, Doctor."

"This looks to be of good quality, similar to what we burn in our hearths in England."

"This is not from around here. Porter gets it from a dealer in town. It's mined out west around Bear Creek, I think. It's better quality coal than the local product. Burns hotter."

Our conversation migrated over many topics from there. Jasper was repairing saddles and other leather work, while Josiah sharpened knives and axes on a grinding wheel that he powered with a foot pedal. A lull in the conversation gave me an opportunity to ask about the neighbors, Mellon and Crowder.

Mellon was described as a "fine fellow and good neighbor. Last winter, Stephen and Sarah both got deathly ill and were bedridden. Mellon came down and stayed several days

---

72 Editor's note: Coal comes in a variety of compositions ranked by hardness and BTU content. Eastern Montana has enormous deposits of both sub-bituminous and lignite coal which have a lower BTU rating than the bituminous coal mined in south central Montana.

nursing them back to health. Best cook there is," said Jasper.

"Don't be ridiculous," Josiah said as he gave his brother a scowl.

"Best man cook," answered Jasper. He fed Sarah and Stephen chicken soup for four days."

"It was good," injected Josiah.

"And I think it saved their lives. That and some herbs he had which broke their fever," continued Jasper.

"Crowder is just the opposite," said Josiah bitterly. "He is an ornery cuss. Got a lot of money and he tries to bully people."

"With considerable success," added Jasper. "He bullied us right out of the ranching business."

"How so?" I asked, my curiosity piqued.

"Remember we told you about the blackleg infecting our cattle?" Josiah asked.

"Yes," I replied.

"Crowder was the cause of it. One of his heifers got diseased and got mixed in with our herd. Before we knew it, our cows were all infected."

"How did you know that?"

"We found a dead heifer with his brand on it in a coulee next to where our cattle were grazing. Crowder's cattle were all on the other side of his ranch, probably five miles from our cattle. That sick heifer didn't wander over to our place on its lonesome."

"What are you implying?" I asked.

"Not implying anything," Josiah said. "Just saying that when we had to put the place up for sale Crowder was the first one in with an offer."

"We were lucky," said Jasper returning to the conversation. "Porter heard about the sale and he came in and topped Crowder's price. If Stephen hadn't shown up, Crowder would have gotten the land and kicked us off to boot."

"Crowder is the most possessive, greedy man I know," Josiah said, his enmity clear and his face flashing in rage.

"Porter buying your land and foiling Crowder's plans must have angered him," I said.

"It did," answered Jasper. "But interestingly, it didn't seem to last too long. I don't know why, but Porter can get along with him."

"Nobody else can," injected Josiah. "He's a bastard."

If Holmes were here he'd be very curious about Stephen Porter's relationship with Crowder, so I probed the issue cautiously.

"That's interesting about Porter," I said. "He can get along with Crowder even after besting him in a business transaction."

"Stephen told me he knew Crowder from before."

"Oh," I said, hoping that Jasper would continue.

"They grew up in Illinois, somewhere around Moline. That's all I know."

The men finished their work and we made our way back to our respective dwellings in preparation for supper. Holmes arrived just as the sun was setting, his body rigid from the cold. Mrs. Porter was kind enough to brew him a strong cup of tea which he drank as he thawed out next to the parlour stove. We were alone so I quickly gave him a report of what I had learned. I asked about the success of his trip to Glendive, and Holmes merely nodded and said that he had cleared up some issues in his own mind.

About that time the Maier brothers came in and Holmes asked Josiah for a weather forecast.

"The pain in my knee is starting to lessen, Mr. Sherlock. The cold is going to break. Probably not tomorrow, but a day or two after that."

"Most encouraging, Mr. Maier. I don't believe I've encountered such cold and wind in many years. It reminds me of a visit I once paid to Kirkwell in the Orkney Islands of Scotland. Wind so ferocious a man couldn't stand up in it."

Following supper and after the hired men had departed, Holmes pulled Porter into the parlour for a private conversation.

"I made some inquiries when I was in Glendive," he said, "and discovered that you're not the only one to have lost cattle. According to the sheriff, ranchers between Billings and Dickinson are reporting mysterious cattle losses. There was another incident last night near Hysham."[73]

"What does that mean?" Porter asked.

"It means that the thieves have departed the area and any chance that the Doctor and I have of exposing their identity has vanished. To further complicate things, when I was in Glendive I received a cable from Mycroft who begged that I return to London post haste. Apparently, the Chancellor of the Exchequer cannot explain the absence of five million pounds sterling from the treasury. We must depart for Britain tomorrow."

Porter was clearly distraught and visited with Holmes about what steps might be taken by local law enforcement officials. Holmes provided him with several ideas, and Porter thanked us for our effort.

---

73 Editor's note: Dickinson is a city in western North Dakota. Hysham is a small farm town about 60 miles east of Billings, Montana.

In the morning, Holmes thanked Mrs. Porter "for her most excellent hospitality" and explained, per our arrangement with her husband, that we were being called back to St. Paul to look at some property near that city. We also said our goodbyes to Jasper, Josiah, and each of the boys. I read to Adam very briefly one last time. We departed mid-morning.

Once we were well away from the ranch house I asked Holmes where we were going.

"To St. Paul," came his curt reply.

I could see by his eyes that his mind was fully engaged and there was no point in my trying to engage him in further conversation.

I took up residence in Dion's Saloon next to the stove. Mick Devlin was behind the bar, and he and Holmes engaged in some quiet conversation while I read. Holmes then disappeared for several hours and returned to the tavern around 5:30 p.m.

"As our American friends are wont to say, Watson, it's time to saddle up. Our train east will be here momentarily."

On board, I started to settle in my seat and get comfortable for a long night's journey. Holmes, as was his practice, liked to walk through the train looking for faces he recognized. He'd started the practice several years ago to insure that we were not being followed. For a period, Moriarty[74] had us under almost complete surveillance and we engaged in a variety of stratagems to lose his agents. It was easier

---

74   Editor's note: Moriarty is Professor James Moriarty, Holmes' greatest enemy, a criminal mastermind whom Watson described as the "Napoleon of Crime." Holmes ultimately killed Moriarty at Reichenbach Falls, in central Switzerland, in a case Watson called "The Adventure of the Final Problem."

for Holmes, the master of disguise, than it was for me. Frequently I had to simply outrun them, no mean task for a man of my age and girth.

Just as the train started its forward motion Holmes came back into the coach and invited me, in a voice loud enough to be heard by those sitting nearby, to come back and join him and Mr. Adair. I needed no further encouragement. Adair was a grain merchant in St. Paul and close friend of James J. Hill. We had enjoyed his hospitality on two previous occasions, and the man was one of the few I'd met in America who had a truly cultivated palate when it came to wine. His wine cellar was most excellent.

I exited the car behind Holmes, and on the platform outside, Holmes said, "We get off here, Watson."

"Are you daft, Holmes?" I replied. "This train must be going twenty miles per hour. We'll break our legs. And our luggage?" The minute I said luggage, I knew how feeble my entreaty sounded.

"Don't worry about your portmanteau. Devlin has taken care of that. Remember to roll when we hit the ground."

With that comment Holmes pulled me off the train onto the frozen ground adjacent the track. I rolled. Fortunately, we were in a grassy meadow and after taking inventory of the condition of my back and limbs, I climbed to my feet with a small boost from Holmes.

"Now what?" I inquired.

"We follow the tracks back toward Glendive. Devlin will meet us."

We walked about 300 yards by my calculation where we found a road crossing and met Devlin. Holmes and I climbed into the back of the wagon and covered ourselves with a heavy canvas tarp. The wagon ride was but a few minutes' duration and Devlin ushered us into his home. After fortifying the two of us with a hot cup of coffee laced with rye whiskey, Devlin brought our luggage and we piled on extra clothes. All Holmes said was "it might be a long night."

Well after dark, Devlin led us through the streets of Glendive to the railroad yard and we took up position between two long strings of cattle cars parked on sidings. Around 8 p.m. we heard the sounds of a switch engine draw near and followed it as it backed onto one of the tracks with the cattle cars. We hurriedly climbed aboard the second car in the string, and maintaining perfect silence pulled ourselves up against the front wall. Through the slots in the wall I spotted a trainman walk past the car followed by the sound of a coupling being disengaged. The trainman then walked forward to the engine and in a few minutes we were underway.

The train gathered speed and I saw the section house at Colgate siding, which we had investigated three days previously, flash by on my right.

Devlin said, "You're right, Mr. Holmes. It looks like we're going to the Hoyt, Marsh, or Conlin siding."[75]

About ten to fifteen minutes later the train began to slow and Devlin said, "Hoyt." Holmes nodded. The engine dropped the three cattle cars, pulled back on to the main line, and returned to Glendive.

We got out of the car and went into the section house, which was more of a hut about eight feet wide and twelve

---

75 Editor's note: The names of three railroad sidings between Glendive and Fallon, Montana.

feet long. Thankfully, it had a stove, box of kindling wood, and full bin of coal.

Devlin made a fire and it quickly drove the chill out of the room. There were two windows in the room—one facing east in the direction of the track and the other to the north facing the river. Holmes stood in the corner, alternatively looking out one window and then the next, quietly smoking his pipe. Devlin, ever thoughtful, had brought along a canvas bag containing his bottle of whiskey among other things. While Holmes smoked we enjoyed a companionable drink. Holmes finally took notice of us and I asked him what we were going to do.

"We wait," came his terse reply.

Devlin and I moved the room's benches close around the stove and we retired for the evening. This was the second time since coming to Montana where Holmes pulled the ruse of leaving town, only to steal back in the dead of night and set up watch for our felonious quarry.[76]

I slept soundly, disturbed momentarily as either Holmes or Devlin periodically restoked the fire. I doubt that Holmes slept at all as he kept watch through the night.

The next morning Devlin pulled some flour, salt and baking soda from his bag and melted snow from a small drift on the lee side of the building, and we supped on pancakes and a gritty coffee made by heating coffee grounds in water, what I refer to as vagrant coffee and what Montanans call cowboy coffee.

Holmes then posted me to guard duty at the windows

---

76 Editor's note: See "The Ghosts of Red Lion" as reported in *Sherlock Holmes: The Montana Chronicles.*

while he lay down and slept. Devlin occupied himself feeding the fire and whittling on a piece of firewood. By noon he had carved a reasonable facsimile of that character called Father Christmas in England and Santa Claus in the United States.

In the late afternoon as the sun began sinking from the afternoon sky, Holmes doused the fire in the stove and we turned down the lantern. Just before dusk he called Devlin and I to the window where, across the river in the meadow running upslope from the river bank, we saw a hay wagon making its way in our direction. One cowboy drove the wagon and a second tossed small bundles of hay off the fan-tail. Upon reaching the river it turned around and retraced its course back to its place of origin.

Holmes smiled, nodded his head and said, "The game is afoot. It shouldn't be long now, gentlemen."

It seemed long. With the fire out the section house cooled off quickly, and Devlin and I were soon pacing around to keep our feet warm. Holmes, whose immunity to cold is legendary, at least with me, stood quietly by the window.

It was a bright night with a full moon. Around nine o'clock Holmes drew us back to the window. Very faintly in the distance we were able to observe three cowboys driving a small herd of thirty to forty cattle in our direction.

When they approached the north river bank, the three of us left the building and took up position in some nearby trees.

The cowboys pushed the cattle across the river ice, onto the south bank, and into the cattle cars. Afterward, they dismounted, tied their horses to a railing attached to the section house, went inside, and started a fire.

We moved up close to the windows and peered inside.

I was shocked, no horrified by what I saw. Sitting around the fire were Jasper Maier, Thomas Mellon, and a stranger whom Devlin identified as Abel Anderson, the railroad station master from Fallon, the next town to the west. Our timing was perfect. Mellon, like Devlin, had thought to bring along a bottle of spirits and the three henchmen sat down to talk.

"A good night's work, gentlemen," said Mellon.

"Too cold," answered Jasper. "Josiah said it was going to warm up but he was wrong."

"It will tomorrow," Mellon said. "That knee of his has never been wrong before."

"Thomas, if you'll beg my pardon, I can understand why you would steal from Porter. But why steal from yourself?" Jasper asked.

"To take away any suspicion of my involvement in Porter's theft. When I report that I am also a victim, nobody will suspect me. It also makes me a little more money. After Porter's cattle disappeared I insured mine for twenty dollars a head. We sell the cows to the abattoir[77] for thirty-five dollars apiece and collect an additional twenty dollars from the insurance company. All that money tastes very sweet indeed."

"My God, Holmes," I said in a hushed voice, "My Webley is in my portmanteau."

"No worries, Watson, Devlin has his Peacemaker."

With that, Devlin cranked the handle on the door, jumped through and leveled his pistol at Mellon's chest. He then announced, "There's been a change of plans, Thomas.

---

77 Editor's note: A slaughterhouse.

Meet Detective Sherlock Holmes and his able assistant, Dr. Watson."

"I thought so," Mellon cursed.

"Devlin, you bastard," hissed Jasper.

Holmes then produced several pieces of a stout twine from Devlin's canvas bag and instructed the three felons to "turn around."

The thieves never moved, and instead stood there eyeing the three of us as if assessing their chances for escape. Mellon's right hand slowly moved toward a pistol on his hip.

Devlin fired his Peacemaker, and when a Colt 44 goes off in a small room it sounds like an artillery piece. Mellon yelled and grabbed his face, and all three of the desperados buckled at the knees. Devlin had shot the wall behind them, but some of the muzzle blast must have caught Mellon.

After disarming and tying up the rustlers, Devlin and Holmes talked quietly outside the door. Then Devlin departed on Mellon's horse, a powerfully built dark brown stallion.

At exactly 11:42 p.m. that night, the night freight appeared from the east and pulled to a stop next to the siding. Holmes donned Jasper's overcoat and cowboy hat and went out to talk with the engineer. The train then departed, continuing its run west without the three cattle cars.

Throughout the night Holmes and I took turns tending the fire and keeping watch over our prisoners. In the morning I boiled some coffee as Devlin had done the day before and gave each of the prisoners a cup. Unfortunately, we had used up the other provisions the night before and there was nothing else to eat. My hunger was becoming palpable.

The sun had just cleared the horizon when I heard the

sound of a steam engine in the distance, and looking out the east-facing window saw the small switch engine which had ferried us to Hoyt the night before, returning with yet another cattle car and caboose. It pulled onto the side track in front of the three loaded cattle cars. Once stopped, four armed men emerged from the caboose while Devlin, two other riders, and four saddle horses descended from the cattle car.

After introducing Holmes and me to Sheriff Dominick Cavanaugh, Devlin and his mates opened the cattle cars and freed the livestock. Holmes counseled with the sheriff, no doubt giving him the particulars of the case. Soon thereafter, the prisoners were loaded aboard the train.

I heard the sheriff tell Devlin to "take Mellon's cattle over to Porter. It's partial compensation, and we'll get the rest later." Holmes joined me and asked that I return to Glendive with the sheriff and write out a full statement of what had transpired last night. He then joined Devlin and headed toward the Porter Ranch.

After locking up the three ne'er-do-wells, the sheriff asked me to join him for a meal. He and his wife lived in an apartment attached to the jail. I was grateful for my first food in two days. I then walked back to Dion's Saloon, ordered a brandy despite the early hour, and waited for Holmes and Devlin to appear.

Devlin arrived just before noon with Porter, who briefly paused to thank me for my assistance before hurrying off to the sheriff's office.

Holmes arrived just before 4 p.m. Devlin brought some nourishment to our table, and after having his fill Holmes told us how he solved the case.

I chided him a bit first by remarking, "You seemed to have solved this case more by old fashioned police work than by deduction, Holmes."

"Quite to the contrary, Watson. After hearing Devlin's description of what happened, I quickly formed several hypothesis and then used my powers of observation and deductive skills to craft a series of answers that led the case to its successful conclusion.

"I first hypothesized that a crime had been committed and its commission was undertaken by local residents. I ratified that notion on our first ride out to Porter's house. This land is so scarcely populated that no one from the outside could perpetrate the deed without running afoul of the topography and climate.

"Second, I reasoned that if 167 head of cattle were missing, they had to be moved by railcar. It's the only method of conveyance that could quickly remove the cattle from the scene of the crime. Had they merely been trailed to some other location, there would be plenty of signs leading to their whereabouts.

"Making the cattle seem to disappear in mid-air was a bit of genius," Holmes said as he paused to fill the heel of his pipe with some shag tobacco and set it to fire.

"How was that accomplished?" Devlin asked, taking the words right out of my mouth.

"It was quite easy. The partner in Fallon, Mr. Anderson, simply opened the headgate and sent water from the Yellowstone River down the irrigation ditch. Jasper diverted the water into the meadow where it froze. When the cattle were herded across the ice they left behind little evidence of their movements. Then, when the weather turned warm the ice melted and any sign that the cattle had been herded toward the river and railroad tracks disappeared. They were aided unwittingly by Josiah, whose rheumatic knees provided Jasper, and hence the criminal conspiracy, with an accurate weather forecast."

"You said Josiah was an unwitting participant, Holmes. I find that hard to believe. He and Jasper live together. He had to know what his brother was doing."

"Not so, Watson. I don't know if you deduced it, but Josiah is hard of hearing. I noticed it at that first luncheon when we were introduced. He speaks loudly, a common characteristic among men who do not hear well. When he talks with another he turns his head to the right so that his left ear is directly toward the speaker. I tested my theory about his hearing when we left the ranch house after our meal. I snapped my fingers right next to his right ear and Josiah didn't react."

"Still, Holmes—"

"There's more. This morning when I returned to the Porter Ranch, I took a few minutes to look through the Maier's cabin. I found a bottle of laudanum in the cupboard. It's my theory that when Jasper planned one of his midnight escapades he fed Josiah some of the potion. Coupled with his lack of hearing, it was bound to insure a good night's sleep."

"When did you conclude that the cattle were being trailed across the ice to the railroad?" asked Devlin.

"The first day, when Porter showed us where the cattle were when they disappeared. If you recall, I spent considerable time walking up and down the ditch and doing the same thing in the meadow. I observed that the ditch bottom was moist west of where we were standing and dry to the east. There was a similar pattern in the meadow below. The ground was still wet from the melting ice where it had been flooded but dry outside the flood zone."

"And the railroad?" continued Devlin.

"Simply a matter of bribery. Anderson slipped the train crew a few dollars for dropping off the cars. Then instructions were left for the engineer of the west-bound night freight to pick up the loaded cattle cars and take them to their destination."

"Which was?"

"Butte. There isn't any other town big enough where a slaughterhouse could quickly dispose of that many cattle."

About that time we heard a train whistle, our signal that it was time to leave. Devlin ferried us back to the train station and helped us get our luggage aboard. Porter showed up just as we were about to leave and he and Devlin offered their profound thanks.

For the second time in three days I settled into my seat, looking forward to the trip back to the east coast and on to England. As usual, Holmes searched the train cars in search of a friendly face but found none and took up residence in the seat next to me on the aisle. As he withdrew his pipe from his coat pocket, I put down my book and congratulated him for being the only English policeman, official or unofficial, in his case, to solve a cattle rustling crime. "It's another mark of distinction in your already illustrious career," I added.

"Thank you, Watson," Holmes replied, but his affect was flat and I could tell that he was troubled.

"Old chap," I said, "something seems to be bothering you."

"Nothing more than man's perfidy," Holmes replied.

"Perfidy is your business."

"It is indeed, Watson, but I find some examples of it particularly odious."

"I am in disbelief, Holmes. This incident was nothing more than common theft, a subject in which you're well experienced."

"Theft, indeed, but also betrayal."

"You're upset over Jasper's treatment of Porter. He buys their ranch and gives them a job and Jasper repays him by attempting to ruin him."

"That's certainly part of it. The Maiers, Jasper in particular, were of the belief that Porter conspired with Crowder to create the blackleg epidemic and drive them from their land. I only learned this morning that Porter and Crowder are half-brothers, and Jasper knew of that relationship from his youth. Recall that the Maiers said they grew up in Iowa."

"Yes," I replied.

Holmes continued, "Crowder and Porter lived a few miles away, across the Mississippi in Illinois. When Porter showed up to buy the Maier's ranch, contrary to their public representation, they viewed it as a conspiracy and wanted retribution. Jasper bided his time and one day he met Thomas Mellon and soon a criminal partnership was formed."

"You've seen countless cases of betrayal, Holmes," I said as I turned and looked out the window at the darkening landscape. The sun would soon set and we'd ride the night through North Dakota.

"True, Watson, but there was a fourth member of the conspiracy and it's her perfidy I find particularly troubling.

"No!" I exclaimed.

"Indeed, Sarah Porter."

"And how do you know this, Holmes?"

"From what I observed and what you told me."

"I told you?" I asked, puzzled by such a suggestion.

"Please recall that when we first ate with the Porters, Sarah explained that she baked every Sunday afternoon."

"Yes. In fact, she said she didn't need to bake this coming Sunday because her lads had been sick and had eaten very little."

"And the day Mellon arrived to talk with us—"

"She baked bread and a cake that morning," I said, finishing Holmes' sentence. "Furthermore, she knew Mellon was coming to their home."

"Yes, no doubt Jasper was the communication conduit, and during lunch do you recall how vivacious she was?"

"Oh yes, ebullient would be an accurate depiction of her mood," I said.

"That made me suspicious," Holmes said, "and then you filled in the missing piece of the puzzle when you reported upon your conversation with the Maier brothers."

Anticipating Holmes' next statement, I said, "They told me how Mellon had nursed Sarah and Porter back to health when they had become seriously ill."

"No doubt a bond of affection was formed. Stephen Porter is an honest, industrious and fair man, but he doesn't strike me as particularly demonstrative."

"Now that you mention it, Holmes, I don't recall seeing any outward display of affection toward her or the boys."

Holmes continued. "After Devlin and Porter left the ranch this morning to come into Glendive and meet with the sheriff, I searched the Maier cabin as I previously reported, talked with Josiah, and satisfied myself that he was not involved in the conspiracy notwithstanding his antipathy toward Porter. I also talked to Mrs. Porter and laid out my theory of her complicity. She looked me in the eye, Watson. For the longest time, she simply looked into my eyes."

"Where she saw nothing but the gray depths of steely resolve," I remarked.

"She admitted to an affair with Mellon as I had surmised. A romantic spark between the two was kindled when Mellon came over to nurse the Porters back to health when they were ill. It took some questions from me, but she finally confessed to her role in a plan to ruin Porter which would allow Mellon to acquire his land. Once penniless, Sarah planned to divorce Porter and marry Mellon."

"Well, that plan is clearly in arrears now! I surmise that you told the sheriff and Porter?"

"No, I didn't, Watson. I gave Sarah two choices. The first being that I do exactly as you have just said. In that case, Porter would divorce her and take the children. No court would entrust the lives of four young men to a woman who had fallen so far, and she would be left without a home or family, and probably no means of support save prostitution."

"And the second option?" I asked.

"That she could forget Thomas Mellon and Jasper Maier and have no further contact with either man. Of course, that won't pose much of a challenge since both men will be in prison for a long time, if they aren't hung. In this part of the world, cattle rustling is viewed as seriously as murder. Then, I told her that she had to stay with Porter serving him as a good wife and mothering their children to adulthood. At that time, if she chose to leave Porter she could do so.

She hesitated, but accepted my second proposal."

"I think you may have saved that last piece of decency and good in this entire sordid affair, Holmes." After pausing momentarily, I continued. "I like these American women, Holmes. They have energy, spirit, and cunning, much more so than the fairer sex of Britain. But alas, it seems to lead far too many of them astray."

"The price of independence is eternal vigilance," added Holmes.

"Or something like that, Holmes," I answered, clearly confused by his meaning. The train began to decelerate. We were entering another station. The sign above the door said Beach, North Dakota. We were, indeed, heading east. We were going home.

About the Author

John Fitzpatrick is a native of Anaconda, Montana.
For the past thirty years he has worked as a lobbyist for the
metal mining, telecommunications, and utility industry.
He resides in Helena, Montana.

Also by John S. Fitzpatrick

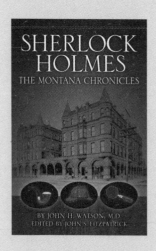
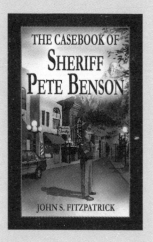